just *like* heaven

USA Today Bestselling Author

TRILINA PUCCI

Cover Design: Ashes and Vellichor

Photography: Michelle Lancaster, www.michellelancaster.com

Formatting: LJ Designs

Editing/Proofing: One Love Editing, Rebecca Fairest Reviews, My Brother's Editor, All-Encompassing, Rumi Khan

Printed in the United States of America IBSN: 13-9780578989174

Chapter One

"**H**ey, guys," Aubrey calls, looking over at Piper and me.

I glance over my shoulder, realizing I've lost myself in a bunch of vintage magazines displayed neatly in a cart outside of a quaint little boutique bookstore.

"Check this out."

She holds up a piece of paper that looks like some kind of advertisement. Piper walks over, resting her chin on Aubrey's shoulder, reading whatever's in her hand. But before I can peek at what they're staring at, Aubs looks up at me, smiling brightly.

"We have to do this."

I shake my head, holding out my hand for the paper, wondering what the hell she's talking about. Instead of showing me, Aubrey grabs my outstretched palm.

"Just keep an open mind, Sut."

She wags her brows, opening the french door to the tea shop behind her, making a bell chime above the door.

"What does the paper say, Aubs? Hand it over."

I roll my eyes, already knowing this has "*dumb idea*" written all over it, but that doesn't diminish the grin on my face.

She passes it to me just as she lets my hand go, turning toward Piper, who's already lifting the top of a metal container to smell what's inside. I gaze around the dimly lit shop, past black walls and Turkish rugs to a gold-painted Victorian buffet. It's stocked with dried herbs and leaves, all in glass apothecary jars.

My eyes drop down at the creased white paper.

Tea leaf readings. Today only. $10.

I glance up as Piper says, "Aubs, just give me your ten, and I'll be happy to tell you that you're about to meet the love of your life and win the lottery."

We giggle, but we're silenced as someone behind us clears their throat. The three of us swing around simultaneously to deep-set dark brown eyes staring back at us, so dark they almost look black.

The old woman smirks, pointing her finger at Piper, all her metal bracelets jingling as she does.

"No lottery. But maybe true love."

Piper nudges me as I reach for my hair, fidgeting. Aubrey pushes through us, bold as ever, her ten-dollar bill readied in her hand.

"Ten, right? I'm so in."

The woman accepts the money, then motions to the small table near the bay window. Streams of light filter in, blocked only by the shade from the trees outside. She points to a seat, saying, "Sit," before walking around to the other side of the table, sweeping her long skirt up before seating herself.

Aubrey plops down onto the chair as Piper and I stand behind her with piqued curiosity, glancing at each other and trying not to smile. The woman flips over a gold-rimmed porcelain teacup, pouring in water and adding some herbs. My nose scrunches up at the smell, but she looks up, making me dart my head down.

Whoops.

Aubrey takes a whiff and laughs, "Gnarly," but the woman says nothing as she places a deck of tarot cards on the table.

Piper furrows her brow. "I thought it was a tea reading?"

Those dark eyes flick up, the hint of a smile on her lips. "It is."

Piper's eyes swing to mine, both of us still trying not to smile, watching as she shuffles the cards before looking at Aubrey and saying, "Drink. All of it at once. Then turn the cup over."

I'm staring, fascinated, as Aubrey gulps the tea back, doing what she's told.

The woman lifts the cup, staring down at the broken pieces of herbs strewn over the table. An indent forms between her eyes as she flips over a card. She stares at it, a heart with three swords stabbed into it.

That can't be good.

She goes back to the leaves and then flips another card, her hand immediately covering it before she shakes her head.

"What does it say?" Aubrey blurts out. "Is my future that dismal? Great. There goes my hope for Chase."

"Don't make her state the obvious," Piper chuckles under her breath, but the woman's head lifts, eyes locked on mine.

"This card." She holds up the heart with the swords. "It means heartbreak." I dart my eyes to Piper, slightly freaked-out that the woman is staring at me so intensely. "And this one—" She holds up the one she'd covered. A grim reaper dressed as a knight riding a horse. "—this means death, endings."

"But I didn't drink the tea," I whisper, not knowing what to say, drawing my arms behind me.

"Mon amie, the stars and moon are already in motion." She drops the card in her hand next to the other, my eyes following. "Your love will end tragically—he won't save you."

I lift my gaze, words stuck in my throat as she looks deeply into my eyes.

"But *you* will save him."

Chills explode over my body, eyes searching hers, almost feeling like I want to cry. Like I can feel the end of a story I've never read.

Piper grabs my hand, giggling, "Oh my God," before covering her mouth as she pulls me out of the store. I glance back at the woman, who's watching me the whole way out. Aubrey joins, laughing hysterically.

They're both speaking at the same time as I blink, trying to make sense of what just happened.

"What was that?" … "She was so weird. Your love will end tragically…um, okay, freak."

Piper wipes a tear from her eye from laughing so hard as we hurry down the street before our feet slow, and their amusement tapers off.

Aubrey smiles, holding up the ten-dollar bill that she apparently took back, shaking it. "Let's get cupcakes since I didn't get my fucking leaves read by the witch."

Piper claps her hands with a gleeful "Yes. Sugar is life" as I smile, turning toward the store, still weirded out. I shift my face to Aubrey's to say something, but my words are cut off.

"Holy fuckballs, who's that?" Aubrey snaps, grabbing my hand and pointing toward the street. My head follows, goose bumps blooming over my fair skin before my eyes land on a car full of guys passing in a matte-black Mustang.

Whoa. They do *not* belong here.

It's like one of those movie moments—the car rolling by slowly, my breath held as I lick my lips—locked in a moment I'm trying to memorize and live at the same time.

The sandy-haired driver has a cigarette dangling from his full lips. He lifts his chin, showing off a jawline that looks like it could take a punch or makes you want to run your tongue over it all the way to the tattoo on his neck.

Jesus, he's the definition of bad ideas with one hand on the steering wheel as the other hangs lazily out of the window. His fingers, adorned with thick black rings, tap to the beat of the music filtering from the window.

But if the music isn't enough to draw scowls as they come to a stop at the crosswalk, his foul mouth does the job.

"It's rude to point," Piper offers, lowering Aubrey's finger. "But damn. When did *Sons of Anarchy* move in? That's hot."

Hot isn't the word. That's too tame for them. I don't even need to completely see them to know that.

The engine growls, idling, making me blink rapidly from my trance. I tug my hand from Aubrey, stepping forward, and loop my arm around a black lamppost, my curiosity urging me on for a better look.

With my mouth slightly agape, I let the tip of my sneaker hang over the edge of the sidewalk. I look stupid, but I don't care. It's not every day that a bunch of tattooed outsiders find themselves in a place like St. Simeon.

"Holy shit. St. Simeon just became interesting." Aubrey laughs behind me, pulling me backward.

I'm nodding, captivated by the tattoo on the driver's hand, trying to make out what it is, as two women make their way across the crosswalk. The Miss Manners duo all but clutch their pearls as they stare at Main Street's newest fascinations through the windshield.

From where I stand, I can only see the driver's profile.

"Ugh. I can't see his whole face."

Aubrey clutches my hand, settling shoulder to shoulder with me as the car's engine revs—making me jump, Aubrey laugh, and the women move faster.

"Animals," she snarks, shaking her head.

The driver flicks his cigarette toward the street, laughing as one of the women gasps.

He's an asshole, not an animal. But that laugh—so deep and carnal. Piper comes up on the other side of me, staring up at my face with a grin.

"I smell the need for a confession coming on. No hate. That jawline alone puts him in my dream rotation."

I giggle as Aubrey exhales, "Jesus," and fans herself.

"It's a good thing we go to Catholic school—because those dudes' vibes were immaculate, and staring at them definitely got me pregnant."

Piper reaches behind me, shoving Aubrey's shoulder. "You have to be a virgin for that…"

"Shut your blasphemous mouth. I am still a virgin because anal counts in the tally too, bitch."

They start playfully sparring back and forth, but I'm not paying attention. My eyes are on the set of taillights turning the corner. Until the feeling of someone watching me has my head shifting to look over my shoulder.

The woman with those dark eyes and even darker words makes the sign of the cross before walking back inside the shop.

"Dad?" The door slams behind me as I walk inside my house. "Mom? Hello? Anyone?"

"Sutton," I hear my mom call from her office off the entryway. "In here."

Peeking my head inside the door, I see her sitting at her desk, papers littered across the surface. Her sleek blonde tresses shine like she's in one of those hair commercials as her blue eyes affix to mine.

"How was your day, kid? Aubrey and Piper exhaust you too much with all the shopping? I still don't understand why you need to shop for clothes this much when you wear a uniform most days."

I shrug with a smile. "What about all the free-dress days and the dances? And don't forget the wild parties and secret trips into the city we take and never tell you about. And the most obvious is summer. I can't just wear a bathing suit every day. That's indecent— so say the nuns."

She piles a manila folder on top of the impossibly high stack next to her.

"And yet, you own enough to do so. Just make sure everything is front page appropriate."

I roll my eyes, walking inside as she gestures for me to sit down.

"Back to your day."

Plopping down on the chenille armchair in front of her glass desk, I relax back, doing what we always do. She pretends to listen as I speak, and I only give her the headlines. It's almost like a real family.

"Well, in order, it was boring. Boring. Boring. Then way less boring."

Her perfectly shaped brows raise. "Oh yeah? Definitely start with the less boring part, please."

I wrap my hand around the ends of my long copper hair and pull my legs up to sit crisscross as she takes another file from the stack, looking it over.

"Well...you'll never believe what I saw downtown today. There were these boys—well, not really boys—and also this super-strange lady giving like tarot slash tea leaf readings. It was weird—"

Before I can finish, my father bursts through the doorway, tossing a newspaper onto the desk as he stalks toward it.

"Did you see this?"

My mother scrambles for the paper as my head shifts between them. My father's face grows crimson as his voice gets louder, making me jump.

"Read it."

I stare at my mother's surprised face before I look over at the fury scrawled over my father's. The words on the tip of my tongue are swallowed because I'm too scared to draw his attention.

She shakes her head.

"This is a commercial real estate announcement, Baron." Confusion mars her brow. "I don't under—"

"Look at the goddamn name, Elizabeth," he barks, cutting her off. "Look at who bought up all those properties across the tracks."

My father slaps the paper from her hand back to the desk, stabbing his finger on it, and I quickly cover the shriek that shoots from my mouth, drawing their attention.

My father straightens, motioning toward the door dismissively. "A moment, Sutton."

I stand quickly, nodding as I walk toward the door, hearing, "That scum takes my town over my dead body."

Chapter Two

Sutton

G olden sunrays bathe my cheeks as I lift my face toward the sky. Eyes closed. Mind quiet. My Doc Marten–adorned heels bounce off the cement wall I'm perched on as the chatter from my friends becomes muffled.

I take a deep breath, drawing in the ocean air, and feel my shoulders relax. A smile begins to bloom on my lips as tiny birds chirp their songs and the leaves on the nearest tree rustle.

May's always warm on St. Simeon, but this year it's as if summer's come early. I can almost smell the scent of the coconut oil that'll replace all the musty library books and taste the cherry Popsicles that'll become my only communion—no more nuns, homework, or mass on the first Friday instead of pep rallies.

One more week and goodbye, junior year.

"Sutton, are you listening to me?"

A faint breeze carries a stray copper tendril over my lip, getting it stuck on my gloss as I soak up the moment. I brush the strand away as Aubrey's voice cracks through my daydream.

"Hello?"

Shh, I think, but my smile gives away that I've heard her.

Piper tsks. "No. She isn't. Her head is in the clouds, as usual. A penny for your thoughts, Sut. Although, I bet I can guess."

I don't move from my sun worship as I answer.

"If you must know, I'm thinking about how this is always my favorite time of the year. There's something kind of sexy about it. You know?" My hands grip the cement as I tip my chin a bit higher. "It sounds weird, but it's like all of a sudden, the sun comes out, and everything comes to life. Like the world becomes more vivid. Even the stars shine brighter."

There's silence, and then they both laugh.

"Oh my God, you dreamy bitch." Aubrey gently pinches my arm. "Open your eyes. I need you on planet Earth. Stat."

She's only half-joking. My friends are used to me. They should be, considering our whole lives have been intertwined since birth. We're the three musketeers, minus the swords and the unknown fourth member. *Why do people even say "three" musketeers? It's so misleading.*

"Hello. Eyes. Open."

Knowing I got lost in thought again, I grin as a contented sigh drifts from between my lips. My chin lowers, emerald eyes reopening, ready to join the conversation with a laughed, "What?"

Aubrey holds her phone to my face, showing me her Instagram feed. *Ah, that's what.* There's a photo of a senior she likes named Chase. His arm is wrapped around a girl she despises, named Chloe. The caption reads:

All my sunsets belong to you.

"Gross," I answer like a good friend. "And ironic, since that photo was taken in the middle of the day. Sunset?"

"Exactly," Piper adds. "You dodged a 'dumbass' bullet. He's totally the kind of guy that doesn't know the diff between *your* and *you're*."

We're nodding as a hint of a smile graces Aubrey's face before disappearing just as quickly. I frown down, sticking out my bottom lip, but she rolls her eyes, acting like she doesn't care—even though she's still scrolling.

Boys are dubious creatures. They always assure you that they mean what they say but never seem to do what they mean. Aubrey looks up, attempting to mask her feelings.

"Whatever. He's a shitty lacrosse player anyway. And a terrible kisser. He basically tried to french my tonsils."

Piper lies over my lap, propping her chin on her hand as we both watch Aubrey pull shades from her bag and squint into the sun before putting them on.

"Aubs—" Piper offers, extending her other hand, but Aubrey ignores the gesture, changing the subject.

"I'm fine. I'm so ready for a tan *and* for all the families that come to summer. I wonder if we'll see those Hillcrest boys again? Which one did I think was cute?"

Piper glances up at me with a smile but answers Aubrey. "Um... both."

Aubrey smirks. "That's right. Choices are the key ingredient to a happy life. You can write that down."

"Whore," Piper mouths, eliciting a chuckle from me.

"I saw that. And speaking of whores." Aubrey closes in on me, motioning with her chin over my shoulder and whispering, "Hunter's here."

Piper stands, looking behind me, but I don't dare do the same. I can't.

I know my cheeks are already red.

Hunter is *that guy* at St. Simeon-Burr Catholic Prep, Burr for short. He plays every sport and wins. Excels academically. He's the one everyone listens to and wants to emulate.

And to add insult to injury, Hunter has flawless hair, a perfectly tanned six-pack, and is blessed with eyes almost as seductive as his pedigree.

He's the All-American golden-boy type.

And last week, that golden boy called me Freckles.

It was a two-second interaction, but enough to be kind of memorable. I was on the field taking some last-minute makeup photos for the yearbook. One minute I'm hidden behind my camera, and then the next, he's right there next to me.

"Want to take my photo?"

I keep my eye against the viewer, heart racing, trying to play it cool.

"I didn't realize you were in Band too."

He laughs, and I sneak a quick glance, still pretending to take photos. His thumbs are tucked under the straps of his backpack. And—Oh. My. God—he's shirtless. I'd shake his parents' hands if I could. Well done, Kellys.

"I'm not. I was at swim practice."

Lacrosse, crew, swim—he really does do everything.

I don't answer, clicking at nothing because what else am I going to do? Hunter doesn't move or offer anything else as he stands next to me, making the butterflies in my stomach flutter like a tornado.

We may have known each other our whole lives, but I've never been on his radar, like ever. And I'm starting to feel grateful because I feel too nervous to speak.

"So?" he laughs, bumping my shoulder. "Are you going to talk to me or what?"

Swinging my camera lens toward his face, I click without warning, grinning when he jumps.

"Hey. No fair. You didn't tell me to say cheese."

I lower my camera and shrug, chewing the inside of my cheek. His smile grows, gleaming white teeth on display. Hunter steps in closer, crowding my space, but I don't back away, feet rooted to the turf, lump in my throat.

He bends forward, his face so close that I stop breathing.

"Well, whaddya know? I like 'em. A lot."

He straightens as he presses his thumb to his bottom lip and sweeps it across. My eyes obediently watch.

Hunter's feet carry him backward a few steps before he turns to leave. When he does, my body finally unfreezes, heat burning my cheeks as I call out.

"Wait. What does that mean—you like 'em?"

Hunter looks over his shoulder, giving me a wink. "See you around, Freckles."

Laughter from under a sprawling oak tree draws my attention, quieting the memory. A group of freshman boys in khakis are huddled together, playfully shoving each other while taking quick glances at some girls in tartan plaid school skirts like mine.

"Sut." Aubrey nudges me. "Hunter's so hot. You need to secure that boy."

"Leave her alone. Maybe she's not into him, Aubs. Not everyone wants to date a god."

"Zip it," I hiss, watching her wink.

Aubrey spins around quickly. "Oh my God. He's totally looking over here. Smile at him or something, Sutton. Go. Do it now."

I shake my head quickly. "No. Nooo. No way. That's dumb."

Piper speaks to my profile, keeping her lips together to pretend she isn't talking.

"Just, like, look over your shoulder. Like in a movie, all slow and hair flippy. Give him a tiny smile. Trust me, it works in every Netflix movie."

I take a breath, trying not to laugh. "Oh sure, if it's good enough for Netflix. Because that's real life. I mean, maybe if he were Jacob Elordi—"

"Get in the car, Elle!" Piper growls, quoting *The Kissing Booth* and making us laugh before adding, "Just do it, chicken."

Aubrey pokes me. "Do it, ya dirty virgin."

Ugh, she had to go there. It's the equivalent of a double-dog dare.

A groan rattles my chest. "I hate you two so much. Like a tremendous amount of despising is happening inside of my body right now."

"Yeah, but our hymens aren't begging, pleading, to be broken."

Piper laughs as Aubrey sticks her tongue out at me while I attempt to hide my smile.

I seriously dislike being the only one of the three of us with absolutely zero experience. Maybe not zero. Fingers, sure. Kissing, yes. Even a good dry hump has happened. But I'm sans all the rest of the goodies in the sex department. And it sucks. Times are starting to feel a bit desperate over here because, at this rate, I'll be a forty-year-old virgin.

Then again, that almost seems like a better idea than flirting back with Hunter. Because Piper's right. I am too chicken. Especially with Hunter—because, Jesus…he's Hunter.

Rubbing my lips together, I hope for the bravery I need before steeling my spine. Another giggle escapes. *This is so dumb.*

My forefinger picks at the Tiffany blue polish on my thumbnail as I swallow and casually glance over my shoulder, trying to ignore Aubrey moaning, "Oh, Hunter. Yes. Right there. It's so big. Put it in my butt."

I scream and turn back, laughing, shoving Aubrey's shoulder.

"Would you stop? You're a child. I hate you. Do you want me to be a virgin forever?"

Piper's still grinning as she makes a "zip the lips" motion to a more subdued Aubrey, who just winks at me. I take another deep breath and sweep my hair over my shoulder, going in for the kill, but as my cheek touches my shoulder, it's not Hunter I see.

My bottom lip draws between my teeth as everything around me goes silent. It's like two hands are holding the sides of my face, locking me into place—right onto the boys from the wrong side of everything.

I haven't seen them around since that first day, but I also haven't forgotten any detail either. I bet everyone that was there remembers. It's impossible to forget. It was the most exciting thing to happen in St. Simeon since forever.

Those boys driving on Main Street were a greasy smudge on a high tea white dress. A Wednesday tainted by inconvenience in the elitist eyes that followed them down our fancy tree-lined streets.

Streets chock-full of French bakeries like St. Honoré Boulangerie and picture-perfect window displays. All worthy of a magazine spread. All unwelcome to them.

But here they are, thirty-six days since they made their debut driving down that street, standing on the basketball court on our side of town.

"He's smiling, Sutton," Aubrey whispers.

I swallow, eyes ticking toward Hunter, because I know that's who she's talking about, before slingshotting right back to where they shouldn't be.

They don't look like any boys I've ever seen. Not even the ones from the side of town I'm not allowed to visit—their side. Two of them look older, but one seems about my age. Are they brothers? No. There's zero family resemblance.

My eyes roam over them, their backs to me, wondering if any of the boys I know could ever grow up to look like that.

The one that's hot in a "street" kind of way—lean with an angular jaw and black shaved hair—like a guy that would be in a fight club, laughs loudly while taking a practice shot. My eyes follow him as he jogs toward the ball, laughing as he easily fights off the one who looks my age.

That guy seems easy in charm, armed with a dimple that would make you drop your panties on the first date, and long cross earrings. Nothing about him screams religion, so that's definitely for looks. He lifts his cap, exposing tousled honey-brown, curly hair before twisting it backward. The motion makes his bicep flex as he snugs it back onto his head.

Damn. Hello Vinnie Hacker look-alike.

I'm mesmerized, caught in the moment, staring at them until Baseball Cap calls, "Calder," toward the sideline. My eyes shoot to the profile I haven't stopped thinking about—the driver. He turns, giving me his whole face. Dark lashes imprison stormy blue eyes laid out for adoration on smooth tan skin.

Suddenly, my throat is dry, like dying in the desert kind of dry.

Even from here, I feel the same thing I felt standing on that sidewalk—tingles up my spine. My heart rate picks up when my eyes lock on Calder, my lips quietly forming the word, cementing *that* name to *that* face.

I bite my lip as Calder swipes a water bottle from the asphalt, highlighting the veins in his forearm. His head swings sideways toward Hunter's group as he twists the lid, and I can't help but shift my focus to Hunter, wondering how he's reacting.

Oh. He's pissed, arms crossed, facing Calder with a look that can only be described as *wrong neighborhood.*

It is the wrong neighborhood. There are courts over the tracks. But Calder commands attention like he's entitled to it, and I guarantee he doesn't give a fuck about who's watching or from where they're doing it. That much is obvious.

This should be interesting.

Calder winks at him, tipping the water bottle back, dismissing Hunter like he doesn't matter. *Don't laugh, Sutton*—not that I would…well, maybe a little—but I'm too busy watching Calder's Adam's apple dip as he gulps, making me do a slow blink. *Jesus. H. Christ.*

My gaze stays locked on him as he tosses the empty bottle in the trash before dragging his black T-shirt over his head. My thighs squeeze together, watching his muscles ripple as he exposes the black band of his boxer briefs that peek out from under his basketball shorts.

"Skins," he bellows, tossing the shirt to the ground.

Calder's painted shoulders are broad but not bulky, more like defined. He looks built for aggression, not gentleness. Even his hands seem as if the softest touch would leave a mark.

That thought makes me shiver, but also, something about it makes me want to stare longer.

"Sutton," I hear Piper say.

Before I can answer, the sound of sneakers squeaking against the pavement invades my ears. The basketball beats against the pavement with a thunderous force, sounding a lot like my heart right now.

"Sutton," she presses, but I'm lost to watching them play.

No. Watching Calder play.

The longer I stare, the more time begins moving in slow motion. I can hear my blood pumping through my veins as all the thoughts in my head die.

Calder's glistening, sweat-beaded body penetrates my focus. He jogs backward, his long fingers flicking at the bottom of his black Nike basketball shorts, tugging them up to his muscular thighs as he crouches, ready to defend his side of the court.

My tongue darts out to wet my dry lips, and I swallow, rocking forward on the wall, fingers digging into the concrete. He's—So.

Fucking. Hot.

My entire body feels tense and achy as Calder steals the ball. He runs it down between the guys for a lay-up, landing back on his feet and combing his hand through the top of his sandy undercut.

What would it feel like between my thighs? I bet it would tickle my—

"Oh my God, Sutton," Aubrey cackles. "You are so horny for the town criminal."

I blink quickly and turn my head, embarrassed. "Do you ever shut up?"

Aubrey's eyes grow wide, amused that she's right, as Piper links her arm to mine, looking in the guys' direction.

"Sutton," Piper teases, making me grin, "the only thing you're getting from boys like that is a felony record and an unwanted pregnancy."

"Mmhmm—" I answer absentmindedly. "You guys are snobs."

I feel a harmless pinch to my arm from Aubrey. "Sutton…Piper. Seriously. Stop staring. People will see. Plus, Hunter'll think you're uninterested."

I linger one last glance at Calder dunking the basketball before settling back on Aubrey's annoyed face, tossing her words from earlier back at her for fun.

"I thought choices were the key ingredient to a happy life?"

She laughs and sticks her tongue out at me, reaching up to tug a piece of my hair.

"Very funny. But I meant good, excellent, non-'possibly' criminal choices." I roll my eyes as she bends down for her bag, saying, "Ooh, that reminds me."

I shrug, looking out at the trees.

"Don't you wonder about them? They've lived here for a month, and they're such a mystery—what does anyone even know?"

Piper shrugs. "Other than they make you want to make bad

decisions? Nothing, I guess. But they're Eastsiders. What do we know about anyone that lives over there?"

Aubrey huffs, squatting and almost falling onto her butt. "Umm, exactly. I don't sit around thinking about those thugs just like I don't ponder all about herpes, and neither should you, bitch."

We laugh at her, Piper rolling gloss over her lips as she looks down at Aubrey, who's still rummaging around in her bag.

"Oh my God. You said thugs? Really? You sound like an eighty-year-old woman." Piper bumps her polo-covered shoulder to my arm. "And who are you kidding, Aubs? You told me you'd let them do bad things to your body after we saw them."

"Oh really?" I beam, eyes jumping to Aubrey, whose own are now narrowed on Piper as she stands.

"Never happened," Aubrey offers, almost sincerely.

Piper raises her brows. "Liar. Liar. Pants not even on fire because you're slutty."

A laugh cracks in my chest, even though I try and hold it back. Aubrey joins in before saying, "I hate you," making us all laugh even more before my head sweeps back over my shoulder to steal another peek.

The ball bounces off the backboard and bounds over toward where Hunter and his friends are. Baseball Cap jogs up, motioning for it back, but Shephard, Hunter's best friend, holds it in his hand, staring them down.

"The ball," he requests, only barely friendly, but nobody moves. *Whoa.*

Piper and I exchange a nervous glance, her whispering, "Are they going to fight?"

All eyes in the park are fixed on them. Piper grabs my knee as Fight Club cracks his neck, stalking toward Hunter's crew. Everyone in the park is buzzing with the anticipation of a battle. Even me, seeing as my mouth refuses to close as I watch with eyes open wide.

"Roman."

Calder's command shakes my chest and halts Fight Club's—now known as Roman—steps. I didn't even realize I was holding my breath until Aubrey laughs, and I suck one in.

"Oh yeah. Not thugs at all. Come on, horndogs. Let the animals entertain the masses. I have a surprise."

Aubrey grabs my wrist, tugging me off the wall, and I nab Piper's wrist, making us a little chain gang as Aubrey hauls us away. But I glance back, only to see Calder staring down Hunter until the sound of the ball bouncing on asphalt becomes a waved white flag.

Damn. That was intense.

Chapter Three

Sutton

Piper and I follow quickly behind Aubrey now that the almost throw-down is over. We disappear behind the bathrooms before coming to a stop.

"What are we doing, Aubrey?" Piper laughs before blanching. "Eww, it smells like pee back here."

I smile, saying, "Boys' side," before dropping her wrist.

Aubrey looks over her shoulder, then puts her finger to her lip, telling us to be quiet, before holding her hand up. She wags her perfectly arched black eyebrows while shaking a small white-and-red square box.

"Look."

I slap a hand over my mouth, laughing as Piper stares between us.

"Oh my God. You stole cigarettes." Piper smacks my arm. "She stole cigarettes."

Aubrey opens the box, and I lift my chin, trying to peer past her hands. She hands a long white stick to each of us before digging around her purse again.

It's so dumb, but we made a pact a couple of weeks ago during a sleepover that quickly became a joint breakdown over how shitty and uneventful high school has been. I came up with the idea of a list of ridiculous stuff we wanted to check off our high school experiences before we graduate.

This is Aubrey's because she's obsessed with Audrey Hepburn and thinks channeling her through smoking will improve her luck with boys. Piper's is to sneak into Manhattan for a whole night because if there were ever anyone who wanted out of this town and into the real world more than me, it's Piper. Mine is to lose my dumb virginity. I'm done with the idea of falling hopelessly in love and sharing some magical experience. It's not happening for me.

So, now I kind of just want to get fucked and move on. Just rip the Band-Aid off so that when my real life starts, I'll be ready for it.

"Dammit. Dumb lighter—" Aubrey mutters to herself.

"Are we really doing this?" Piper questions, looking around nervously.

I get her nerves. But we're doing this. Aubrey lifts her head for a moment, letting out a frustrated breath.

"We're in high school, Piper, and the worst thing we've done is nothing."

"You've done plenty," Piper counters, rolling her eyes, making me laugh again.

"Regardless." Aubrey huffs. "I need a life. We need a life. Junior year's been a wasted experience with boys that don't like me back."

She lowers her voice to sound like my dad. "And lame 'you may only attend parentally supervised parties,' thanks to Sutton's overprotective dad. We finally all got cute at the same time—braces off, boobs on. We can't chance another gap year."

I internally cringe because she's right. The fact that they've lived my miserable party existence with me and never complained makes them the truest ride or dies. And she's right—freshman and sophomore year was like RIP to love. I can't even think about it. I may have PTSD over my hair alone.

"Don't worry, Piper," Aubrey continues. "God will forgive us. And if the extra Hail Mary those witches made me say counts today—then my soul is safe." She gives us a wink. "At least until next week."

I bump a hip to Piper's, who smiles back, giving in. Aubrey looks inside her bag again before holding up the lighter victoriously.

"Got it."

She steps in closer, the click sounding around us as I lean forward. I'm trying to act like a natural, even though I don't know what I'm doing.

Piper's watching me, pointing a finger toward the butt.

"I think you have to, like, inhale really big to make it stay lit."

The burn filters into my mouth as I take quick draws like I've seen my father do with his cigars, but it doesn't stay lit.

Aubrey smirks, clicking the lighter again to relight mine.

"I bet your criminal shares these with the girls he sleeps with, like after doing the deed—they lie there naked and share a cigarette, letting the high they feel fade away as they smoke."

"No, like a deep inhale," Piper instructs, taking hers and pretending to inhale dramatically to show me.

So I suck in, hollowing my cheeks as the tip glows red, just before my chest heaves, rejecting my stupid idea and leaving me in a coughing fit.

Piper starts smacking my back. "Oh my God, Sutton. Are you okay?"

Aubrey cackles as I open my mouth to speak, only to heave out another cough just as footsteps accompanied by a husky voice turns the corner.

"Oh fuck," Aubrey whispers, still laughing, shoving the pack back into her bag and hiding the evidence of our stupidity. We're like stooges, turning in circles and bumping into each other as I keep coughing.

"You good?" The rough baritone makes us freeze. Aubrey's laughter murdered.

Rich chocolate-brown eyes stare back at me—Roman.

He's focused on me. And what was so hot about him from far away feels intimidating now. Especially since his question might've seemed friendly, but *he* definitely isn't.

Roman's glare shifts to Piper, making her shrink back, and then to Aubrey as if he's working out everything that just happened. I push into Aubrey, taking her hand in a vise grip, forcing us to take a step backward, when my attention's stolen by a chuckle.

The other guy, Ball cap, strides up, propping his elbow on Roman's shoulder, his thumbnail finding his teeth as he stares at us, a smirk on his face. He leans into Roman, saying something in his ear—something that faintly sounded like "Dibs on, Red" before Roman says, "Chill, West," under his breath as he looks back, drawing his bottom lip between his teeth and letting it out slowly.

My heart is racing, not because I'm scared, but I'm also not stupid—they feel unrestrained under the guise of civility. I swallow, looking between them, feeling overwhelmed by the intensity of their stare.

Hold on—West, and Roman. That means… *Shit.*

Goose bumps explode over my body because my eyes know just where to go as Calder rounds the corner. The bluest pools I've ever seen fix on me, arresting my lungs like my heart, making the cough that wants out burn worse.

Calder looks at his friends, giving nothing away before turning back to *me*—not *us*—his blue eyes never drifting from mine. The black T-shirt he took off earlier is draped over his shoulder. All of his smooth olive-colored skin is on display underneath the intricate details of the raven on his chest.

"Sut, we need to go," Aubrey whispers in my ear, but I don't know what's wrong with me. My eyes refuse to look away from his.

I'm slowly tugged backward, my feet begrudgingly moving. Aubrey's hand tightens around my wrist, her nails accidentally digging into my skin, and I wince.

Calder's jaw tenses, eyes dropped to where she's holding me before he brings them back.

I swear to God, I almost twist from Aubrey, but another step has me exhaling and then another forcing me to spin around. I blink, rubbing my lips together, feeling my heart begin to slow, just as a rough hand wraps heavily around my other wrist, turning me to stone.

My head swivels in time with my hand being lifted, a faint "*Oh shit*" heard in the background.

Calder bends forward, close to my face, eyes level to mine, as he brings my palm toward his face.

My lips part, watching him bring his mouth to the cigarette held between my fingers. *I'm still holding the cigarette. How the hell did I miss that?*

The light blond stubble under his bottom lip shines in the sunlight as he nabs the end between his teeth, drawing my eyes to his lips that have the faintest glisten as if he just licked them.

His brows draw together as he stares at me, making him look like some kind of fallen angel. Like the ones from the Catholic Church's stained glass windows—the angels with blood on their swords and anger in their eyes as they fight for the heavens.

Seconds that feel like minutes tick by as Calder says nothing, eyes locked on mine, stealing all my rational thought.

Because he has that same storm behind his eyes.

And as strange as it sounds, it makes him beautiful, like an exquisitely broken soul at war with himself and everyone else around him.

He gives a slight tug for me to release the smoke. But I'm liquified—a total waste. Completely lost to him. His fingertips snake up my palm, making me draw in a breath before he weaves his thick digits between mine, forcing my fingers to spread and release the cigarette.

My chest rises and falls too fast—way too fast. But I can't control it.

As he lets go of my hand, Calder's lips drag slowly up my fingers, and my eyes almost roll into the back of my head.

If he saw, I'd never know because Calder is unreadable, staring down at me at his full height, with *my* Marlboro Red between his lips.

He sucks in the tobacco, releasing a plume without so much as touching the damn thing, eyes still on mine, unwavering.

Oh. My. God.

Calder pulls the cigarette from his lips between pinched fingers, letting his eyes drift down my body, giving me a once-over. Then he turns, leaving me in a puddle, and walks into the men's bathroom.

Not one of them looks back even once. Even as laughter erupts behind me, accompanied by "Did that just happen?" and "What the fuck?" pelting down simultaneously.

But I don't have any answers. I'm dumbstruck because Calder just lived up to every fantasy I've had of him since the first day I saw him.

Chapter Four

Sutton

"Whoa. Where's the fire?"

My feet skid to a stop, and my hair swings across my face, but I smile brightly, hoping to avoid a lecture about rushing. My father's standing in the marbled entry of our home, arms crossed over his chest, dressed in one of his signature black suits. I knew he was flying in from DC today. I just didn't think he'd be home right now.

"Sorry, Dad. I wish I could stay, but Piper's qualifying meet is about to start. Aubrey and I promised we wouldn't miss it. She needs her cheering section so she can kill it and level up next year. Mom said it was okay."

He's nodding, but there's worry on his face. His eyes dart to the already opened front door, then back.

"You can take the town car. My driver's still here."

I look over my shoulder to see the driver carrying his bags inside.

"It's okay. I'm good to drive myself."

He holds up a hand. "Sutton. Hold on. While I was away, I heard there was some trouble at the park on Thursday. Some boys from Eastside."

I shake my head and shrug as if I don't know what he's talking about. *Snitches get stiches, Dad.*

And technically, there wasn't any trouble. Nobody actually fought, so I'm not lying.

He checks his phone, ignoring a text before walking toward me.

"Three brothers. You're sure you didn't see anything?"

So they are brothers.

My head shakes again.

"I'm surprised. Those Wolfe boys caused quite a ruckus at the park you kids like to hang out at. I know there had to be some talk."

His last name's Wolfe…it suits him.

"Nope. No talk."

More like a morbid fascination dipped in obsession from the amount of conversation that's happened at school.

I shrug, keeping my eyes up so he doesn't catch on to my little white lie. Lying isn't something I often do with my father, but yesterday is on a *need-to-know* basis. He definitely does not need to know why I left and didn't see everything. The lecture on smoking from the man on the Senate Health Committee would be one of epic proportions.

"Sutton. I'm sure someone said something. Did you see them at the park?"

I nod, shifting my stance and drawing an arm behind my back, trying to think of a clever subject change as I answer.

"I think so. Maybe. I don't remember. I was busy hating on a boy that Aubrey likes while we scrolled Insta. Hey, speaking of social media, Mom said you made huge waves on the Hill this week, even made the cut for Trevor Noah's Twitter."

A rare grin graces his face. "My task force to combat organized crime was approved. We're set to go after the lowest forms of humanity—starting with the O'Bannions and their Italian counterpart, the Sovranos."

"Wow, that's great." *Mission accomplished.* "And now the press can stop hammering you about meeting your campaign promises."

He steps in front of me, staring down, dismay on his brow. "So, I take it from all this bait-and-switch that you *did* see the ruckus. Nice try though."

Shoot.

"Define ruckus—because if you mean Hunter Kelly and his band of merry preppies marking their territory, then fine, yes, I saw. But boys will be boys, right?"

He chuckles, saying, "Good," looking pleased. Of course he does, because there's nothing more appealing to a walking legacy than misogyny. My father is a good man, but elitists will be elitists.

"But if you mean anything else, then sorry, Senator, I know about as much as you." I hook a thumb over my shoulder. "As much as I'm enjoying this inquisition, I seriously have to jet."

He's already waving me off. "All right, smart-ass. Get lost. But stay out of trouble. I will not tolerate poor press."

"Okay," I answer, only half-heartedly rolling my eyes, but he gives me that look. The one that says he's serious.

I nod, knowing he means what he says.

"Okay, Dad." When he narrows his eyes at me, I smile, adding, "I promise," and crisscross a finger over my heart.

Aubrey swings her jet-black hair over her shoulder. "Dude. Piper smoked everyone. I'm so proud."

I smile, agreeing, "She did amazing. I don't even know why she was worried."

The smell of chlorine infiltrates my nose as we stand in the walkway between the bleachers and the pool, waiting for her to dry off and get dressed.

Aubrey looks around the pool, rolling her eyes as she spots Chloe before turning her attention back to me.

"Do you think she's cuter than me?"

"No. Not at all. She's cute. You're gorgeous. There's no comparison, Aubs."

It's a good pep talk, but I'm also not lying. Aubrey's beautiful, armed with delicate features, an aristocratic nose, and soulful brown eyes—all bestowed on her by her Brazilian and Japanese descent. Sometimes I'm jealous of how effortless her beauty seems.

Too bad for her she doesn't feel the way she looks—superior.

"Hey," she says, mischief in her eyes, "there's a party tonight. And it's at Hunter's. Tag's throwing it. Now that he's on probation from Yale, he has too much free time on his hands. Yay us."

My head's already shaking as I sidestep water droplets launched off a swim cap as some girl removes it. Tag is a notorious douchebag slash former god at St. Simeon. He's also Hunter's older brother.

"A Tag party is out of our league, Aubrey. Like, way out."

She grabs my elbow, hauling me over to the bleachers to sit, whispering, "Sutton. This is a once-in-a-lifetime opportunity. Tag's parties are legendary."

"No way. First off, the senator would never let me go. In case you've forgotten, he'd be saying no because everyone remembers what happened at Tag's parties. Sex, drugs, and more drugs. Again I say—out of our league."

"Oh my God." Her voice rises. "Can you please think outside of the box and stop being such a perfect daughter. I swear, if I left our social existence up to you and Piper, we'd be fucking doomed."

A throat clearing makes us sit up straighter. Aubrey gives a tight smile, looking over my shoulder.

"Sorry, Sister."

Three nuns in full habit, cloth sweeping the wet ground, pass by. Their glares issue a silent judgment, no doubt having just heard Aubrey's foul mouth. But she doesn't care, giggling as they walk out of earshot.

I smile but narrow my eyes at her.

She waves me off.

"Come on, Sutton. We don't have to do meth, dude. And as for your 'rents, tell the senator you're sleeping over at my place. My parents are gone for the weekend, and our new housesitter will cover so long as I line her pockets. Piper can say the same. Nobody will know. You promised."

God, I did. I promised to make our party life happen, but I was tipsy after we'd snuck vodka shots back to Piper's room during our sleepover.

One day I'm positive Aubrey will become an evil genius, masterminding the world like her PR exec mother. But today, she's just a pain in the ass.

"This is a terrible idea. And, might I add, how every unsolved murder begins. Girl lies to parents. Girl goes to a party, only to never be seen again."

She slaps her hand on my leg. "First off, shave your legs. Second, that shit only happens in like the Bahamas."

That makes me laugh as she continues.

"Third, we need a social life, you little weirdo. And *you* need to go and fucking—" she shoots her head over her shoulder to make sure the sisters are still gone, opting to whisper anyway. "—and fucking play tonsil hockey with Hunter. There's no man left behind, Sutton. It's your turn to pop that cherry. And with the hottest guy at fucking Burr. We decided."

I blow out air, making my lips flap.

"Who says Hunter wants to even do *that* with me?"

Her grin is evil because she knows she's got me on board. Of course she does.

"I say. Hunter's fucking DNA says. Man up—we're getting you laid tonight. He's absolutely perfect, and you know he collects virginities the way that nerdy-ass dude you liked freshman year collected Pokémon cards."

I'm frowning, trying to hold back my smile as Piper slides up next to me, staring down.

"So? Are we partying tonight and watching Sut ho out with Hunter?"

My mouth pops open as I look between them, unsurprised but still shocked. I groan unconvincingly because they roll their eyes.

"One of these days, I'm getting new friends. Mark my words, bitches."

I stand at the same time Aubrey does, and Piper links her arm through mine.

"Lies. You'd die without us. Plus, we love you too much to let you go. Now, let's talk strategy."

Chapter Five

Sutton

"**I** can't believe you two talked me into this. If we get caught, I am fully blaming you. Fully. I'll say you drugged me and brought me here."

"Noted." Piper smiles, brushing my hair over my shoulders. "Now, remember the plan. We get drinks. Mingle. Ignore Hunter, and then talk to whatever boy is the closest to him."

Suddenly, panic sets in, and I scrunch my nose.

"And we know this will work because?"

She puts her hands on my bare shoulders. I was feeling brave earlier when I chose to wear a strapless top and high-waisted jeans. But now I feel exposed.

Aubrey looks over her shoulder as she pushes the front door open, letting all the noise spill out.

"Boys are like dogs, Sutton—they hate it when someone else plays with their toys. That's how we know it'll work. Trust us. Plus, you look like a fucking goddess."

My face shoots to Piper's, who's grinning, her lips folded between her teeth.

"Fantastic. I'm a beautiful chew toy," I mutter, but Piper looks thoughtful.

"Beautiful chew toy sounds like a Billie Eilish song."

We laugh as we walk inside. People are scattered around in small groups, holding red Solo cups, talking and hanging out, music subdued in the background. Eyes land on us and leave just as fast as we make our way through the entry, only adding to how awkward I feel.

None of this should be a big deal, but it is for me. I've been complaining about being left behind. But sleeping with someone, in theory, is totally different than doing this shit in real life. *Do I really picture myself all sweaty on some random bed with a bunch of people downstairs? Do I even imagine doing it with Hunter?*

At first, I thought I'd just find some random guy, but then Hunter came out of nowhere. I didn't really see him coming. I mean, it's not as if I'm socially unacceptable. I'm not. I'm a catch, but guys like Hunter run in a faster crowd than I do, which is both a pro and a con.

A pro for him is that he's managed quite the reputation for taking virginities. In the same breath, he seems to leave the girl feeling grateful rather than discarded. It's so weird. But there's never been a complaint lodged, so when he started talking to me, I figured—why not.

A con is that I'll be relegated to the basic bitches of the world that all lost it to Hunter Kelly. That's not really a club I want to join.

But eye on the prize and a means to an end and all.

The other con is how all my bravado is beginning to taste like bile.

Come on, loser, get it together.

Piper's head swings back to me, all smiles before returning to the front.

I got this. It's fine. There's no right way to do it, and if I keep trying to plan it, senior year will suck. College will suck. And then I'll be on my deathbed, just me and my virginity, together forever. BFFs.

No. Hunter's a perfect choice, and if the rumors are true…he's hung. That's a plus, or so I hear. *Ooo, but maybe it would be better the first time with something more midsize. Like something I could have a better handle on.*

Oh my God. What is wrong with me?

"You holding up okay, Sut?" Aubrey laughs, intuitively knowing I'm in my head, as she takes my hand to pull me farther into the house.

I nod in answer, half a smile on my face as we snake through some people. The crack of a cue ball makes my shoulders jump as my eyes swing to a room with an arched entryway, watching some college guys tease the girl they're with. Shifting my head to the other side, I take in a large living room with more people that look way older than us, and worry starts to grow.

"I don't see any other people from our class. You think they'll let us stay?" I whisper into Aubrey's ear.

She points, making me turn my head toward a glass accordion door that's opened to the backyard.

"Whoa."

Kids are everywhere, flanking the rectangular pool that's illuminated by red lights. Past them, stairs lead out to the beach where a bonfire's raging and even more people are partying.

"Jesus, all of Burr is here. Probably Eastside Public too."

Eastside? *Maybe West goes there since he looked younger. Or maybe they all do.*

My dad's voice pushes to the forefront of my mind. *"If they come anywhere near you, I want to know."* No way would they come to a party like this. Then again, they did come to our courts.

Piper smiles at me. "This is a rager. You still think this was a bad idea, Sutton?"

Definitely not now. *Not that I'm hoping to see them.*

"Time to party," Aubrey interjects, stopping us in front of a big silver keg.

Our eyes collectively land on a guy I recognize as a senior named Phillip.

"Ladies." He grins. "Thirsty?"

"Absolutely," Aubrey answers way too seductively, making me and Piper laugh.

"Well, ask and you shall receive, gorgeous."

He hands us each a cup, eyes lingering on Aubrey before Piper pulls her a few feet away, closer to the back doors, with me in tow.

"Pace yourself. He's a skeeze, and everyone knows it," Piper snarks. "I'm only taking the drink because I watched him pour it."

The honey-colored liquid sloshes as I bring it to my nose to sniff, half-joking.

"Um…mine smells like shoe. Is that normal?"

Piper sticks her tongue out at me.

"You drink it. You don't wear it," Aubrey jokes, taking a big gulp, and then she looks at us. "Well? Am I doing this alone? We're here. Finally. All in, sluts."

Piper giggles before holding up her cup, saying, "All in," and takes a drink. She looks at me when she finishes, having chugged the whole thing. So I lift the beer and wink because there's no way I'm doing what I came for without a little liquid courage.

"Bottoms up, and cherries popped."

They both squeal, but as the rim touches my lips, I'm rammed from behind and sent flying. My knees buckle, hands hitting the ground as the cup goes flying but not before I'm drenched in cheap beer.

"What the fuck, dude!" Aubrey yells, shoving some guy.

Piper's at my side in a split second, helping me to stand, darting her glare back behind me as she says, "Are you okay, Sut?"

A slightly slurred, deeper voice behind her cuts in. "Hey, sorry, chick. That was my bad."

"It's fine," I mumble, looking down at my ruined and partially see-through top as I wipe my cheeks.

"Do you want another drink?" the idiot says, making me blow out a frustrated breath.

Piper snaps her fingers. "Dude, get the hell out of here before I—oh."

The change in her tone has my head jerking around to see perfectly tousled hair and an awfully familiar smirk.

Hunter's smile grows, and I turn bright red as I pat the back of my hand over my mouth. His eyes dart to my outfit, then back to my face.

"You look wet."

I smile. I can't help it.

"I feel wet."

Oh God—put the words back in my mouth. My embarrassment isn't helped by my shitty friends that laugh.

"Come on. I can help."

I raise my brows as he takes my hand.

"You can borrow a shirt, Freckles."

Duh. You horny weirdo—he wasn't going to fuck you right here.

"Oh. Yeah. Okay. Cool. Thanks."

"Yeah, you go get that shirt, Sutton." Piper smiles, and Aubrey joins in. "Yeah, take your time choosing the right one. We got all night."

I'll kill them.

Hunter turns, joining both his hands behind his back, holding mine in between them, as he leads me away. *Oh my God* begins running consecutively through my head, as if I'm hyperventilating.

I glance back over my shoulder at Piper and Aubrey, who are doing different versions of hip thrusts.

A giggle escapes before I turn back, knowing they haven't stopped but still trying to play it cool.

Hunter says hello to everyone as we make our way through his massive living room decorated in white—all white. It's sterile. But I bet his parents boast about the clean lines and minimalism. It's something I've heard my mother say, and it seems to fit.

As we walk, I begin to notice the number of curious faces each time they see whose hand he's holding. *Are they surprised he's into me or that I'm into him?*

Or maybe they're all hearing the soundtrack of my life right now—*Another One Bites The Dust*. I have to bite my lip to stop the laugh that wants to shoot out over that thought.

Hunter takes me up the stairs and down a long hallway until everyone from downstairs disappears and we get to what I assume is his bedroom door. He grabs the brushed-gold doorknob, pausing to look over his shoulder at me.

"Have you ever been in a guy's room?"

I chew the inside of my cheek before I tease, "Yes. But the door had to stay open."

He laughs, and I bite the tip of my tongue before I add, "Then again, I don't plan on spending time in yours either. So you can shut it since I'm just here for the free shirt."

Lies. Throw me on the bed and do me.

He nods, eyes dropping to my lips before he opens the door, leading me inside. It's exactly what I expected. Trophy shelves line the wall, and posters of the Olympic crew team hang like collages. There's even a Yale banner.

He really is a perfectly packaged St. Simeon heartbreaker.

Whole Pinterest boards could be made from this room, and

they'd all be called "hot guy aesthetic."

The thought makes me chuckle, causing Hunter to look over from where he's standing, next to his bed. He jumps onto the mattress, lying back with his hands behind his head.

"Closet's over there," he offers, motioning with his chin.

Wait. What? Seriously?

"Cool. Thanks."

I wrap my long copper hair around my hand, crossing my legs before I turn around and close the distance to his walk-in. Every few steps, I glance back over my shoulder, watching him watch me and wondering if I'm really only getting a shirt.

"Hey, Sutton."

My eyes swing back to his.

"You can have anything you want. I hope you know that."

And we're back. I lick my lips and nod. Heat blooms on my cheeks as Hunter runs his hand over his stomach, so I walk inside the closet to hide. Oh my God, I'm such a nerd. That was the moment to say, *"Great, I'd love the assistance of your dick. Thanks so much."* But instead, I'm hiding.

I'm like one of those yappy little dogs—all bark and no bite.

But this is so weird. *What am I doing?* Maybe I should just date him and see where it goes. Like, let it all unfold naturally like a normal person. Ordinary people don't put their virginity on a to-do list.

I smile to myself, wallowing in the ridiculousness of this moment as my fingers brush over his perfectly arranged T-shirts, all hung by color. *Okay, Hunter, a little anal but not a deal-breaker.*

He laughs from inside the room, so I lean sideways, peeking out of the doorway. Hunter waves from the bed, remote in hand, and I pull back, kind of embarrassed.

He's so cute. Like so fucking cute.

I'm out of my depth here. The last guy I did anything with

quoted Star Trek when he fingered me. I can't even hear anyone say "Beam me up" anymore. This is why girls should never read. I've been stuck in all the smart classes, limiting my damn dating pool. *Supermodel tastes, MIT budget.*

Focus, Sutton. I pull my phone from my back pocket, shooting off a text to the group chat.

Me: Spiral in effect. How do I do this? I'm failing. Thumbs up, I take off my clothes and walk out of his closet naked. Thumbs down, I pretend to have a seizure and sneak out when he goes for help. Vote now.

I don't bother to read the responses because I know it'll be two thumbs up—they're assholes. Then, taking a deep breath, I exhale, feeling my chest grow cold.

Shoot. The cold, damp shirt sticking to my skin reminds me that I need to change. I work quickly, untucking it from my jeans and peeling it off as I give myself a mental pep talk. My nude strapless bra is relatively dry, but I use the least wet part of my top to pat my damp chest.

"So gross," I say to myself, lifting my head to inspect Hunter's shirts when I hear footsteps.

"Hey, I have some smaller T-shirts on the top shelf—"

Oh my God. Hunter's voice is too close. I turn back and forth, panicking, reaching for anything just as he walks into the closet, making us both freeze.

His mouth opens, then closes as I cling to my bundled shirt in front of me, eyes popping out of their sockets.

"Oh my God. Turn around."

He exhales as he spins around quickly, bringing his palms to the back of his head. "Oh, wow. I'm sorry."

I jerk a plaid flannel from a hanger, shrug it on, and work quickly to button it up. I'm swimming in it because Hunter is much bigger than I am, but it's better than him seeing way more of me than he should until I've talked myself into it.

"Okay," I breathe out, tucking the front into the top of my jeans. "You can turn around now."

When he does, all he does is smile. I sweep my hair over my shoulder and wrap it around my hand, feeling awkward and nervous.

"What? Why are you looking at me like that?"

"You look different, Sutton."

My brows draw together, head diving to the front of me to inspect myself.

"What does that mean?"

"It means you don't look like the other girls." He cracks a small laugh. "No. I don't mean that...wait. I do, but not how it sounds. Damn."

If *what the hell* was a face, it would be mine. He takes a step closer, shoving his hands into his pockets.

"You've always been pretty, Sutton." I must call bullshit on my face because he adds, "Yeah, I've noticed. Our whole lives, actually. But there's just something new—"

I'm smiling again.

"New?"

His fingers fall between strands of my hair before he cups my head.

"Something different. Something special, Freckles. You're not like the other girls."

I'm staring up at him, bated breath, eyes closing as he leans in torturously slow. *It's happening.* Hunter Kelly is going to kiss the girl—me.

The sound of a door banging open paired with the music filtering in has my eyelids fluttering open and Hunter freezing centimeters from my lips.

"Shit," he exhales, and he's so close to me that his minty breath feathers my face.

I keep my eyes on him, willing us to happen. *Just kiss me. Come on, you got this, champ.* He licks his lips, saying, "Goddamn, that mouth is tempting," before barely brushing them against mine.

"Hey, dick. I don't care if you're jerking off or fucking that chick you brought up here. Quit. Now. Basement."

Fuck you, Tag—or Cockblock, as I will unaffectionately always remember him—I think as he bangs on the wall. Hunter touches his forehead to mine, groaning as he cradles both sides of my face.

"Favor?"

My head's already nodding.

"Go find your friends and check in, then meet me in the last cabana before the dunes. You can't miss it. It's at the very end of the deck. Give me fifteen minutes, maybe twenty. I want you all to myself tonight, and every night after that, Freckles."

What?

He brings his lips to mine, giving me a chaste kiss, so I close my eyes, but he pulls back just as fast when Tag yells again, "Hunter. Now, you pussy. It's business."

All I hear is, "We're happening, Sutton. Those lips are mine," before he's gone.

I can't speak. My mouth won't move. The only thing I can do is burn red as I stand inside Hunter's closet. The moment his door shuts, I break out into a little dance.

I can't believe this is happening. *Holy hell. This is actually going to happen.* Freaking out, I reach for my phone.

My fingers fly over the keys until I realize that neither of them responded to my other message. There's not even a Read receipt. Crap, I must not get service in here.

Walking out of the closet, I give myself a once-over in the standing mirror before heading out of Hunter's room. I make my way back the way we came, taking the stairs slowly, using the height to scour the open spaces for my friends. But I don't see them.

As I reach the bottom, I bump shoulders with a girl, offering a passing "*Sorry*" as I keep searching the crowd for Aubrey and Piper. But the girl I recognize as Tiffany Astor huffs while glaring at me, so I stare back.

She doesn't even go to St. Simeon. Guess the parties at Madison are no fun—but no surprise there. All-girls schools aren't known for their party atmosphere.

Tiffany's friend whispers into her ear, and Tiffany grins, but something about it makes me feel momentarily self-conscious.

Only briefly because it's obvious they're talking shit about me. And frankly, that's none of my business. I adjust the baggy shirt on my shoulders, and they laugh, glancing over at me again. Yep, over it.

I push past, hearing, "Nice souvenir," making lines form between my eyes before I turn around and smile because I realize that she thinks I fucked Hunter. *Not yet, Tiff.*

"Thanks. I really earned it. My knees are a wreck."

They stare at me, shocked and probably a little surprised, so I add, "I know. This isn't how the mean girl dynamics are supposed to work. But I'm a smart girl. So that bullshit doesn't work on me. In the meantime, don't worry, Tiff. I'm sure Hunter will let you know when you get called up to the big leagues. But…it'll be when I'm done with him."

I hear a familiar laugh, making me smile, so I turn and walk away. Piper sounds like a hyena. It's unmistakable. But her blonde pixie cut and perfectly winged eyeliner paired with a waifish stature give her a Natalie Portman look, so no boy could ever hold her laugh against her. I work my way toward the front, where I saw the pool tables earlier. I'm looking down, rolling up my sleeves, as a pool stick drops in front of me, blocking the way, making me jerk back.

"Excuse me?" I frown before lifting my face.

Piper grins, reaching her hand out for me. "Shephard, quit. Stop being a dick."

He lifts the stick and turns, smacking her ass and making her jump as she yelps. My eyes pop open as I dramatically blink.

"Um, I've been gone for like, what? Twenty minutes. How did this happen? When? Where's Aubrey?"

She shakes her shoulder and lifts a shot. "I forgot how to pace myself. And Shep's so cute."

Her cough is muffled by the back of her hand before she blows out, smiling at me again. Oh, man. Piper's tipsy.

"But Shephard? Really?"

My nose scrunches. It's not that Shephard isn't hot. He completely is. But he's just so frat boy to Piper's indie rock. Then again, I'm about to do it with the possible future president of Alpha Beat-off Pi.

Aubrey throws her arm over my shoulder, coming out of nowhere, and presses a kiss to my cheek. "So? Spill it. Was it the best five seconds of your life?"

I look between them, my smile already beaming. "We're meeting in a cabana. Hunter said he wanted me all to himself, tonight and every night after." They quietly squeal. "But—"

Aubrey's finger comes to my lips, quieting me. "No."

Piper covers Aubrey's finger on my mouth with hers, shaking her head. "Absolutely no. No matter what you're going to say, the answer is no."

I nod, and they narrow their eyes but take their hands away, glaring at me, so I shrug as I'm handed a shot by Shephard.

"Okay. Fine. No buts. I'm nervous though." Piper pushes the shot glass toward my mouth, so I throw the liquid back, feeling the burn in my throat.

Shephard comes up behind me, putting his arms around us. "Can I join? We can braid each other's hair, practice kissing…you know, *wherever* you want me to french you."

"Eww," we groan simultaneously, all shrugging him off as I add, "Get off…alone."

"Sorry." He laughs, tickling Piper. "I forgot you've been claimed. And Aubrey's just a bitch."

"True," she answers, putting her hands on my shoulders. "Are you ready?"

Piper comes up behind me, wrapping her arms around my waist, her head on my shoulder.

"This is your choice, Sut. No means no, even to us, and to our dumb list."

"Shot me," I say to Aubrey. Her eyebrows rise as she hands me another. "I'll see you in a bit. I have plans in a cabana."

Aubrey reaches across and gives Piper a high five as I let the liquid slide down my throat with ease.

"'Kay, I'm going before I lose my nerve."

They're nodding, smoothing my shirt and my hair. I let out a harsh breath and smile goofily before spinning around and heading directly to the last place my virginity will ever be a reality again.

Chapter Six

Sutton

A shaky breath leaves my lips as my feet hit the steps outside and pad down slowly toward the cabanas. Three white tents, drowning in the shadows, sit between the edge of the deck and the bonfire that's illuminating the debauchery happening on the beach.

The crowd is way bigger out here. There's a mix of faces I recognize and others that I don't. The lit rectangular lap pool also seems to have attracted a following. Because while it was empty when we first got here, there are now people playfully splashing around in makeshift bathing suits. *And, oh, even some couples making out.*

"Electric Love" by BØRNS beats in the background, setting the mood under conversation and laughter as I slip between people, trying to keep my eye on the cabana prize. Despite my bravery, my eyes flick over each person I pass, wondering if anyone can tell what's about to happen to me. But nope. Of course they can't.

I'm carrying the secret of all secrets while hiding in plain sight. It's kind of exciting. Like I'm getting away with something I shouldn't. My fingers find the ends of my hair as I walk, playing with it as I hide my smile, but the closer I get, the more the butterflies erupt in my stomach.

Sliding around a group of cute college-age guys—*they must be Tag's friends*—I offer a quiet "Excuse me." Their eyes roam over me as one of them raises his beer, giving me a small, appreciative salute. It makes the smirk I'm hiding harder to keep hidden.

I really have been missing out by not coming to more parties.

A few more feet and a few more people navigated, and I'm standing at the top of the three cedar stairs that lead to the sand—and out to the cabanas.

Wait. Which one did Hunter say to go to? Shit. I forgot.

I toe off my checkered pink Vans, bending down to hold them in my hand before walking toward the nearest one. There are only three, so if I have to Goldilocks it, I will.

My bubble-gum-pink-painted toes sink into the ground, causing my steps to drag and forcing me to sashay so I don't kick up sand. It's cool on my bare feet but not cold. With each step, I make my way deeper into the dark, only pausing to look over my shoulder once.

It's strange how lives intersect and collide. Something monumental is about to happen to me, but it's just a regular Saturday night to someone else. It almost makes what I'm about to do seem insignificant, and I guess, in a way, it is. Millions of people do it with strangers every day. It's not anything transcendent.

It's just sex, no big deal—a physical transaction. *A regular Saturday night.* But a tiny piece of me still kind of wishes that it was magical or even earth-shattering. Just like a part of me wishes

Hogwarts was real or that lying in the sun would turn my ginger skin tan and not into cancer.

I blame movies. The ideas about the "sexiness of sex" being sold are so false. I know because my dumbasses made me watch way too much porn over the last two weeks. Piper called it a CliffsNote for my "snack"—the grossest name for my vag.

And even the stories I've heard, once they both started having sex last year, cemented the facts. Sex is awkward, sometimes uneventful, and not like the second installment of the movie *After...* there is no Hero Fiennes Tiffin in real life.

There's only a Hunter—hot AF, doesn't read, but wants to eat my snack.

I shake my head with a chuckle, pulling myself out of the kind of thoughts I lose myself in way too often, and shift my head back to the darkness.

Circling around to the front of the tent, the heavy canvas fabric that's usually tied off is closed for privacy. Crap. He beat me here. I stare at the front, rolling my shoulders, hopping up and down like I'm prepping for a fight. *Be casual. Be cool. Don't be yourself.*

Am I ready? Yes. *Am I really?* Yes.

Okay. Game time.

The waves crash, mixing with the music from the party as I slide my hand between the draped material, pulling the front back just enough to duck inside.

My voice is barely above a whisper. "Hunter?"

It's pitch-black, only a beam of moonlight coming in from a slit at the top, turning a shadowed figure from black to dark gray.

"Hunt—"

Faint noise slowly seeps into my ears, growing louder, crawling underneath my skin, spreading heat through my body. It's wet and sloppy like— *Oh my God.*

My entire body freezes, eyes wide, and panic sets in. The scene on display in front of me slaps me square in the face.

A guy's hand is dug into some girl's hair, gripped so hard that his knuckles are white. The front of his jeans hangs open, the silver buckle on his belt making a clicking sound each time he shoves his hips forward.

I blink a thousand times, feeling stuck, fixed on what's happening as he groans, making my body tense as I press my lips together.

He slows her movements, groaning, "Fuck, yes. Suck it," boring into her like the world has disappeared. But I see and hear everything. All the filthy sounds of arousal dripping and slapping from her mouth with each thrust.

He shoves deep inside her mouth, rhythmically, breath ragged.

"Take it. Fuck, yes. That's it. Gimme that fucking throat."

The command in his voice pulls a whimper from the girl on her knees, triggering him to move faster, grunting, rutting into her, making her take it deeper without any gentleness or remorse. God, he looks like an animal.

That's the only way to describe it because I've never seen anything like this. This isn't a blow job. He's fucking her mouth.

My eyes won't budge. And my feet won't move. Not even when she gags. His breath becomes ragged as she bobs her head faster and faster.

"Yeah, baby. Hollow those cheeks. Suck that cock, slut."

Another moan has her hands gripping his hips, mine doing the same to my jeans.

"Yeah, you're a dirty bitch. You like to gag like a little whore, don't you."

His head drops, and I imagine his eyes growing heavy, jaw slack as I lick my lips, lost to the sexual carnage.

The muscles in his forearm strain with ferocity as he presses himself forward, swaying, lost to the feeling. My teeth find my bottom lip, watching as he lifts his chin, displaying his angular jaw.

Aggression oozes off him as he grips her hair harder, using her to get off without restraint. My chest rises and falls as stars begin speckling my vision. His other hand grabs the chair in front of him, making it rattle just as a raw, animalistic growl erupts from his throat and the face hidden by shadows leans into that damn moonlight.

West.

Dropping my shoes, my hands slap over my mouth as I stumble backward out of the tent. A string of "*I'm sorrys*" leaving my lips.

Holy shit. My mind can't catch up as I make a hasty escape, stumbling over myself, traveling further into the dark toward a group of rocks on the beach.

I whisper to myself, head swinging around, only half looking to see if anyone is witnessing my spiral. "Jesus Christ. What am I doing? Oh my God, Sutton. What the fuck?"

Did that just happen?

My body's still flush, warm in places it shouldn't be. I can't see Hunter like this. For fuck's sake. I'm so out of my depth.

The thoughts in my head refuse to calm down as I rake my hand through my hair, the other reaching for my cell phone, pulling it from my back pocket. My breath is moving too fast, keeping my chest from slowing down. Fuck. Am I going to hyperventilate?

A huffed laugh leaves me as I talk to myself again. "Oh my God. Get it together, hypochondriac weirdo." But humor swings back to panic just as quickly. My hand comes to my chest, rubbing a tight spot in the middle as I put my other hand down on my knee, bending over to take deep breaths.

The cell I've brought to my eyes spotlights my face as I blink, beginning to calm as I scroll the messages looking for my group chat. I let out a deep exhale before I stand.

Holy hell. I'm going to need a Snuggie, eight bags of chips, and three days of true crime shows to counteract this train wreck of a night.

Impatient thumbs hover over the keyboard as I wander around in a circle, trying to figure out what to text Piper and Aubrey, still saying shit under my breath. "Oh yeah. Let me lose my virginity in a tent. Sure. Who cares? It's not a big deal. Gah, you fucking loser."

How am I supposed to be ready for sex in a cabana with Hunter when I'm about to have a fucking heart attack over a blow job I wasn't even giving?

Me: Code Blue. Plan B. I don't care what. But get me out of here. Burn the house down if you have to. This is a Liam Neeson Taken kind of situation. Help. Me. Hos."

I'm staring at the screen as laugh emojis fill it.

"Assholes." I groan.

Me: I just watched West get a blow job…

Nope. Delete. That dies with me.

The cell in my hand drops to my side as I tip my head toward the sky littered with tiny, bright explosions. The white dots twinkling down mock me with their perfect existence.

I wanted to see those—just not like this. Fuck my life.

Closing my eyes, I take one last deep breath and open them to stare at the moon. That globed, elegant, bold full moon is nothing but a curse. Nothing good happens when a moon like that is out because it's the only thing allowed to be beautiful, so it curses all the moments that could be.

First Tag cockblocks, now West's actual cock is blocking me. Cursed. And cursed.

A whoosh of air breezes past my lips. "I hate you, moon."

Chapter Seven

Calder

S he's staring at the moon—berating it. Who does that? It's weird. But I haven't stopped watching her since she began because it's equally as mesmerizing.

From the rock I'm seated at, I watch her dramatic little moment unfold, lifting my cigarette to my lips, readied to light it as she whispers.

"I hate you, moon."

My chest shakes, a laugh trying to break free as the lighter clicks. All that wild red hair swings in my direction as I give an exhaled, "Don't stop on my account."

Her eyes grow wide. She's frozen in place but only for a millisecond until a bloodcurdling scream explodes from between her lips.

"Whoa," I rumble, launching from my rock, tossing my smoke to the ground as I do. "What the fuck are you screaming for?"

She's moving backward, obviously scared. So I nab the belt loop of her jeans as she shrieks, swatting at my hands, and yank her flush to my body, wrapping her in one arm, the other slapping over her mouth.

"Chill out."

Her squeal is muffled under my palm as she tries to squirm, eyes squeezed shut. But she can't move. I'm three times her size, and I've got at least a hundred pounds on her. There's no escaping.

"Open your eyes. It's okay."

I shake my head as she does, feeling her chest rising and falling against me. Those big green doe eyes pierce into mine. She's looking at me the same way she did the other day. It's unnerving, like I can almost feel her thoughts. Because they feel like mine.

Who are you?

Her breathing slows as I blink, following the brown speckled pattern over her nose. There's just enough light for me to see them.

Waves crash onto the shore, bringing a breeze with it, making a few strands of her hair blow over my hand, replacing the smell of my cigarette with something I can't place—*grapefruit, maybe?*

She clears her throat, and my brows draw together. Fuck. My hand's still over her mouth.

"I'm not going to hurt you. I'm gonna let you go. But no more screaming. All right? I have no interest in fucking up a bunch of preppy assholes attempting to protect you from nothing. Cool?"

I feel her smile against my palm.

"Nod if you understand."

She does, slowly, then picks up speed. My hand peels away, and I watch as she licks her lips and takes a deep breath. Lips that look like—fuck me, her mouth is built for kissing. She draws in her bottom lip between her teeth, letting her gorgeous eyes peek up at me from under the blackest lashes.

Goddamn.

I brush away the hair that got caught up on her face, still staring down, our breaths matching in rhythm.

"Sorry," she whispers, "You scared me."

"It's my fault. But you and the moon were having a deep one-on-one, so I was trying not to interrupt."

She blushes, and my chest hollows, lips parting. That's a good color on her. Absentmindedly, she begins playing with the strings on my hoodie, staring at my chest.

"Oh my God. It's so embarrassing."

I swallow hard, fingertips curling into her back, suddenly realizing that I've still got my arm around her.

"Uh…it's not." I let her go, stepping back but only a small step. "What are you doing out here anyway? Cuz I know it's not to smoke."

Her cheeks stain red again, and this time I want to reach out to see if her skin is hot too.

"Weren't you listening?" She laughs, playing with the ends of her long locks, looking up at me from between those long-ass lashes.

I lick my lips, trying to hide my smirk. "I was, but I wasn't going to say anything."

"Oh my God, stop. You were giving me my dignity." Her eyes roll with a grin. "Joke's on you. I have none anymore."

She's teasing, so I do too.

"All right, then tell me who you're meeting out here so I can bury him befo—"

She cuts me off with her fingers against my lips. "Shh." She shakes her head.

The smile on her face makes me do the same. We're locked on each other, underneath a blanket of stars, nestled in the darkest sky. Her hand stays against my lips as I exhale, warmth enveloping her fingers. Fuck, I can't stop looking at her. It's like every piece of her calls to me. Like magnets.

I want to tug her closer—die in that fucking grapefruit scent as I run my nose up her neck. My eyes drift down her body. One I know is innocent, but looks are deceiving because the way that she weaponizes shyness should be illegal.

I almost feel guilty over the defiling thoughts that are doing their worst inside my head.

Before I think twice, not that I've ever been guilty of that, my tongue slowly runs up the pad of her finger. And she fucking shivers, making me feel drunk on her.

Her hand draws back, lips parted by a quiet gasp. But I encircle her wrist, a half-smile pointed in her direction.

"Tell me your name."

Chapter Eight

Sutton

My entire body's short-circuiting, still feeling the slickness of his tongue over my fingertips.

"Huh?"

Calder's grin peeks out as I open my mouth, realizing what he's asked, but nothing comes out. *Hmm, do I give you my name? On this night...with this moon?*

I whip around, before glancing over my shoulder as I start walking away. There's amusement in Calder's make-me-quiver kind of deep voice as he follows behind.

"Hey. Hold up. Tell me your name. Don't do me dirty like that…" He chuckles. "What would the moon think?"

I laugh, looking back at him again, as we near the porn tent, before spinning to face him.

"The moon is a wicked bitch. She curses everything."

He stops in front of me, biting his lip, making butterflies lose their minds in my belly. My hand comes to my stomach, hoping to calm them as I feel a strand of my hair being gently tugged.

My smile matches his. Or his matches mine. I can't tell. It's like we're feeling everything at the same time, in this exact moment, with identical depth.

He bends down, catching my eyes that start to drop as I lose myself to that thought.

"Then I guess I'll have to ask you again in the daylight. Wouldn't want us cursed."

God, he has the smoothest lips. They look soft, as if they'd glide over mine like satin. Why doesn't anyone have lips like this at Burr? My question jumps out before I can stop it.

"Do you go to Eastside?"

"No."

His head tilts left as he raises his hand to the base of my neck, weaving his fingers through my hair, massaging while he watches.

"So, you're older, then?"

Oh my God. Am I panting?

He nods, his grip becoming firmer as he forces my chin up. My breath is useless because it's barely there anymore.

"How much older?"

Calder's tongue drags over his lips as he stares at mine. *Oh, sweet Jesus, I want that in my mouth.*

"Nineteen."

Calder gives me a tug, forcing my feet closer, the heat of his body devouring me.

"My turn."

The heart that I think is still in my chest starts beating out of control. He swallows, and my back arches ever so delicately toward him, repeating his words.

"Your turn."

He smirks. "How old are you?"

"I'm a senior."

Going to be… Same difference.

His face lowers as my eyes close. But instead of his lips pressing to mine, Calder runs his nose up my jaw. He inhales, leaving the barest touch of his lips against my earlobe. "Do you really believe in curses?"

I can't move because my whole fucking body wants to shake. "Maybe."

"I don't." He pulls back, locking eyes with me. "Tell me your name."

I'm about to surrender in this little game we're playing, feeling lost in Calder's magic, when his attention's stolen by the sound of someone snapping their fingers behind me.

I'm released, my body suddenly cold.

Looking over my shoulder, my eyes land on Hunter as he rounds the corner, and my heart stops.

He stops dead in his tracks, looking between us.

Oh shit. My head swings back and forth, feeling the air change, tension sweeping over us.

Hunter extends his arm, calling me over. "What's going on here?"

I shake my head because the words aren't coming out. They can't. They're held hostage by the fact that Calder's still holding a strand of my hair, eyes back on me. Zero fucks given to Hunter.

"Fuck off, little Kelly. She's busy. Go play somewhere else."

Calder lifts my hair to his nose, inhaling, and I blink up at the sincerest blue pools as he grins.

"I like your shampoo."

This time I laugh, sweeping my hair over my shoulder, away from him. Avoiding the growl that leaves his throat as I take a step back, I put distance between us, even when his fingers graze my hand, because this could get ugly fast.

Like he said before, there are more than enough juniors and Roman numerals inside for Hunter to call on. I won't be the catalyst for a throw-down between the two schools here.

Calder stares at me, crossing his arms, but I shrug, turning my attention to Hunter, who's mimicking Calder's pose.

The sound of fabric swishing open draws our collective attention, West chuckling as he walks out. His arm is slung over the girl who was just on her knees, and she's staring at him like he's a god.

West's eyes meet mine immediately, then drop to my bare feet. His smile broadens so much that the shine should sparkle on his teeth.

"Hey, Cinderella. You left something in the tent."

He holds up my pink Vans, giving them a shake. Jesus. I reach out, snatching my shoes, the whole tragic night hitting me in the gut again.

"Thank you." I point at the tent, my cheeks turning scarlet. "And sorry about the plus-one—"

I shift toward Calder, walking backward as he starts following me, pointing to myself. "Sutton. And I promise no more screaming."

He laughs, but I spin to Hunter, who looks like he's got plenty to say to me. I hold up the sleeve of his flannel that my hand's folded over. "Thanks for the shirt and the offer. But I've had a weird night. I'm just going to go."

I take four or five quick skips on the balls of my feet over the sand before I look back. The expressions on their faces pull a burst of laughter from my chest. *The thoughts they must be thinking.* I can almost tell what each is thinking—one with a smirk, the other a scowl, and West looking at that girl's boobs.

As I turn, Hunter calls my name, but it's Calder's eyes I lock with.

"See you in the daylight."

"I cannot get over that you saw that dude get a blow job."

Aubrey shimmies her sweats over her hips before reaching up to put her hair in a messy bun. I shake my head, trying not to laugh, falling back onto the bed.

"It was so embarrassing. And loud. Eww. I'm still cringing all over again at what a perv I was."

Piper throws a pillow at me. "Yeah. I mean, I was super pissed when you made us leave, but this story is so worth it."

Aubrey snuggles up in her bamboo chair swing, grabbing her water. "So what happened after the criminal let you go?"

I roll my eyes. "Don't call him that. He's nice."

Their heads turn to stare at each other before they begin taunting me. "Oh, sorry. Are we offending your boyfriend?" Piper puts a hand to her chest. "Oh no, Aubrey, don't talk about her true love that way."

I scream-laugh, flipping them off. "Fuck off, please, and thank you. And for your information, nothing happened. Hunter walked around the corner, and I left. It was embarrassing. I died. And now we're here."

It's a lie. And I meant to tell it. Guilt blooms, growing and compounding because I just lied as if I do it every day—with a smile on my lips, never skipping a beat. But I don't want to share him.

Aubrey wags her brows.

"What are you going to say to Hunter now? Like how will you explain? We need a plan."

Piper inserts a terrible idea, and they start bickering back and forth about what I should do. And I'm happy to let them because my thoughts are elsewhere.

I may have said nothing happened with Calder, but the truth is it feels as if *everything* happened with him. Like I woke up for the first time in my life. But how do I tell them that I have a hard-core crush on someone they so lovingly refer to as the town criminal?

They'll just tell me it was lust—that I was horny. And yeah, of course I was. Calder's insanely hot. The lips, the eyes…the damn tattoos. He's the inspiration for ruined panties everywhere. But there was more, an attraction I've never felt before him.

I let my teeth find my bottom lip.

He felt epic.

My phone dings from across the room, and I push up to my elbows, staring at it.

Calder doesn't have my number, but everything else tonight has been bizarre—what's one more thing? The girls stop talking as my phone begins dinging over and over, turning their attention to my face before they both scramble to get it.

Piper nabs it first, tossing it to me and laughing as Aubrey jumps on her back.

"Piper! We can't trust her to make her own decisions. What are you thinking?"

I'm giggling, opening my texts, offering, "It's Hunter," as I scroll to the top of the chain.

"Duh," Aubrey mocks, jumping off Piper's back.

They walk over toward the bed, but my smile begins to fade with each step.

"What's he texting?" Piper nudges as I sit silently.

Hunter: I'm drunk, and you're not here.

Hunter: Why aren't you here, Freckles?

Hunter: Is it because you're slumming it across the tracks?

Hunter: Whatever. Fuck it. Do you. I like my toys brand new anyway.

Hunter: Tiffany says hi.

I drop the phone on my lap, looking up at my friends. They read the messages from over my shoulder, so I don't have to say anything.

"Can I really be pissed? We aren't anything to each other."

I don't say that he kind of lost his opportunity to bang me the minute Calder asked me for my name. Yet still, what a douchebag.

Aubrey shakes her head. "Yes, you will be mad. Fuck him. He's so gross. Tiffany Astor is not a flex. Monday morning, I'm telling everyone he had mold on his cock, and you didn't want to touch it."

Piper's nodding. "Mold allergies are a real thing. I've heard of that. We hate him. For life."

I start to laugh before I grab a pillow, covering my face, and groan, falling back.

Fuck. This. Night.

Chapter Nine

Calder

"**K**eys," Roman calls, holding his hand up as I toss them, a smile permanently planted on my face.

Like the fucking puppy he is, West pushes past me, calling dibs on the front seat, but I ignore him, pulling back the black leather bucket seat and motioning for him to get in.

"Bro, I called it."

My eyes shift to his.

"Come on, dude. I'm always in the back."

"Get the fuck in, West. It's where the kids sit. It's safer."

Roman chuckles as West flips me off, climbing into the back. I push the seat back, settling in at the same time Roman does.

The Mustang growls, engine revving as I hang an arm out the window, looking back at the house before we pull out of the driveway.

See ya later, Sutton.

We pull out onto the main road as Roman keeps glancing at me.

"What the fuck has you acting like you took a hit of the shit we were just selling?"

I don't answer, looking in the side mirror, then out the window. West leans forward from the middle of the back, propping his arms on the seats.

"There's a girl. The redhead from the park."

My palm comes to his face, pushing him back as he keeps fucking talking, shoving my hand away.

"And she's kinky. She was watching—"

I turn in my seat, bumping Roman's arm and making us swerve as I reach back, slapping West's face before he can finish.

"Shut the fuck up, or you walk home."

West doubles over, having avoided most of my hand as I point to him before falling back into my seat.

"Oh shit," Roman bellows. "Is our Romeo in love?"

"Gimme a break. She was hot. That's it. That asshole was busy," I chuckle, pointing back to West. "I wanted to be too."

I shift my face toward the blurred houses to hide any evidence of my lie. Because it was more than that. I've never felt that kind of attraction. I wanted to bust that little fuck Hunter in the mouth when he called her over. Maybe I will the next time I see him.

West lifts his face to the sky, sounding feminine. "Ah, Calder. Yeah, do me."

I lean down, turning the music up to offensive, drowning out the torment. Roman breaks out into laughter, shoving my shoulder and hitting the gas as we wind around the cliff—guided only by headlights and the moon *she* hates shining down on the ocean.

West howls, standing up in the back, gripping the headrests as we whip around corners, my hand slapping the side of the car.

This is life. Wild, free, and filled with the possibility of Sutton.

West drops back on his ass, and I lay my head back, wind whipping my face as my eyes close.

The first day I saw her wasn't at the park. It was earlier. The guys and I were coming back from a run my Pops sent us on. We were parked at a red light talking about playing some ball later. Sutton was walking into the church next to her school, Immaculate whatever. She was with those friends of hers, laughing as her wild red hair flew around her face.

They were in those ugly fucking skirts that are too long and plaid. But unlike her friends, who'd rolled those shitty things up short enough to show the goods, hers hit her knees.

She was all buttoned up in her white shirt and virtue.

Just a good girl—only willing to get on her knees to pray. And the most dominant part of me wanted to make her dirty.

What the fuck is it with men? We see something clean and want to run a smudge down the middle.

Sutton is pristine.

And the whole time we stood out on that beach, all I wanted to do was run my grease-stained finger down her body. Through her folds, pressing inside her warmest places until she forgot that *good girls* exist because all she craved was my dirty fucking mouth.

I can almost picture it.

I'm pulled from my thoughts as the sound of tires over the train tracks mark our re-entry back onto our side of town. The side where white picket fences need repainting and people cut their own lawns.

My eyes lower to the mirror, watching her side grow smaller.

A town like St. Simeon is an illusion—a mirage. It doesn't really fucking exist. Their side is the same as ours—corrupt, cruel, greedy. We just don't have the luxury of hiding it all behind five-hundred-dollar sunglasses and afternoon polo matches.

Not that I ever would.

It's better to be the wolf than the bitch that hides in sheep's clothing.

But are you hiding, Sutton? Will I find out that you're exactly what I hate—just some rich girl trying to slum it.

Something deep inside of me, something I refuse as fast as it brims, tells me that we're already cursed if she's from that side.

We don't need the moon.

Roman lifts his chin toward a liquor store, and I nod, suddenly feeling like liquor would be a perfect idea.

"Calder."

My father's voice carries through the garage walls, so the guys and I separate as we walk through the yard with a nod. I walk inside the ample space, looking past all the cars he likes to collect.

There are six in here, and the 1970 Plymouth Hemi 'Cuda is up on a custom lift. My eyes drift over the sleek body as I walk the row of cars toward where my old man is seated.

"What's up, Pops?"

He's wiping his greasy hands on a rag as he looks up at me with a sun-worn face behind dark eyes.

"Any trouble at the Kellys' tonight?"

I shake my head. "No, Pops, we made sure they were stocked with product and happy."

"Good. Good. Keep those boys happy. I don't need to remind you how important this arrangement is."

"No, Pops. You don't."

"Okay, you boys get a good night's sleep. We have church in the mornin'. It's time we met the town and I said hello to that goddamn thorn in our side, Senator Prescott. And your souls would do well with a little prayer."

Every once in a while, my Pops' Irish lilt leaks out in his speech.

He hates it. It reminds him that he doesn't belong. And for a man like my father, knowing your place in this world is of the utmost importance.

It's one of the reasons Roman and West have the Wolfe name.

Roman's mom was a drug addict, who overdosed, and his dad was a deadbeat. At three, he was left alone eating spoiled leftovers and sitting in his own shit. So a woman brought him to our house— not child protective services or the cops.

To us.

Our way of life is different than most. Loyalty is up there with God. Roman lived on our block, which meant that he already belonged to our family in a way. It meant that he had a place in this fucked-up world.

On the other hand, West tried to pick-pocket my dad four years ago on a Boston subway. It amused my Pops so much that he gave him a place with us because there's always honor among thieves.

"I expect you three ready tomorrow. Bright-eyed and goddamned bushy-tailed. No fucking around, Calder. Tomorrow's business. God first—then business."

I give him a nod. "All right, Pops."

He turns away, standing and popping the hood of the Camaro he's working on, dismissing me. So I turn, making my way out to the yard, toward the small house in the back.

When we moved, none of us wanted to. Boston's home. We know it like the back of our hands, raising hell, dodging cops, and running those streets. But our lives are not our own.

Family means more than the people you're related to. It's loyalty and allegiance.

Roman and West declared theirs years ago. But for me, I was born into it. Baptized in blood as my mother was gunned down—me in her belly.

This life was chosen for me, and I'll die never knowing anything else.

West looks up from the couch as I open the front door.

"Everything good?"

I nod. "We have a curfew. Business in the a.m.—church."

"Shit." He jumps up. "I'll get the shot glasses. That way, we get lit faster."

Roman shakes his head, tossing me a beer, but I crack it open as I head toward my bedroom.

"I'm wiped. I'm gonna pass out."

West grabs the counter, pretending to jack off. "Sweet dreams, bitch."

My middle finger is all I give as I walk into my room, shutting the door behind me before dropping to the mattress on the floor and downing my beer.

I lean over, grabbing a leather-bound notebook from the floor, and toss the now empty can down. My back hits the bed, and I open to the place I wrote my last thoughts.

The cigarette was nice, but she's the only thing I wanted to inhale.

Fuck. I toss the journal, kicking off my shoes as I reach over my shoulder and drag my hoodie off, remembering how she played with the strings. And the look on her face, tempting me to give her the kiss her lips prayed for.

"I should have," I breathe out, lying back to shove my pants off, eyes dropping to my dick.

It's hard, bobbing against my stomach, wanting me to strangle it as I picture her pert tits bouncing in my face or that perfect ass bent over the hood of my car. I dig into the pocket of my discarded jeans and pull out my phone, tapping the very first playlist. I lift my palm to my face and spit into it before wrapping it around my cock.

Air hisses between my teeth as I wind my palm down over the veiny shaft, chin tilting up toward the ceiling. My muscular thighs separate, one knee bent as I close my eyes, pushing into my hand.

Goddamn, I want this girl bad.

I want my hand in her hair, holding her over the hood of my car for anyone to see just to prove they can't fucking have her. She's my wild beauty.

Mine to ruin, to fuck, to have.

My jaw drops open as my breathing gets heavier, each tug turning my exhales more ragged. The side of my ass indents with her pulse as I jack off to the vision of her.

I can see her—legs open, that sweet cunt glistening, begging me to give it pleasure.

"Oh fuck. Spread those legs for me."

I push inside of her, enveloped by her warm pussy. It hugs my cock, quivering as I stroke the soft walls.

"Yes. Take it deep."

Moans fall out of her mouth as she's controlled, my hand gripping her soft mane. I fuck her like an animal, thrusting inside, over and over, listening to her scream my name, begging God to make me let her come.

With each thrust, her silky-smooth ass bounces, screaming to be marked as her cream soaks my cock.

"Say my name."

I'm jerking my cock harder, lost in the fantasy of fucking Sutton. Knowing just a taste of her would send me over the edge. A lick of that sweet pussy coming all over my tongue as I ate her from behind.

"Oh fuck," I grunt as my body contracts, warm beads of cum spurting onto my stomach and cascading onto my hand.

My eyes stay closed as my breathing slows, not ready to give up my fantasy. The memory of her walking away tonight pushes to the forefront of my mind as I let out a rough breath and open my eyes.

"See you in the daylight."

Chapter Ten

Sutton

"Sutton, honey, we're going to be late to mass."
I'm nodding even though my mother can't see me as I text Piper back from the hallway upstairs.

Me: I don't care if Hunter wants to apologize. He was a dick. What happened to we'll hate him forever?

Piper: Nothing. Don't kill the messenger. Shephard told me to tell you.

Me: I see. Shephard told you…mmhmm. Someone wants to get flocked.

Piper: Don't start. That's a terrible pun. I'm just saying—be prepared because Shephard said Hunter's on a "land Sutton" mission.

Piper: You should've just texted him back—boys always want the ones that get away.

Me: 😊 See you soon.

I shove my cell in my purse, hearing my father call this time with his *I'm irritated* voice, so I hustle.

"Sorry," I answer, bounding down the stairs. "I was just grabbing my purse."

My mother's brushing over my father's lapels before he turns toward the door with an annoyed glance at me and heads out to the waiting limo. She offers me a smile as I follow, wishing I'd overslept at Aubrey's so that I could've skipped today.

The idea of asking for forgiveness rather than permission is beginning to grow on me. I need to try it out more because this scene is the same every week.

We dress in our Sunday bests, sit on a hard wooden pew, and deal with my father's mood until we're back home. Then we all complain about going, only to be reminded by the guy who put everyone in a bad mood that the constituency demands it.

I'm not sure either of my parents are particularly religious. Still, according to Baron Prescott, God serves the highest purpose—he helps elections.

"So," My mother pats my knee as we settle into the back of the limo. "How was the sleepover at Aubrey's last night? Anything I need to know?"

"Uneventful." I half-smile, turning my head toward the window. *That lie's going to cost you half a rosary of prayers.*

My parents begin talking about some fundraiser they're organizing for the town. I swear my mother does it on purpose to relax my father as I stare out the window.

Life is so weird. Last night was supposed to change the trajectory of my life. I was supposed to be different today—defiled and happy.

I mean, I am different, but it's not because I slept with Hunter. A smile drifts over my lips, thinking about the way Calder played with my hair. My mother says something about Marianne Kelly, Hunter's mother, so I stay zoned out, hating to be reminded of him again.

Such a jerk.

"Sutton, darling?"

My eyes lift to my mother's as I come back from my errant thoughts.

"Sorry, I was—"

"Deep in thought," she interjects.

I nod.

"I was saying that Marianne Kelly called me this morning to tell me all about how smitten her son is with you. Apparently, he messaged her while she and Mr. Kelly are in London. Why haven't I heard anything about this from you?"

My face scrunches up. *Low blow, Hunter—getting the parents on board.*

"Which boy?" my father interrupts. "Because a college dropout isn't someone I want my daughter entertaining."

My mother waves him off, and I wipe my hands over my cornflower-blue knee-length baby doll dress.

"Doesn't matter which one. The feeling isn't mutual. And most specifically, for Hunter."

"Now, wait a minute," my father counters. "Hunter's a star athlete. Wants to go into politics and has the name for doing it. I vote to give the boy a chance."

My head swings between my mother and father. *Since when did my love life become a democracy?*

"We aren't voting. Hunter's a whore. I'm uninterested."

Stern consternation—that's the look he gives me. But I hold my ground. My father may be a professional bully on the Hill, but I have zero interest in a group decision here.

Can it, Senator. It's what I wish I could say but never would.

"You should save that kind of speak for your friends, Sutton. And a word of advice—boys don't like to be caged in. Bide your time, let him fly, and he'll remember you when it matters. Hunter Kelly comes from the kind of family who's worth your while."

Oh. My. God. I should open the car door and jump—my future is bleaker than death. *Let him fly? When it matters?* I'm going to puke. I have to physically force my eyes from rolling back into my head. It's not often I get these lectures, but when I do, I become convinced that I'll be victim to a modern-day arranged marriage—a politically advantageous one.

There has to be a Netflix show documenting how I can escape.

"Geez, Dad." Sarcasm drips from my mouth. "I'd hoped this kind of matchmaking would start in college. You know, our families would summer together, forcing us to be around each other, planting the seed until we cave. Only to realize we don't even like each other. The only thing we have in common is that our families are maniacal institutions powered by greed. So we make the ultimate sacrifice and join the ranks of loveless marriages throughout history, having two-point-three kids and a golden retriever named Chardonnay."

The snort from my mother tells me she enjoyed my little speech, but the unappreciative eyes sitting across from me—they do not share the same sentiment.

His phone chimes, and he looks down, finally losing the scowl. "I like to get the ball rolling early. Sue me. Elizabeth, let's have the Kellys over for dinner next week."

This time, I do roll my eyes.

The car slows in the parking lot, pulling to a stop at the curb. The three of us sit in uncomfortable silence before my father nods at me.

"Try and be pleasant today, Sutton. It is a house of God, after all."

My father is let out first, leaving my mother to raise her brows at me.

"What?" I shrug. "He started it. And do not invite the Kellys over."

She grins, patting my cheek. "Give him a break? Between re-elections coming up and this whole town thing, he's hitting the ceiling. More than ever, you need to be a team player."

My hand falls over hers, stopping her from exiting.

"What town thing?"

The smile I'm given is the one she reserves for the press. "Nothing you need to bother yourself with. If it's pertinent, you'll know. Until then, be the daughter we know you are and make friends with Hunter Kelly. You don't have to marry the kid, but his family's name is an ally I'd like your father to have. I'd hoped you'd want that too."

And just like that, I'm effectively schooled by one Elizabeth Prescott, senator's wife and bloodthirsty attorney-at-law.

"Yep," I whisper under my breath, following her out and joining my father's side.

Friendly waves from my father and gleaming white smiles from my mother flank me as we walk the long wide cement path toward the mini Gothic cathedral modeled after Westminster Abbey. But unlike the abbey, the entry for the cathedral isn't ground level.

Three sets of dark wood doors flanked by arches stand at the top of a grand stone staircase. It's a statement, just like the manicured lawn on either side of me that stretches out along the width of the building.

"Remind me," my father whispers as we walk the pathway toward the front. "The new priest is…"

"Father Paul," I answer discreetly, letting my eyes travel past the archways where families are entering under the stained glass.

There are those angels.

My mother whispers something catty about someone's dress to me as Piper waves from the front lawn, and I smile back.

My nerves grow with each step forward because I just want to make it through the morning without seeing Hunter. It's clear our friendship is out of my hands, but I can at least hold out for today. Especially if he plans on making a big deal about last night. I can't believe he got his mother to call mine. Ugh, I should castrate him for that.

I'm searching the crowd, hoping to spot Hunter so I know where to avoid, when "Hey, Freckles" fills my ear from behind.

"Oh shit," I gasp, spinning around as Hunter takes a step back.

My mother's face shoots to mine. "Excuse me? What did you just say?"

Hunter's grin gets my narrowed eyes as I cover for myself.

"O…ceans of people…" I motion around as my cheeks turn red because I'm positive she knows exactly what just came out of my mouth, but I lie anyway.

"Doesn't it seem like a bigger turnout than normal? I bet Jesus is so happy."

My father stares down at me before giving a nod toward Hunter. "Nice to see you, Hunter."

"Sir. Mrs. Prescott." He smiles like a portrait of charm.

I hate him.

"What do you want, Hunter?" I huff, pointing toward the church. "Confession is that way."

My father clears his throat, drawing my eyes.

"We seem to have the local press here today. So, stop being yourself and smile. And for God's sake, Hunter, apologize for whatever you did to this girl—because she holds grudges. She still hates me for telling her she was allergic to dogs so that she'd stop asking for one. It happened when she was three."

My mouth drops open as my father's name is called. "Senator Prescott. Sir. Could we have a photo?"

"Absolutely." He beams, escorting my mother toward the front steps of the church, where Father Paul is standing.

Hunter stares at me, reaching for my hand, but I link it behind my back with the other.

"Freckles."

"It's Sutton. Or do you call all your toys that so you don't have to remember our names? Although, you seemed to know Tiffany's last night."

He lets out a deep breath. "Jesus Christ. Can we just start again?"

I draw my brows together in question because I'm not really sure I want to. But as he starts, I don't stop him because far be it from me to rob him of begging for forgiveness.

"Listen, I was a dick because I got jealous." His eyes lock with mine. "Not an excuse, just an explanation. But I thought you liked that asshole, and I got mad and tried to hurt your feelings. My ego is fragile. It's a '*my bad*' kind of thing, and I swear I won't do it again. But you have to give me one more chance to let me prove it."

My teeth find the inside of my cheek because that was unexpected honesty. A lot of it. He steps in closer to me.

"I know the truth probably makes me look worse than the shit I pulled last night, but I'm fucking scared that you've decided to pass on me. Because I like you, Sutton. Like more than any other girls I've dated."

"You've dated people?"

I say it teasingly, but it's the truth. Hunter doesn't date.

He tugs my hands from behind my back, holding them at my side. "See, it's because of stuff like that. You give me shit. Call me out. I like it."

A smile peeks out, even though I try like hell to keep it away. Now he's laying it on thick.

"Nuh-uh. Nice try, but you've officially dipped a toe into '*that guy*' status with 'you call me on my shit.' I mean, we've spoken like, what? Three times? And now you're in love with me? You want me because I turned you down."

He smiles, not even ashamed to admit that I'm right.

"Maybe. But that's not the only reason. I also think you're funny. Pretty. Smart. Unexpected. And hard to get just makes winning your heart that much sweeter. I like you, Sutton. And not that you care, but I didn't touch that girl last night. Because I couldn't stop thinking about you."

I shrug, but he bends down slowly until his mouth is almost touching mine.

"Forgive me? Let me win you over?"

An exhale leaves my lips as I step back. "I'll think about it."

His grip tightens around my hands as I start to tug them away, and he locks eyes with me.

"You can like him. It's fine. Just like me more."

As he lets me go, my heart picks up its pace because I *do* like Calder, and Hunter knows it. And that fact makes me feel a lot less high-and-mighty—because who was the player first? Me.

I lick my lips, hand wrapping around my hair. "Like I said, I'll think about it."

His jaw tenses, a glint of mischief in his eyes as he groans.

"Fuck. You're killing me, Freckles."

The church bells ring, signaling the start of mass. So, I look back over my shoulder toward the steps as Hunter chuckles and says, "I should probably watch my language. We are in front of a church."

As my head swings back to him with a grin on my face, I pause, seeing my father standing close to another man, his hands fisted at his sides. He looks angry, and that's unlike him.

What the hell? My father never cracks. Ever.

"I don't think it counts until you're inside the building," I murmur, my focus fixed on the scene.

The photographers are nowhere to be seen, and more and more, the steps to the church are becoming empty as people filter inside. But my father and the stranger both stand their ground.

Whatever's happening isn't good.

"I'll see you later, Hunter," I offer as I make my way over toward my mother. I feel him following, but I don't care because my focus is on my mom. She's standing at the bottom of the church steps, a few feet away from my father, with a look of concern marring her face.

What the hell is going on?

The closer I get, the more I can feel the tension hanging thick in the air. I'm staring, taking the stranger in because he's familiar, although I've never met him.

He's the same build as my father and looks around the same age just not aged as gracefully. His hands are covered in tattoos, probably attached to more, hidden under his expensive suit.

He looks like...

Harsh words spitting from my father make me bristle and pay attention.

"This is no place for you. St. Simeon will not fall to your drugs and filth."

"Senator, you don't have a say here. And you know it. This town is as much ours now as it is yours. The sooner you accept that, the better it'll be for everyone."

"You piece of shit. St. Simeon is my advantage. You and Connor O'Bannion would be smart to remember that this isn't the only hill I run."

O'Bannion? How do I know that name? The memory of my father talking about a bill targeting organized crime flitters through as I come to stand next to my mother. *They're talking about the Irish mafia.*

"Mom, what's happening?" I whisper, glancing over to see Hunter walk past us, eyes darting to mine before he heads up the stairs.

As if sensing me, my father looks over his shoulder. "Elizabeth.

Take Sutton inside."

She takes my hand, patting it as she turns me to take us away. But I tug back, not wanting to leave my father alone.

"We should stay with him," I rush out, but she drags me up the steps, her words harshly whispered into my ear.

"That man is scum. He and his sons will infest our community with drugs and crime and happily ruin everything your father's built. He's an enemy of this state and your father."

"Who is he?" I breathe out, stumbling a bit as I'm forced to take the stairs too quickly.

"A terrible man, in the O'Bannion crime family…Tyler Wolfe."

Wolfe? As in…

My head shoots back over my shoulder as we reach the landing, mind swirling as the pit in my stomach grows so big that all the butterflies that were once there are sucked down, dying in the darkness.

Honey-blond hair and broad shoulders stand above the rest, calling my eyes as Calder comes to stand right next to his father.

No.

My mother's arm wraps around my waist just as Calder's eyes— ones that match the color of my dress—stare up at me with the same tragic recognition.

"Come, darling. There is nothing but trouble down there." I shift my head to look at her. "I forbid you from ever being around them, Sutton. Tyler Wolfe and his boys will be ruined and run out of this town. Your father will see to it. Promise me you'll stay away."

I nod, glancing back at the boy with a storm behind his angel eyes and the devil in his soul, watching him watch me. Feeling just as lost in him as I was last night.

"Then I guess I'll have to ask you again in the daylight. Wouldn't want us cursed."

But we are.

"Why does it have to be you," I whisper to myself, watching Calder's face grow dark as a hand weaves through mine.

I lift my eyes to Hunter, who's looking down at me, and I pull my hand back.

"Come on, Freckles. Sit with me?"

I nod, not really knowing what to do, as we turn and walk inside, but Calder never stops watching me. I know because the goose bumps don't go away until the church doors close.

Chapter
Eleven

Calder

Her last name's Prescott. What the fuck.

The heavy church doors slam shut, cutting me off from Sutton and throwing me back into reality. Goddammit. If I didn't know any better, I would think I'd been set up.

Baron Prescott is not only my father's enemy but the loathed opponent of the Irish mob. He's a goddamn dead man walking, and I was almost in bed with his daughter. At least I was hoping to be.

That girl's a siren's call—fiery red hair, with eyes greener than envy luring me right off a fucking cliff. Although by the look in her eyes, that wasn't her intention. The regret she hurled in my direction hit me square in the chest as she stared me down.

It felt a lot like Sutton wished she'd never met me, but I'd do last night over again a thousand more times if it meant I could have another chance to kiss her.

I should've fucking kissed her.

West leans in, nudging me. "Dude, Red is Senator Prescott's daughter."

I shake my head discreetly, letting him know to shut the fuck up. This isn't the time or the fucking place to clue my Pops in. Not that there ever will be. Last night goes to my goddamn grave because if Pops finds out, there are only two outcomes: I become a liability or an advantage. I don't like either.

My father snaps his fingers, and Roman, West, and I turn, following him back toward the black SUV waiting at the curb. The guys that work for my father jump out, opening the doors for us, but I hang back, gripping my neck with one hand, a singular thought on repeat.

"Pops, you mind if I stay back?"

What the fuck am I doing?

Roman and West look at me and then at each other as our dad walks toward me, searching my eyes.

"Everything okay, boy?"

Fuck, this is stupid and reckless. There's no way in hell either of us could ever cross this line. But I have to see her. One more time.

I nod, letting my hand drop from my neck. "Yeah. I just want some time to think. Church always makes me think about, you know—"

His face grows stern, understanding that I mean my mother.

Using her as my lie is the lowest of the lows, but if anyone would've understood the part of me that's still human, I think it would've been her. It's also the most convincing lie I can tell my Pops because he harbors the same sadness.

My mother was beloved in our community. Spent all her free time at the small parish by our home, volunteering and helping the nun's with their garden. Looking back, I think it was her way of balancing the wickedness of life. When she died, that church and the people in it made sure I always carried her with me.

Forgive me, Ma.

"Go. Take the time you need. Lena was a godly woman, taken too soon." He pats my face. "Men like us don't deserve peace, but we can pray she gets it."

He turns around, walking back to the car as I stare at his back. I stand in my place, watching as the door closes. I don't move until the SUV turns the corner, just to make sure they're gone before I cut across the lawn next to the church, diving in deep to my bad ideas.

My hand glides over the wall as I sneak around the side, stopping at the first door I come to. *Come on, be open.*

It clicks as I twist the knob, the sound of the priest giving the reading filtering out. I slip into the hall next to the main room, shutting the door quietly as I look around, no plan in mind, just fucking winging it.

My head shifts up and down the hall, scoping shit out. "*What's the next move, asshole?*" I walk quickly toward the stairs by the front, looking over my shoulder to make sure nobody's coming. I'll head to the balcony and try to spot her and then figure out what the fuck I'm going to do next.

As I near an archway that connects the hall to the main room, I take a deep breath before darting past, hopefully unseen. I come to the stairs, taking them two at a time until I'm at the top.

The sound of people lowering the benches to fall on their knees to pray rattles the room, echoing against the walls, keeping my footsteps quiet as I enter.

Sun burning through the stained glass touches everything in the room, creating pockets of light that show tiny little specks of dust floating in the air. I walk by two confessionals sitting side by side, along with an organ that shows its neglect.

It's as if nobody comes up here.

The small balcony juts out, overlooking the congregation below.

So I duck down, sliding onto the organ's bench, staying somewhat hidden as my arms rest on the gold-leafed wooden rail.

Prayed responses fill the room as I scan it for the girl I shouldn't be looking for when she suddenly stands.

Making me do the same.

Sutton walks toward the altar and takes a wine goblet from the priest. She turns, smiling, taking her place to help with communion, as row after row of people stand, lining up in front of her.

Look up. Come on, Sutton. Look. Up.

Each person steps forward, taking a sip, and she wipes the goblet before handing it over again as I shift my head, trying to keep my eyes on her around all the backs of heads.

Look up.

Some old man pats her shoulder, making her smile bright, and I can't help but get drawn in. It's the way she smiles…with genuine goodness. Goodness I don't possess. This is her world, one where old men say nice things and people at least pretend to have a heart.

What the fuck am I doing? We don't just come from two different worlds. More like parallel universes. What the hell am I going to do? To say?

My eyes drop as I take a step away, feeling something I can't explain. It's like being shown the sun and then imprisoned in darkness.

Our fathers are enemies. Our lives are predestined—doomed from the start.

Except there was this moment.

An amazing fucking moment when she smiled at me with all that same goodness and I forgot who I was.

I've never hated my last name until now.

I turn, shoving my hands into the pockets of my dress pants, feeling the weight of disappointment on my shoulders.

You walk the fuck away. Forget this girl. Because if you do one good thing in your goddamn life, it'll be to leave Sutton Prescott alone.

A heavy exhale leaves my body as I head back toward the stairs, but the sound of footsteps lifts my face just as her green eyes come into view.

She stops at the top, staring at me, blinking. My head shifts to the balcony, pointing to where I just saw her.

"What are you doing here? How'd you get here so fast? I just saw you—"

"I ran," she rushes out, brushing her hair from her face. "I saw you. So I pretended I had to pee. Then I ran here."

My eyes drop to her chest, seeing it rise and fall quickly, then to her hand, the wine goblet still in it.

She ran.

"You're supposed to give that back." I grin, making her smile.

She drops her eyes before coyly looking up through a forest of lashes. "Why are you up here and not down there?"

"We came to the earlier mass. Is that what you're asking?"

She shakes her head. "No. Are you up here for me?"

Yes. I take a step closer, not on purpose, but her body calls me to it.

"I had something to say to you."

Her eyes urge me to speak, hungry for the words on the tip of my tongue. But more footsteps have her spinning around, then back to me. Her fingers press over her lips as she hurries toward me, pushing me backward with one hand, wine sloshing in the other.

"Go. We have to hide."

The petite hand against my chest presses me backward as I smile, taking the wine goblet from her.

"Nobody's coming. It's from the hall downstairs."

She opens the door to the confessional, shoving me inside as she takes the other side, the one where the priest usually sits.

I'm laughing to myself, ready to walk back out as she whispers, "Shh. Shh. Shh. Please. I just want another second."

Another second...with me. That's all it takes to seal my fucking lips.

We sit in silence, each on our own sides of the box, separated by a wooden partition with small clovers carved out, giving me just enough of her face. The footsteps fade, leaving us alone again, and a sigh of relief leaves her lips. My eyes close, gripped by the sweetness of the sound.

Sutton's face comes closer, exorcising all thought from my body as I stare at her delicate profile. What is it with this girl? I don't think straight around her.

I'm sitting in a fucking confessional, hiding, staring at her face through a partition.

My eyes dart to the goblet in my hand, and I bring it to my lips, downing the rest of the wine as she whispers, "What are you thinking right now?"

She's so close that I can see her lick her lips after asking. I wipe over my lips with the back of my hand before I speak.

"That I'm a criminal... What are you thinking?"

She answers without hesitation, touching the partition.

"That I'm a liar... Why are you a criminal?"

I bring my fingers up, almost touching hers, but hover, tracing them in the air instead.

"Because I was born that way... Why are you a liar?"

"Because I promised I'd stay away from you."

Her hand drops away, but I linger, still lost in the memory of how her skin feels.

More silence stretches out until she whispers, "What did you want to say to me?"

Everything. Nothing. Fuck, I don't know.

"Would it matter?"

"No. But do you still want to tell me?"

"Yes."

The answer leaves my lips without permission because I'm no longer in control of my mind or body. I'm possessed by that same goddamn thought from earlier.

"Get out."

My fingers scramble over the door, searching for the handle, swinging it open quickly as I step out.

I'm already reaching for hers as she yanks it open, but before she can exit, I grip the nape of her neck, pulling her flush against me, sealing my mouth over hers.

Her gasp is swallowed by my tongue dipping inside, taking the exact fucking thing I wanted last night—a kiss.

But this one's rough and forceful. Because I'm willing to steal something undeserved and leave her lips swollen from the fucking possession I feel.

I want to burn my mark into the softness of her mouth—more than I've ever needed anything.

My head twists, taking from her as she grips the front of my dress shirt. Her fingertips curl around the fabric, pressing her body as close as possible, melting into me.

She tastes like regret, but I'm happy to suffer through it because I've never felt a bigger high.

We kiss, untamed like we could tear each other apart, until all the sounds become muted and the darkness of our eyelids takes over. Our tongues glide and dance over each other's, slowing, teasing, just until we're on the brink of need before diving in recklessly for more.

Her lips drag over mine, tongues moving in rhythm, breath stolen and given until we're the only goddamn thing that exists.

Fuck. I've kissed her my whole life—it's what it feels like.

Music floats around us, ethereal and angelic, as she runs her hands up my chest, wrapping them around the back of my neck. My head tilts in the other direction, hand rooted in her hair as I deepen our connection again.

The priest begins the benediction, but I'm not paying any attention until she tries to pull away because I'm fucking desperate for her.

As she does, my mouth finds her jaw, forcing her head to the side to give me more room. I lick and suck down her smooth neck, wanting to mark her as I run my tongue to where her shoulders meet. Goose bumps erupt as I growl into her flesh, hearing her sigh my fucking name.

"Calder."

I'm drawn to a complete stop, eyes meeting hers as I swallow hard. Because of the way she just said it. Fuck. Me.

The shit I'm feeling right now scares me. I barely know her. But right now, hearing my fucking name said like a goddamn prayer from those sweet lips—I'll kill any person that tries to take my place. There's no doubt in my mind. That's the power this girl holds over me.

I want to keep what I can't have.

Walk the fuck away before you actually burn it all to the ground.

Even as I think it, I'm so fucking spun that my mouth's hanging open, wanting more of hers, leaning in as she shakes her head.

"We can't."

"I know."

Her mouth meets mine, body arching toward me, hands in my hair before she pushes me away again.

"We really can't."

"I really know."

I yank her forward, wanting more seconds, but her palms cradle my face, forcing me to look at her as she whispers, "Be someone different."

I can't.

"Don't give a shit." I counter, but the look on her face says it all.

She can't.

My brows draw together, and I let my hands fall away as I step back from her.

She doesn't say a word, stepping out of the confessional, tucking her hair behind her ears before walking back toward the stairs and disappearing back to where she came from.

"Hey. Where the fuck did you disappear to today?"

I look up from where I've been hiding out—the passenger seat of the convertible GTO marked with primer—to see Roman walking toward me.

"Nowhere. Just had some shit to deal with."

The journal in my hand snaps shut as he raises his brows, opening the driver's-side door and sliding in.

"That *shit* wouldn't have to do with a certain little redhead, would it?"

I rest my arm on the door, not answering, so he smirks.

"You know Pops will have your ass. She's not worth that."

I chuckle. "You don't have to worry about me. I know my place. There's no pussy in this world that changes that."

"But—" he presses.

I hate that he can always read my mind. When we were kids, people used to always say that we thought with the same brain. Probably because every single one of our ideas was bad. But even then, Roman and I were always on the same page.

"But—" I groan, dropping my head with a grin. "She was—I don't fucking know. It was like for a hot minute I got out of the grime. You know?"

His brows draw together, and he grips the steering wheel as he stares out the front windshield.

"That's a dangerous game, C. Dudes like us need this life because, without it, we don't make sense. You start going around forgetting who the fuck you are, and shit's gonna go south."

He's right, and I know it. But that doesn't mean I don't hate it. My head falls back on the seat, as I begin tapping the leather journal on my knee.

"Like I said, you don't have to worry. I know my place."

Roman half-laughs. "How many more times are you gonna say that shit before it becomes the truth?"

I stare out the window, jaw tense, not answering because the truth is I don't know. I know my place isn't with her, but I also can't shake the feeling that hers is with me. Goddamn. That kiss... For a few precious moments, she made me forget about the blood on my hands and the gun at my back. Because all I felt was her.

But that's what makes Roman so fucking right. This *is* a dangerous game because there is no "out." Not for real. Sutton's a lie—a mirage, just like the world she lives in. Because the only way out of my life is in a body bag.

My head turns to Roman to say just that, but the door to the garage swings open, hitting the wall as West stumbles in, face busted open.

"What the fuck."

Blood drips down his cheek from a gash over his eye as Roman and I jump out, over the doors.

"What the fuck happened?" Roman barks, grabbing a rag from the tool bench and pressing it to West's head as he sits on a chair.

He's mumbling, barely able to speak through his swollen mouth, but I bring my hands to his face anyway, forcing him to look at me.

"Who did this?"

He stutters, trying to speak, palming his ribs as he coughs, before looking at me, ragged breaths between his words. "Some college guys on bikes…down by…down by the wharf."

Motherfuckers.

"Are they still there?"

Roman doesn't wait for the answer, walking toward the racks and pulling a bat down. West nods, and my eyes meet Roman's.

"Help me get him in the car."

He shakes his head. "He can barely walk."

West groans as I pull him to stand, but Roman grabs my forearm before letting go quickly.

"He's all fucked-up, man. Leave him here."

My eyes lock to West's, gritting the words out from between my teeth.

"You wanna stay behind?"

He drops his face to the floor, not answering, but I tug it back up.

"You never let another man fight your goddamn battles. I don't give a fuck how bad it hurts—if there's breath in you, you fight. To the fucking death if it's your time. But you never roll the fuck over. You understand me?"

He nods, stepping out of my grip, lifting his chin before ambling toward the car door like he should. But as I follow, Roman's hand on my shoulder stops me.

"You gonna run this by Pops?"

I shake my head, looking over my shoulder.

"I don't need permission to protect my fucking brothers."

Roman doesn't move, eyes searching mine before a smile breaks out over his face.

"Then let's fuck shit up."

The minute the car skids to a stop, my feet hit the pavement, bat in hand, nothing but violence in my fucking veins. Adrenaline buzzes like an electric shock as we rush toward three assholes in their pussy-ass leather gear standing next to and on some bikes.

"Which one?" I roar, flipping the bat from head to handle, pointing it in front of me.

West motions toward the guy in the middle, wearing a leather jacket with racing stripes. But all three start to square up laughing as we walk toward them.

You're gonna eat this fucking wood.

"You do this to my brother?" I growl as he flips me off like he's going to fucking do something.

He doesn't get a chance to try because the first crack knocks the motherfucker off his bike. The second splits his skull. My chest heaves as I look over the two still standing frozen from fear.

"Who's next?"

Roman rushes the guy to my left just as I'm encased in a bear hug from behind. Fuck. I'm tossed to the ground, feeling the asphalt embed in my arm as all hell breaks loose. It's like everything is on fast-forward. I shoot to my feet, toe to toe with some wannabe fucking biker, lifting my fists before throwing down.

Everyone's swinging, kicking, brawling—trying to kill each other.

Two more guys make their way out of the bar they were squatting in, running up on us as Roman knocks some cocksucker out. Obscenities fill the air as their yells get louder with each blow we deliver. A crack to my jaw makes me spit blood as I grin because I don't feel anything but invincibility.

And the need to kill.

"You'll have to do better than that, pussy."

The dude comes at me again, but I throw my fist into his throat, hearing him immediately gasp for air and fall to his knees. My head turns to see West with the bat I dropped, using it like a fucking meat cleaver on the guy he pointed out.

"Ro," I bellow, pointing to West as Roman brings his boot down on another guy's ribs.

He nods, stalking over to make sure West doesn't kill the guy, as I throw a heavy kick to the guy on all fours, still searching for air. But as I do, a roar comes my way.

I'm charged, picked up off the ground, tumbling down back on the concrete again. Two hard punches land against my cheek, but it's like fuel to the fucking fire. I grab the dude's hair, knocking my skull into his.

"Fuck," he screams.

I push him back, straddling the piece of shit as I hurl punch after devastating punch into his face.

"You think you can touch my family," I roar. "You're a dead man now."

I grab his hair, yanking his head up before smashing it down on the concrete over and over. All the anger inside of me pours out. I'm drowning him in it.

He spits blood to the side, head flopping down as my knuckles come down, splitting open—my blood swirling with his.

But I don't stop because this is who I am.

The person I will never escape. The man I'm meant to be.

There is no goodness. No soul. No gentleness.

I'm an animal.

I throw one more punch before I'm hauled off, Roman yelling in my ear.

"Cops. We gotta get out of here."

I shove off Roman, throwing a boot into the guy's ribs.

"Fuck them. Let 'em come."

"Calder," Roman yells, tugging on me, but I kick the guy again.

Roman grips my shoulder, smacking my face. "Enough, C. We can't risk cops—Tyler would kill us. Or West. We gotta go."

He's walking backward as I stand, breathing hard, mind fighting with emotion until I nod, stumbling into the present, and follow.

West is moving slowly as we walk past him, so I throw his arm over my shoulder, hearing him say, "I fought, Calder. I wasn't a pussy," before he drops the bat, spitting up blood.

My words are breathless as we rush toward the car.

"Good job, West. You can rest now."

I swing the car door open, pulling the front seat forward to let West lie down in the back as I look out over the carnage. Preppy assholes are laid out, slowly trying to get to their feet, except the one I was fighting. He might just be knocked the fuck out. Or he might be dead.

I don't give a fuck either way.

This is my place—in the streets, as judge and executioner.

I look down at my hands, trying to remember what she felt like. But all I feel is the sting from my cuts and slickness from blood replacing where her hair lay softly across them.

"Get the fuck in, Calder."

I do, shutting the door as Roman peels out, shifting his face toward mine.

"You good?"

"Never been better."

Chapter Twelve

Sutton

Aubrey's staring at Hunter from her desk, deep in thought, which worries me. What is she plotting?

She blinks, pulling out of her thoughts and shifting her head to my questioning face.

"Sorry, I still cannot get over the fact you saw that West dude get a blow job—I know you said you were cringing, but it's kind of hot. And I'm here for it."

Of course that's what she's thinking about. Perv.

I shake my head, trying not to laugh. "*I* can't get over the fact that you're still thinking about it. Four days later."

"Shh," Piper whispers from her desk.

Aubrey rolls her eyes. "Whatever. It's been in my spank bank reel since Saturday."

Piper glares at Aubrey, making me fold my lips under as she answers the look.

"Oh, calm down. I'm sure Twisted Sister had some fun in her day before she locked it up for Christ."

We start giggling, garnering a slap on the table that forces us to face forward in our seats. Aubrey stares at me, opening her eyes wide and mouthing, "I hate her," as I smile.

My eyes drop to my desk, the moment washing away as I stare at my nails. The sound of a dry-erase marker fills the room. I don't look up, spreading my fingers over the desk and pressing my fingertips into the hard surface, drifting quickly into the memory of Calder's chest.

I haven't thought of much else since Sunday. That kiss left its mark, leaving me burning in all the right places. But I meant what I said. We can't.

Even if I wanted to change my mind, I couldn't. After my mother questioned if I'd ever met Calder and his brothers in the back of the limo, my father was crystal clear with his expectation.

I was scared she saw right through me when I lied, but it wasn't her I needed to worry about. It was my father. He'd erupted, grabbing my arm as he yelled.

"Sutton, you will stay far away from those boys. They're trash. I won't have my daughter mixed up with those lowlifes. This isn't a suggestion. It's a goddamn order. I will not be disobeyed. Am I understood?"

I wanted to protest and tell him Calder was nice, that he was misjudged, but we'd both know that'd be a lie. Calder admitted as much in the confessional. And for the first time in my life, my father scared me.

Think about him just enough but not enough to forget his name or yours, Sutton. It's what I've repeated over and over in my head every single day.

Especially last night. I lay around, letting my hands roam over my body, remembering every single delicious moment. Hoping if I satisfied my urges, I'd exorcise him from my mind.

I imagined his eyes on me, his smile against my skin, hands on my waist, chest pressed to mine…fuck…the way he wove his hand into my hair before kissing me. I thought about him until all I could chant was his damn name.

A wisp of breath breezes past my parted lips as I trace the swirl pattern on the wooden desk with my fingertip.

"Psst. Psst."

I look up, still lost in thought, as I draw my curved pout between my straight teeth, trying to recreate the perfect sting of our first kiss, but my eyes meet Hunter's.

"Psst."

He smiles from a few seats up, so I half-smile back, feeling Piper pinch my back. I ignore her, almost irritated over being interrupted, but I know she won't stop. They've been bugging me all week to talk to him. I suppose Wednesday's the breaking point.

They almost died, swooned to death, when I told them how he apologized before they jumped right back on the Hunter wagon. I can't be mad. Of course they did—he's Hunter Kelly. A week ago, I would've laughed if someone said that dating him would feel like settling.

But it does because it is. Calder's lips made it that way. Which is fucked-up because Calder is a rule I can't break. There wouldn't be any forgiveness afforded me.

In this world, rebellion is quietly ignored so long as it never affects real life.

You don't date the son of a crime boss for the Irish mob when you're the daughter of a senator. *No matter how much you think about him.*

Hunter waves a note at me, quickly putting it behind him on Shephard's desk. Shep looks up, and I see Hunter whispering something to him before their heads shift in my direction. Shephard glances at Sister Christine, and when she turns to write on the board again, he tosses the note on my desk.

"Open it," Piper whispers.

I cover it quickly, sliding it down onto my lap and unfolding it to read.

Ditch with us to the beach. Don't say no, or I'll cry. I promise you the most epic day. And don't say you'll think about it— time's up, beautiful.

I look up at him, and he's feigning puppy dog eyes. Oh my God. I laugh. I can't help it. But I have to cover a hand over my mouth, faking a cough because Sister Christine is glaring at me.

"Sorry, Sister. Tickle in my throat."

When she looks away, I hand the note over my shoulder to Piper, hearing a whispered "Hell yeah" before she passes it to Aubrey, who stands and puts on her sunglasses.

"Can we go now?"

Piper starts to laugh, but before Aubrey's yelled at or expelled, the bell rings. We all stand, gathering our things, and file out, laughing and joking, only me trying to avoid the nun's glare.

The minute we're in the hall, Shephard snags Piper, mauling her with attention as Aubrey shoots her attention to Hunter.

"Where to, fearless leader?"

He grins, throwing his arm over my shoulder, but I shrug it off. He gives me a slight pout but answers Aubrey.

"Cross Point Beach. Everyone drops what they don't need and meets at the park in ten minutes before the next bell. I'm driving."

"What about bathing suits?" Piper cuts in. "And regular clothes for later. Girls don't carry an extra pair of basketball shorts and a hoodie in the back of our cars."

The guys laugh, but Aubrey waves her off. "My house is on the way. We can stop there, and you two can take whatever from my closet."

"Perfect." Hunter smiles.

The girls link hands as they walk away, Shephard by Piper's side. But I'm still playing catch-up.

My teeth find the inside of my cheek, gnawing as I think. Nobody else has parents that will care or be home to get an absence call, so they can do this stuff. If I ditch, the school will call my father. And he won't care that it's the last week.

Hunter tugs on the bottom of my polo.

"Hey. Freckles. Stop worrying. Just tell your dad you're hanging with me. Trust me, he'll be fine with it. I'll even talk to him if you want."

My head draws back as we walk to my locker.

"Wow, such an inflated ego. Also, how'd you know that's what I was thinking?"

He nudges my shoulder. "Not inflated. Great-grandson of a former president, but it's not a competition, so—"

I giggle, but he shrugs.

"He's hoping for a future nomination, right? A chance at the top seat in politics? Who better for his daughter to get cozy with than a Kelly?" Hunter's fingers weave between mine as he nods a hello to someone passing by. "Trying to have fun under a microscope is fucking hard. Trust me, I get it. Of all people, I get you."

I push him sideways, tugging my hand away. "I'll think about it."

He groans as we stop in front of the row of metal doors, and I spin my lock open.

"Don't think. Just call. Give me a chance to win you over. I've got epic plans for today." He puts his head on my shoulder. "Have you ever been kissed underwater? We can make out with the fishies."

I swing my bag to the side, shoving everything in except my purse.

"Is this your big offer? Making out underwater?"

Hunter licks his lips, pushing my shoulder so I'm forced to turn my back against the locker as he stares down at me.

"I'll make you any offer you want, Freckles. I haven't stopped thinking about you, and the silent treatment this week is killing me."

"I've been preoccupied." I shrug, feeling his hand on my waist.

Hunter bends down to my ear, speaking quietly. "If you're not thinking about me, then I hate— Every. Single. Other. Thought."

He reaches into my bag, pulling out my cell.

"Call your dad, Sutton. I'm not waiting any longer for you to decide about us—I'm going to make it so you can't say no."

I'm staring back at him, eyes searching his as he places the phone into my hand. *Oh, Hunter, what am I going to do about you?* There's no real reason for me not to take him up on the offer. Absolutely none. What's the alternative? That I sit around and obsess over someone I'll never see again?

I did that in sixth grade over Harry Styles, and obviously, that worked out well.

Hunter grins as I hit my dad's number. He answers immediately.

"Sutton. I have a meeting in ten minutes."

My hand comes to Hunter's muscular chest, forcing him back so that I can have some space.

"Sorry, Dad. It's just…" I fold my lips between my teeth then decide to just say it. "Hunter invited me to a ditch day—everyone's going. But if you—"

"Hunter's going?"

Are you kidding? Wait, why am I mad…I want to ditch, right?

"Yep. Hunter's going. His friends, my friends. Probably the whole junior class. Actually, that's a lie, but it's still a thing. I didn't want to go without asking." I lower my voice, glancing over my shoulder at Hunter. "I know you and Mom prefer me not to go to these kinds of things. But it is the last week of school, so maybe give me some credit for waiting and calling?"

My father cuts me off. "Everyone needs to cut loose sometimes. And I can definitely get behind a few sanctioned outings. Is Hunter with you, Sutton?"

I blink, wondering who the hell I'm speaking with because this is not my father. My head swings over my shoulder, nodding before I answer hesitantly.

"Yes. He. Is."

"Let me speak to him, please."

"No," I draw out. "Please tell me that you're joking. Are you okay?"

He laughs louder this time, and I feel like I'm having an out-of-body experience. I can count the number of times on one hand that I've heard my father laugh.

"Sutton, if you want to go, I get to speak with the boy that will name your future dog Chardonnay."

Oh my God. Let me die. He has to be drunk.

"Dad," I whisper. "What is going on with you? Do not embarrass me. And for the record, we're just friends."

I turn just as the bell rings, holding the phone out to Hunter's smug face. I don't have to say anything. His arrogant *I told you so* look is enough. He takes the phone, motioning for me to head toward the exit as he brings it to his ear.

"Sir."

I can't hear what's said, but Hunter's answering, "Absolutely" … "You have my word" … "Will never happen" and "I look forward to it."

He hangs up, taking my hand and shoving my phone into his back pocket.

"What did he say?" I breathe out as we rush across the quad.

Hunter looks over his shoulder with a panty-melting smirk and a wink.

"He said I should knock you up. And then he invited me to

dinner this weekend."

"Sutton. Come on. Get in. Right now."

Hunter's yelling from the water, splashing at me even though I'm too far away. Aubrey rolls to her side, looking out at the water and then back to me.

"That boy is so hot for you. I'm glad we gave him a second chance because I'm manifesting prom queen for your future."

I give a half-laugh, propped up on my elbows and staring out at the bluest ocean while white, foamy waves glisten against the shore.

Piper holds her boobs, looking at me and saying, "Do me?" as she rolls up to sitting. I lean over, tying her top for her, giggling again as the guys goof off in the water.

The day is amazing despite the war in my mind.

It's actually been one of those perfectly laid plans. The ones that you know will become a memory that you'll keep tucked inside to pull out when you need to remember a moment in time when you were exquisitely happy.

Piper runs her fingers through her blonde pixie cut and shrugs. "So let's get back to this past weekend. Are you still letting Hunter pillage your treasure?"

Aubrey sits up, tugging down her sunglasses. "Yeah? Because that hymen is still *seriously* intact. Inquiring minds want to know, ho."

I groan, motioning for the sunscreen. Piper hands it over, and I begin applying as I speak.

"I don't know. I'm thinking about it. But I'm leaning toward holding off for a while."

Piper wrinkles her forehead, sitting up further. "Bullshit."

Aubrey, whose mouth is hanging open, laughs.

"Piper. Is our girl about to become a legend?"

She snaps her fingers along with the first few words before adding, "To be the first person—and I say person because everyone wants Hunty's dick—to turn down a god and make him wait?"

Piper's eyes get wide, the grin on her face growing. "That's legend status, bish. Making him fall in love with you and having to wait for the nonny."

Aubrey shakes my shoulders, making me giggle. "Fuck you, Sutton Tensley Prescott. Who knew you had the long con down?"

I roll my eyes as Piper starts laughing, making Aubrey and I do the same because her laugh is atrocious. Only a tiny piece of me wants to tell them all about the kiss with Calder and explain why I really don't want to fuck Hunter. But I can't.

Sometimes when you say stuff out loud, it makes it too real, and I'm not ready to give up the fantasy. Even if I have to give up hope. And I don't care how dumb that is. Right now, Calder's still mine, and I like it that way.

The guys start making their way up the beach to our towels, shoving each other playfully. Shephard descends on Piper, getting her all wet, as she squeals, but Hunter looks between Aubrey and me.

"One of you walks. The other is going over my shoulder. You choose."

Aubrey and I look at each other, grinning before she says, "Stick that bitch over your shoulder. I'm walking."

I scream as I'm hauled to my feet. But it's drowned out by a crackle in the sky. We all look up to the bright orange fire streak climbing toward the clouds.

"Oh shit. Tag must be here. They're over at the cliffs."

Shephard says it like we know what he's talking about.

"He sends up a flare," Hunter offers, grabbing his T-shirt off the towel, "to let everyone around know to come party. The cliffs are gnarly, but Tag and his friends have been jumping off them for years."

He reaches for my hand. "Throw on some shorts. There's a private cove with access. It's close and guaranteed fun."

Aubrey wraps a sarong around her hips as Piper shimmies up her jean cut-offs. But I opt for my knotted T-shirt and shorts before we walk back to Hunter's truck. We toss everything into the bed before Aubrey scoots inside the car next to Piper and Shephard as I take the front seat.

Hunter pulls out as Shep begins talking about all the near-death experiences he's seen when people jump, so I turn to Hunter, raising my brows.

"You guys are jumping?"

"Hell no," Shep barks from the back. "My face is too pretty for a casket. But his ugly mug can."

Hunter smirks but keeps looking at the road. "Don't trip. Although I'm happy to see you care."

I roll my eyes with a grin on my face as he continues.

"There are three levels. I jump from the middle one, and the bottom one is for the girls, mostly. Nobody does the top—it's too dangerous, and only people with a death wish try that shit. It's fine. You'll see."

My eyes are still on him, unconvinced as he pulls onto the small side road that winds down to a private cove. I hear Shephard say, "There's my place, way over there, babe," to Piper.

Babe? Well then. Time to start grilling her for a change.

Hunter parks at the dead end, and I spot Tag's Corvette because his name is on the plate—*douche*—along with a few other cars I don't recognize.

We get out. Hunter comes around to take my hand as we walk down some wooden steps onto the sand. This time I let him, not pulling away. Because would it be so bad if Hunter was the one?

The music gets louder as more people come into view, about

thirty feet away around a fire pit, cutting off my thoughts and drawing a smile on my face.

"How does he have this many friends to hang out with? Don't they have classes?"

Hunter smirks. "The semester's over for them, Sutton. Duh."

"Oh."

I duck my chin to my shoulder, looking out from the cove, hiding my embarrassment before I turn to look at Hunter. A quick kiss is planted against my lips, surprising me, before he lets go of my hand. "Be right back."

I shift, watching him half jog away toward the crowd as a long exhale bursts from my lips, making my cheeks inflate. Aubrey comes up next to me, weaving her fingers through mine as Hunter navigates the crowd. He's giving high fives and happily accepting all the attention he gets as he makes his way over to Tag.

"I fear *stud* is your soon-to-be boyfriend's default setting."

I smile because she's not wrong.

"Yeah, and it's annoyingly hot sometimes. I just—I don't know—"

She bumps my hip.

"You okay, Sut? You've been weirder than usual."

Aubrey can always read me well. I turn my head, looking at my beautiful friend, wanting to spill everything because I don't think I am okay. *How do you stop feeling something?* That's what I want to ask her, but I'm cut off by Shephard.

He holds up the coolers he's carrying toward some logs in front of us.

"Drink?"

He's offering it to Piper, but we all answer.

"Coke." … "Water." … "Vodka." Piper and I stare at Aubrey, who smiles, changing her order. "Geez, fine. Sprite. But there is a whole party going on over there."

He gives us a little salute. The girls start chatting, Aubrey forgetting my weird moment as my eyes begin wandering around. I've lived here my whole life, and I never knew that this cove was even here.

How was I this clueless?

My hand shades my eyes because even with sunglasses, the sun is too bright as I look up at the cliffs that jut out where the cove opens to the ocean.

"Damn. Those are high."

A high-pitched scream comes as someone jumps from the lowest point, shooting down into the water, distant cheers erupting.

Piper links an arm through my free one. "So yeah. That's terrifying. No, thanks."

"Dude. That's the low ledge." Aubrey points out, drawing her finger up to a higher cut out in the rock. "That's the middle—where Hunty said he jumps from."

I nod, giggling a bit at Aubrey's nickname for Hunter, letting my eyes carry even higher.

"Oh shit. There's someone up there."

The girls follow my line of sight. Our lips collectively parted.

Hunter walks up, and the girls release me so he can put his arm over my shoulder. But I don't look at him, fixated on the speck of a figure standing at the top of the jagged cliff.

"Someone's up there," I whisper. "That's the highest point, right?"

Hunter stares up. "Yeah. Get ready to call an ambulance. That dude's crazy."

Shep laughs as he hands our drinks to us, but it's not funny. Whoever's up there could get hurt.

Aubrey nudges me, whispering, "I thought he said nobody jumped from there."

"Nobody does," Hunter answers back, having heard her. "Way

back, like before we were born, some guy died. So everyone knows it's too dangerous."

All of a sudden, the guy in black swim trunks runs toward the edge. I suck in a breath, bringing my fingers to my lips. Oh, God.

The chatter on the beach goes silent. Even the music is turned down as he hurls himself off the cliff, doing a backflip. The kind where your whole body stays long rather than tucking knees to chest.

It's badass, like something you'd see in a movie.

Every person on this beach is watching with bated breath, frozen in place as he drops like he's falling from heaven for what feels like forever until a splash erupts.

Hearts start beating again, everyone collectively returning to life as people slowly stand, their eyes searching the water.

I'm counting in my head, waiting for the guy to surface, but there's nothing. It's too long. It's been way too long. I pull away from Hunter, my feet carrying me closer to the water as my heart begins beating out of my chest.

Reaching behind me, I'm about to tell Hunter to swim out when the daredevil pops up, garnering howls and cheers from the entire beach.

"Whoa," I whoosh out, before looking back over my shoulder.

Hunter and Shep start talking about the guy being crazy, but my eyes are on the water, smile fading inch by inch because as the daredevil swims closer to shore, all I see are muscular tattooed arms slicing through the water.

Shit.

Chapter
Thirteen

Sutton

Aubrey slow claps, drawing our attention.

"Okay, now that the drama's over and that dude's alive, let's swim."

Hunter pats my ass. "Come on, beautiful. Strip. Let's get in."

I turn around, a smile on my face, never breaking stride as I join back in. Because what else can I do? Shephard makes a joke, pulling a laugh from everyone as I look around, pretending to scope out the best log for our clothes. But really, my eyes are back on him.

Calder walks out of the water, droplets streaming down his chest as he makes his way toward the party, and I swear my body goes numb. Why is he here? I stupidly thought we'd never see each other again, but here he is—the walking definition of sin.

The chest I was obsessing over a few hours ago.

"We can put our stuff here," I half mumble, the confessional racing to the forefront of my mind.

I look down, staring at the sand, going through the motions, unbuttoning my jean shorts. I lick my lips, eyes darting over and back, knowing that Calder has seen me.

Because my whole body warms, feeling his eyes rake over me.

I give my hips a shimmy to pull the shorts down, step out, and bend down to pick them up.

Another glance, and I reach for my shirt. I hate and love Calder watching me because it feels unbearable either way. I lift my shirt over my head, left only in a black string bikini. It's smaller than my normal ones, but all Aubrey had are the ones that pretty much show your ass.

Hunter sweeps my hair over my shoulder as I start to sneak another glance, stopping me.

"Hey, you need more sunscreen on your shoulders."

I give a tiny nod, feeling his hand slide the cold cream over my skin. His name is called again, and I know he looks over his shoulder, so I risk another peek.

Calder's eyes aren't on me. They're on Hunter—boring into where he's touching me, Calder's fists squeezed so tight the veins on his forearms look angry.

I shiver.

But not because I'm scared. It feels like I took a hit of the shit Tag likes to smoke. I've felt Calder, and I want more. Even if I shouldn't. But now, seeing the hate in his eyes over another guy touching me just turned me into an addict.

No. Stop. What the fuck is wrong with you? You're a crackhead.

"You okay? You shivered, Freckles."

I swing around, staring Hunter in the eyes, desperate for him to replace the feeling in my body Calder gives with a single look. A small indent forms between his eyes as he looks down at me.

"I know you saw him. Do you think we should go?"

If this is his way of asking *"Do you still like him?"* then I'm going to give him the answer I should've before.

"Do you? Because I'll do whatever you want. I'm here with you."

That's the correct answer, even if it doesn't sit right in my gut.

Hunter rewards me with a grin, leaning in and kissing my forehead.

"Nah, let's stay. I kinda like showing you off."

Shephard calls Hunter's name, motioning with a football before I can push back. He runs a few feet away, catching the throw with one hand, giving me a wink and pointing the ball at me.

"That one's for you. Want another?"

I nod, saying, "Absolutely," before turning back to the sunscreen and the mindfuck I'm feeling.

"Catch" is all I hear before I'm pelted by Piper's shorts, making me giggle and snap out of the wicked amount of spiral brimming the edge of bad ideas.

"Thanks a lot. Jerk."

She comes up next to me, eyes shining as Aubrey closes in on the other side of me.

"You're welcome. Also, you're shit at hiding."

My brows draw together. "What are you talking about?"

Aubrey tugs my hair. "You're still hot for the town criminal. Can't keep your eyes off him. But now we know he really is a criminal, so says Shephard. Apparently, there's a rumor that his dad is in the mob."

I shrug it off.

"Whatever." The girls look at each other, half believing my false nonchalance. "I'm not hot for anyone except Hunter."

Just add another lie on top of the others.

"Are you talking about me again?" Shephard teases, coming up behind Piper just as Hunter takes my hand.

I smile, letting him lead me toward the water, never glancing back once.

Chapter Fourteen

Calder

Red. It's all I saw from the top of that fucking cliff. Wild red hair, carrying in the fucking ocean breeze.

"Dude. That was amazing."

Tag raises his hand to high-five me, but I just look at it before catching the towel Roman throws me. So, Tag lowers his hand, taking a hit off the shit he called us out here for, exhaling his words in a cloud of smoke. "It was fucking crazy. But I got that shit on the GoPro. It'll make for some wicked footage."

I bend down, grabbing the speaker off the sand, and turn up the music before lowering myself down into an empty beach chair. Roman chuckles, passing me a joint.

"Remind me why the fuck we're hanging out with this asshole?"

Rubbing the towel over my head, I smirk. "Because he buys a ton of drugs. And neither of us is trying to hang out with Pops explaining the bruises on our faces. Let's just be glad he's got bigger fish to fry right now."

As I draw in and hold a breath, he grins. My eyes find her again before I exhale harshly, passing the joint back to Roman. She's walking up the beach, looking at me like I'm doing to her. Neither of us is hiding it well. My tongue darts out over my bottom lip, the sting still there from where it got popped a few days ago.

"Speaking of avoiding Pops, did you text West to get his ass down here? I never thought there'd be a day when he went to school for like days in a row."

I nod my head, eyes still on Sutton. *That bikini's too fucking small.*

"Yeah."

Roman's breath is held as he speaks. "Dude. You're fucking dumb. And a glutton for punishment."

"Fuck you. I'm just lookin'."

He chuckles, blowing smoke at me, "Yeah, for fucking trouble."

I shift my face to his. "I'm sitting in a chair. Not balls-deep in her. How the fuck you figure I'm looking for trouble?"

"You can't even help it. This doesn't end any other way than bloody, dude."

I wave him off. "You've been smoking too much. Paranoia's kicking in."

"Naw, that's bullshit. I know what I see. I saw that dreamy-ass look on your face when we left that party, then on Sunday, and again right now."

I tense my jaw, disliking where this is going.

Roman leans in, passing the joint back. "Every damn time we see that girl, you're staring at her like she's the only fucking thing you see. If she ain't shit to you, then why can't you take your eyes off her?"

How am I supposed to answer that? Not with the truth—that she is the only thing I see. *Fuck.*

"Roman. Relax. Nothing's happening." I point my finger at him. "And stop fucking talking about last weekend. It's not your business. Understood."

He laughs, shaking his head.

"Fine, tough guy. I've seen what you can do with a bat. I'm chill. But brother to brother—be careful. Don't ever make it you versus him, C. Because you know who he'll choose."

By *him*, he means our Pops. And I know Roman's right, but I can't stop this goddamn feeling—one that says she's mine. I want her. I'll have her. And fuck anyone who tells me otherwise.

I look over at her again, nodding, barely hearing the rest of what Roman's saying as I take another long hit, but no amount of weed could keep me chill right now. Because the war inside my head just got a victor.

All I see is Hunter's fucking bitch hands on silky skin that belongs to me.

I'm gonna break every bone in his fucking body.

"Calder—" Roman calls, but I'm lost in a fog.

Sutton turns, saying something to Hunter, and for her sake, it better be "*fuck off.*" But my teeth grit so hard they may break because I know it isn't.

He runs a few steps away, her friends coming up next to her as I take my last hit, then hand that shit over to Roman.

"C. Should we bounce? You can't fuck up little Kelly—you know his father is too important to Pops right now."

"I'm good," I snap.

I'm not. Not even a little. I've crossed over from reckless to dangerous.

He hits my shoulder, trying to get my attention off her, but I don't budge. I can't. Hunter walks up, taking her hand, and I lean forward.

Don't you fucking dare go with him. Come the fuck here.

The minute she takes a step in his direction, I stand. Ready. Out of my mind.

"Calder," Roman barks.

I don't answer, taking a step forward.

"Calder." This time he's in my face, hand pushing me back. "Sit the fuck down. I told you—this shit is trouble. What the fuck are you doing? Trying to die? Let that shit go. Let that chick go. Remember your fucking place, bro."

I growl, looking at his face, and nod, realizing what I almost just did. What the fuck am I doing? I gotta get my head straight. And off this girl.

"Yeah. I got it." He frowns at me, but I push him back. "I said I'm fine. I got it."

He exhales harshly, watching me before grabbing some drunk bitch, who laughs loudly as he squeezes her ass and turns her in my direction.

"Here. Use this as a distraction."

I shake my head, but he chuckles and looks down at her trapped in between us.

"You know how to dance, sweetheart…because my brother's lap could use one."

The fit blonde with a set of double D's steps toward me, pushing a manicured finger against my chest until my ass hits the chair.

"Let's help you relax."

She swings around, sitting in my lap, grinding her cheeks against my dick. A deep groan leaves my chest, only because my body betrays my mind. Even still, I try like hell to give in to it.

Roman smirks, saying, "Keep him busy, mama," as he walks away, leaving me with this bitch on my lap and my mind fighting to remain elsewhere.

The high begins to take over, mouth drying, eyelids growing heavy, all my thoughts fading into the distance as taut skin warms under my hands. She's guiding them, rubbing them up her thighs as she circles her hips. But it doesn't feel like what I wish it did.

I pull one away, running it up her back into her hair, gripping at the nape and bringing her back to my chest.

"Make it good, and I'll let you ride my cock for real."

I don't like her on me, or me on her. I want the goddamn redhead in the water with the little prick. *Motherfucker.* I have to walk away and bury myself in as many fucking chicks as possible until Sutton Prescott becomes a girl I don't even remember.

Sutton

MY HANDS COME UP IN FRONT OF ME as Hunter lets go.

"No. Hunter. Don't."

His eyes are narrowed on me, grin in place as he walks back toward me.

"Too late, Freckles. You said you wanted to swim. No takesy-backsies. You're going all the way in."

I'm hauled over his shoulder with a squeal and carried down into the water, hearing my friends yelling and cheering before he tosses me in. I go under, popping up just as fast and letting out a gasp. The water's cold but refreshing, and as I stand, I wipe my hands over my face slicking my hair back.

"You're a dick." I'm laughing as he wades toward me. "But you know that already."

He wraps his arms around me, caging my arms in next to my body. Water laps around us as he stares down at me.

"You really think I'm a dick?"

I shake my head but answer, "Sometimes."

It's the truth. Hunter leans in, his nose rubbing over mine as his next question's asked quietly, but it feels like a bomb going off around me.

"Are you really here with me, Freckles?"

My heart picks up its pace because suddenly, I'm feeling trapped. In the background, I hear Aubrey talking about the girls' cliffs being lower and less scary than she thought, so I turn my head, avoiding the question.

"Are you about to do something crazy, Aubs?"

She smiles, splashing water toward me. "Who, me? Never. Of course I am."

My chest shakes as I turn back toward Hunter, whose eyes haven't left my face. I hate every single thing about the way he's staring at me. Jesus. I can't even look at him—that's how guilty I feel on the inside.

I can't tell him the truth—that I'm trying my hardest to be here with him, but that it takes all the concentration in my fucking body not to look over my shoulder at the boy stealing my every thought. Hunter closes his arms tighter as I lick my lips.

"Last one there has to go first." Shephard howls, then laughs before diving in and swimming in that direction. The girls scream and follow, but Hunter holds us in place.

"Look at me."

God. I can't, but I swallow as I do. "Come on, let's go with everyone."

He shakes his head. "Why haven't you answered me?"

Because I'm tired of lying.

I roll my eyes. "I have answered. I already told you I was."

He turns me around so that my back is against his chest as he spins us to face the beach. His words are whispered into my ear, giving me chills.

"I'm not the dick, Sutton. He is."

I blink, feeling heat crawling up my neck, and not the kind I feel when it's in my core. This is anger.

Calder's sitting in the same place my eyes left him, except now he has company. One with huge tits and a lot of blonde hair, rubbing her ass all over him.

It doesn't matter that I don't have a right to be mad. I'm doing the same thing. I know Calder and I can't happen.

I shouldn't be jealous. Or even possessive.

But I fucking am.

I twist in Hunter's grasp, determined not to care, draping my arms over his shoulders. But I can still see that girl on Calder's lap even though my eyes aren't on them anymore.

Hunter's face is a challenge that I'm ready to meet. Because the hate I feel is so unnatural inside my body that I'm desperate to replace it with anything. Including Hunter.

"I don't care. I told you already. What's the point of all this?"

"Prove it to me, then."

I blink. Hunter drops his hands to my ass, lifting me up to wrap my legs around his waist. And I instantly feel him against my center—hard and ready.

Oh fuck. God, it's as if I've suddenly jumped into the deep end of the pool but didn't know until my feet never touched the bottom.

I lick my lips, gripping his shoulders, feeling nervous as I stutter out my words.

"H-how?"

His lips press to mine, but I don't kiss him back as he says, "Come for me. Right here."

My head shifts around, heart starting to race as he buries his face in my neck, breathing out a half-laugh.

"Our friends are swimming toward the cliffs. We're all alone, and the party on the beach is far enough away, so nobody will see what's happening under the water. I want to make you come, Sutton. Here. For me."

My breath hitches as I feel his hand run up the underside of my thigh toward my core. *Let it happen, Sutton.* His fingers brush the fabric of my suit as his lips find my neck, speaking words into my flesh.

"I want to feel you wrapped around my fingers. Hear you say my name."

I look over my shoulder, needing to see it one more time. It's the only way I'll be able to toe this goddamn line—Calder's hand is on her back, another in her hair, as he whispers in her ear.

My eyelids close halfway as I turn back. Hunter is running his fingers back and forth over and over, teasing me. He dips in under the seam, stroking my soft tuft of hair, making my body contract as his mouth finds my collarbone. I squeeze my eyes shut, trying to rid myself of the memory of Calder kissing me near there.

No. Get out of my head.

Hunter's fingers move down toward my entrance as my eyes open, locked to his.

"You really want to prove to me that I'm the one?"

I'm nodding, panting, willing to lose myself to the sensation. *Just replace him.*

"Yes."

His finger slides over, just barely rimming my slit as we stare at each other.

"Then let *him* hear you say my name."

Oh my God. My mouth pops open as my hands shove against his immovable shoulders.

"What the fuck? No."

His grip tightens around my waist as his eyes narrow.

"Why not? Scream it. Let everyone on the fucking beach hear you. If you don't give a shit about him, then you'll let him know who you belong to."

"Belong to? I don't belong to anyone that would treat me like this."

"We'll see," Hunter smirks, leaning in to kiss me but I draw back, scowling at him.

"Get the fuck off."

"Don't fight this. You know you want it."

His hand begins touching places it shouldn't, making me physically ill. I drive my foot into his thigh as I shove my hands against his chest, forcing him to drop back into the water as I sink backward.

"Don't ever fucking touch me again."

He's staring at me, not a fraction of remorse on his face. But I am sorry. Sorry that I actually let him touch me.

"Insecurity's a bad look, Kelly." I lock eyes with him. "You had your shot, and you blew it. I'll find a ride home."

"Get back over here, Sutton."

"No," I yell over my shoulder, half swimming, then wading out of the water.

Hunter calls my name the entire time, but he won't follow. Chasing's not his style. I walk out, wringing out my hair over the sand all the way back to grab my stuff, opting to pick my clothes up rather than putting them on. I'd grab my towel, but it's in Hunter's car along with my damn phone.

Fuck.

A growl tears at my throat as tears prick at my eyes because I'm so fucking overwhelmed.

I shake out my hands, trying to calm myself down, but I can't. I feel stupid because I did this shit to myself and hurt because I never saw that coming.

And to add insult to injury, all I want to do is beeline over to the dickhead on the beach chair to tell him what happened. Then demand that he ignore that stupid slut on his lap and take me away from here.

Which is ridiculous because Calder's a figment of my

imagination.

Whatever connection I felt was me alone. That much is obvious. He doesn't seem to be in the middle of any kind of emotional war like I am. And it's just another reminder that I'm a fucking loser— out of my depth and gifted with the shittiest taste in men.

There is no magic. No Romeo. No prince. Just a bunch of dicks, ready to mindfuck you over.

I hate everyone.

Spinning around, I look up to see Piper and Aubrey waving from the cliff, so I wave back, wondering what the fuck I'm going to do. Shephard's still climbing up toward the lowest section, making me actually huff a laugh.

I have to get out of here. I shake my head, knowing precisely what I'm going to have to do. Shit. Securing my clothes to my side, I walk over toward where everyone is hanging to ask Tag to use his phone.

The closer I get, the harder it becomes not to look at Calder. The girl's gone. *Oh.* To West's lap. *When did he get here?* But Calder's in the same spot, drinking a beer. *Is that a bruise on his cheek?*

It's faded, like the one on his jaw. Now that I'm closer, I see that all the guys are banged up, West being the worst.

Calder's eyes meet mine, and I almost forget what I'm here to do. They're so blue, filled with a current that travels directly to every part of my body, but I look away because I'm not that girl—the one that begs for his attention. Nope. That girl is currently dry humping his brother.

Tag turns around, eyeing me as I slide between some people to stand next to him.

"Well, well. If it isn't the one that got away. You've got my brother spun. What kind of magic you got going on down there?"

He drops his eyes toward my stomach, but I know what he's referring to.

"You're disgusting," I snap but point toward where Aubs and Piper are still standing, waiting for Shep to jump. "How do I get there? Because after this conversation, I'd like to hurl myself off that cliff."

I'm really just asking so that I can go tell my friends I'm leaving. He isn't even offended, smirking as I add, "I also need to use your phone."

Tag motions a hand to an entrance at the bottom of the cliffs. It looks a lot like a cave, but he says, "It opens to the other side. There's a path up to all three. Can't miss it, beautiful." He steps in closer, making me step back. "And if you're looking for an upgrade—"

"Shut the fuck up, Tag," booms from behind me, pulling my eyes over my shoulder.

Hunter comes up behind, staring down at me.

"Can we talk?"

I let out a forced laugh, huffing, "Uh. No. Fuck off," before I spin around, heading toward the cave.

Ooo's follow us as the crowd around us splits.

"Sutton," Hunter calls to my back.

I flip him the bird, not looking behind me as I yell, "No."

"Then I guess we're jumping."

Asshole. I glance back, seeing Hunter stalk toward me along with a few of Tag's friends. But that's not what keeps my attention. It's Calder, West, and Roman following at the back.

A pack of Wolfes.

Fuck. Me.

Chapter
Fifteen

Sutton

This isn't happening. Shit. I walk faster as the guys who were tagging along pass me by, jogging toward the front side of the cliff to what I assume is a shortcut. My eyes shoot over my shoulder again, seeing Hunter's closing the distance between us, pissed off and determined.

However, that's not what's making me nervous.

It's the three sets of soulless eyes behind him. Stalking. Not just walking or strolling. They're stalking him—focused and terrifying.

It's one thing to know Calder is dangerous. It's another to see it in action. I squeeze my clothes tighter to my chest as I hurry inside the cave, wanting away from everyone.

I hate Hunter. And Calder.

"Sutton. Just fucking stop."

Hunter's voice is closer.

I shake my head in answer, the light dimming the deeper I get inside the cave, making me shiver.

Halo-like light shines from the exit just around a set of large boulders that hides us from outside view. So I try to pick up my pace, walking between them, but I can't over the hard pebbles.

I wince, stepping on something sharp just as my elbow is grabbed by Hunter, who hurls his meanness through gritted teeth.

"Goddammit, Sutton."

I'm spun around, causing me to lose my balance and fall to the ground, hard. Heat shoots up my leg, accompanied by stinging, just as crimson spreads over my thigh. I shriek, trying to cover the gash with both of my hands, but I can't because Hunter still has one of my arms in his grasp.

Everything happens so fast that I don't have enough time to be scared.

Hunter's face swings to the left, forcing him to let go of me just as a trail of blood splatters over the rocks from his mouth. His body swings in the same direction, landing right on Roman's chest, who lets him drop to the ground before bringing his cold eyes back to me.

Oh my God.

My face shoots to see who hit him, eyes landing on Calder's heaving chest, fists balled at his sides, savagery in his eyes.

Oh my God.

Calder lifts his chin, licking his bottom lip. "Touch her again and I'll fucking kill you."

"Oh my God." This time I say it out loud as my chest begins to tremble. *Am I crying?*

Calder's face meets mine as he squats down, eyes softening. He holds out his hand for me to take as tears cascade from the corners of my eyes. It feels like I can't catch up. I don't understand what I'm seeing.

I stare at Calder's hand, trying to process.

Calder hit Hunter. My head swings to Hunter, seeing him unconscious, then back to Calder. *Why would he do that?* My eyes drop to my leg, feeling the pain. *Did Hunter throw me to the ground, or did I fall?*

"Look at me, Sutton." Calder's voice is calm, drawing my eyes. "Are you okay?"

But I can't move or answer. I'm blinking so fast that I think it's in time with my pulse. I open my mouth, but nothing comes out except stuttered cries.

I swing my head back to Hunter. Oh God, he's not moving.

Calder crawls closer to me, inching in. "Shh. Shh. It's okay. Just look at me. Everything's okay."

My eyes swing back to his. Calder snaps his finger at West as he stares at my leg. "Gimme his shirt."

West reaches down, ripping off Hunter's shirt as he wobbles, groaning and reaching for his jaw.

Calder locks eyes with me as he extends the shirt he's now holding.

"Press it to your leg."

My fingers curl around the fabric, pulling it slowly from him, bringing it to my leg, and pressing down. I gasp when I feel the sharp pain, eyes tearing up again as I shake my head.

"Why? Why did you do that?"

I'm not sure what I'm even asking, but I've never seen anything like this. Boys fight. I've seen that. But this wasn't your typical fight. Calder tried to take Hunter's head off, and if he never woke up, I'm positive Calder would've slept just fine.

He did that for me…I think.

I'm scared, but I'm not sure of who anymore. The boy on the ground or the one in front of me. I just feel blurry and untethered.

"Why are you here?"

His hand comes up, fingers brushing my hair from my eyes

before he answers, making the world come back into focus.

"I'm here because you are."

The deepest inhale attacks me before I let out all my breath in a whoosh. I stare at him, and I know he just knows. He gets that of all the things I don't understand right now—that sentence isn't one of them.

"C'mere, baby."

My arms wrap around his neck so tight that I crush him. The scent of Calder mixed with sunshine fills my nose, so I nuzzle in closer to his neck as he tucks his strong arms under my knees, lifting me.

"Take me away from here," I whisper softly, crying into his skin.

"Put her the fuck down," Hunter groans, but Calder's eyes grow to the darkest blue as he speaks directly to Roman.

"Take him to the top. I'll be there in a minute."

Calder's arms tighten around me, carrying me out of the cave and back into the sunlight as he whispers his words into my hair.

"Sutton. Listen to me, okay. This never happened. You fell after Hunter went to the top. Do you understand?"

I nod against his skin, not lifting my eyes because I want to hide in his arms as he continues.

"Sutton." His voice is gravelly. "Did he hurt you in the water?"

My heart stops. Calder isn't an empty threat—he's a promise.

I lift my face to his bruised profile, wondering how to lie to him because I'm wholly compelled to do the opposite. How is that possible? I almost think, *I barely know him*, but that's not what he feels like.

I've known him over lifetimes.

That's the only real explanation for why the boy I just met makes me feel safer than anyone else. Or how I'll hate myself for eternity because I let Hunter touch me.

Calder feels like magic and forevers.

And if I'm only feeling this way because of this moment, I don't want tomorrow.

"He tried. I said no."

It's the truth without the shitty intention and the last favor I'll ever do for Hunter Kelly. I hear Aubrey yell my name, and my body tenses in Calder's arms.

"It's okay. Just remember what I said." He brushes his cheek over mine. "Do you trust that kid Hunter came with?"

"Shephard. Yes."

Calder nods, coming to a stop as my friends run to meet us. I can feel people looking at me from over by the logs, curious about what happened. My eyes lift to Tag, who's too busy downing beer than to notice that his brother's missing.

"Oh my God. What did you do to her?" Aubrey yells.

But I quickly counter. "Nothing. He helped me. I fell."

She snaps her mouth shut, only looking partially contrite as he wags his hand full of my clothes at her. I didn't even notice he'd grabbed them. Aubrey takes them as Calder shifts to look at Shephard.

"You carry her all the way to the car. And then take her straight to the hospital. The cut on her leg's gonna need stitches."

"Totally, dude, but Hunter drove. Soo—"

Calder's brows draw together. "He's not here though, is he? Take Tag's car. Tell him *I* said to let you. We clear?"

Shep nods a lot. "Crystal, man. Sutton goes now."

Calder holds me out to transfer to Shephard, but I don't let go, forcing him to cradle me again.

"You take me home," I whisper, hiding in him again.

I don't care if people notice or question it. This is where I feel safe.

His chest falls deeply as his mouth comes close to my ear. "I can't. You know that. But no matter what, I'll come to you tonight.

Promise."

I nod before my arms slide off him, switching to Shephard, who says, "I gotcha, Sutton." But it doesn't feel the same.

Shep turns, my friends in tow, taking me back over the sand toward the cars, but my eyes stay on the broad tattooed back, making his way back to the cave.

Chapter Sixteen

Calder

"**H**e tried. I said no."

Bullshit. But I'm not mad that she gave me a half-truth. That angel told me just enough to spare Hunter's fucking life. What did you do to my baby, motherfucker?

I take the last step, cresting the steep terrain, a smirk adorning my face.

"Hey, Hunter."

He spits the blood that's still pooling inside his mouth as he sneers at me.

"What the fuck do you think you're doing, Calder?"

Roman chuckles, looking at me as he crosses his arms, while West grins down from the boulder. They're flanking him, keeping him cornered for me. I walk toward little Kelly, motioning toward the edge of the rocky terrain.

"Well, I was thinking about throwing you off this fucking cliff."

His face pales, shifting between Roman and West before he points his finger at me.

"There will be hell to pay if you do. So stop now, and we can forget this—" He lifts his chin showcasing his busted mouth. "—that this ever happened."

I rub my hand over my jaw, smirking. "Pay to who, bitch? Nobody knows I'm here."

He takes a step backward.

"You think I won't tell my father once I swim back to shore?"

"Who says you'll make it?"

I stop in front of him and stare down before I slap him hard enough to make his fucking ears ring, sending his face flying before grabbing it and bringing it back.

"Do you think that scares me, Hunter? That you'll tell daddy?" My eyes narrow as I smile. "Mine's scarier than yours, and I still don't give a fuck."

He swallows roughly. "What the fuck? I didn't even do anything. She fell. I didn't push her if that's what you think. And why do you even care?"

"I'm sure that's what you want her to believe. But I saw, Hunter. I see what you hide."

I squeeze his face roughly, shaking my head as he keeps begging.

"It was an accident. Seriously. You can't throw me off a fucking cliff over an accident. I could die."

My hand glides over his face to the top of his head, gripping his hair, watching him wince like a pussy.

"You think I'm doing this because she fell?" I make his head shake no. "See. Now you're starting to get it."

Hunter's hands grab my wrists as I pull harder on his hair, forcing him to his toes as he groans, "Then why? This is crazy."

My jaw tenses before the question comes. "What'd you do to

her in the water, Hunter?"

Hunter stills, eyes dropping from mine.

Son of a bitch. He's dead. "You piece of shit."

"C."

Roman says my name like a warning because he heard the switch in my voice, but it's too late for negotiation. The answer's in Hunter's eyes. I don't need the fucking details because whatever it was, he meant to hurt her.

That's all I need to know. Now I hurt him.

West and Roman close in behind me.

I chuckle. "You know what, Hunter? We were just gonna scare you. Because you're right—you're a protected little piece of shit. I can't really hurt you, not the way I want to unless I wanna play Russian roulette with my life. But we both know you deserve a fucking beatdown. So take it, and we'll call it even. Then you forget her fucking name."

I yank him closer, whispering in his ear, "Answer me, pussy, before I change my mind."

Roman grabs my shoulder, but I don't budge, staring down into Hunter's defeated eyes.

"Fine. Okay. Fine."

I let him go with a jerk of his head. He takes a few steps back, wiping the back of his hand over his snotty nose.

"I still don't get why the fuck you even care. It's not like she's fucking prime—she was going to let me finger bang her in the ocean before she freaked out. She's just an uptight wannabe slut."

A chain of *"whoa, whoa, whoa's"* ring out as rage suffocates my senses and brings me crashing into him.

My hand wraps around his fucking throat as I hover over his body.

"You touched her... My beautiful girl. You put your filthy hands on her. And then you call her a—"

I don't say it. Instead, I squeeze, wanting to break his trachea. Hunter's hands slap at my wrist as hot exhales rush from my body.

Roman and West are yelling at me to stop. To let him go. But I can't. A snarl rips through me as my words roar from my chest.

"You don't touch her. She's precious."

His face is purple. A cacophony of failed attempts at air and the deep bellows of my name mix together in the air swirling around me. There are moments in life when you know, way down deep in your soul, that the end of a story is set in motion.

My end has just begun.

Tears fall from Hunter's bloodshot eyes, trickling down onto my hand.

I half blink before my mouth opens with a growl, and I throw him off the cliff. His body hurtles down toward the water below as I lift my head to the sky, letting out a deep, relieved breath, closing my eyes, and seeing only her face.

West leans forward from the back seat, seeing our Pops standing in the garage, arms crossed, with two of his guys.

"Shit, man. News travels fast when you choke a kid out and send him hurling off a fucking cliff."

Roman looks at me, worry set on his face.

"Calder—"

I shake my head. "Nah, don't. I knew what I was doing. That little cocksucker lived—so will I. You two weren't there. You got me?" Roman grips the steering wheel harder, so I add, "Don't you even try to push back about this, Roman. I did this. I'll be the one that takes the consequence. Trust me on this—don't let him see you hesitate when he asks."

The car pulls to a stop, the three of us exiting, giving nothing away as we walk up the driveway and into the garage.

"Pops."

He looks at Roman and West. "Were you a part of this? Don't lie to me."

They look at me as I give them a hard look because he already knows the answer. Tyler Wolfe doesn't ask questions. And I'll bet my life and theirs on this lie—Hunter didn't even mention their names. They each shake their head before answering at the same time.

"No, Pops."

I lock eyes with him. "It was just me. But you already know that."

He nods, motioning to the goons next to him. They walk toward me looking like they're ready for a fight, but neither touches me as they surround me.

Pops keeps his eyes on me but speaks to Roman and West.

"You two get cleaned up. I've got a run for you later."

They walk past me through the garage, but I see the fucking torment in their eyes. They're my brothers. Loyal to the end. Turning their backs on me, wondering if I won't be able to fucking breathe past broken ribs tomorrow, will make for torture. But this is for their own good. Because Tyler's the kind of bastard that will leave the bruises where everyone can see them.

He won't kill me. If he was going to, we wouldn't be standing here. I can't promise the same for them.

Pops walks toward me, undoing his belt, tugging it from the belt loops.

"I don't care about the why, boy. I care that something like this will never happen again."

My eyes stay locked on his. The closer he gets, the more his eyes speak the cruelty he's about to administer. The leather belt wraps around his fist over and over as he speaks.

"If you would've killed him—" He pauses, letting the words he doesn't say hang in the air before continuing. "Well, I guess it's a good thing you didn't."

I offer nothing in return. It's futile. The decision's made. A pound of my flesh is required as retribution and goodwill. That's the service you get when your daddy owns a pharmaceutical company and is more than happy to partner with the Irish mob.

All I can do now is stand here and fucking take it. And hope that it's not bad enough to force me to break my promise to the girl.

"This never happens again, Calder. Do you understand me? Connor promised Michael Kelly he'd give to you what you gave Hunter times three. The next time you decide to be a prick because some little bitch likes that asshole better, you remember that when you think with your dick, it might be the last thought you have. Even if Connor O'Bannion's your uncle."

That little piece of shit. Before I can spout off at the mouth, his fist strikes my ribs once, then twice before my knees buckle, taking me to the ground. The goons grab my arms, holding me up enough to let him continue.

I stare down, head hanging as my father stands above me breathless. Oil stains mix with spit falling from my mouth. Pops brings his mouth close to my cheek.

"Now I'm gonna remind you who's in charge. Because it ain't you, boy. Remember your place, Calder. It's right under my goddamn boot."

His arm raises, the glint of brass on the buckle hitting my eye just before I see black.

Chapter
Seventeen

Sutton

Everyone left hours ago, after spending most of the day doting on me. Piper and Aubrey grilled me about Calder the whole time we sat in the ER. Still, I denied that there was anything to tell, even when I let out an audible sigh of relief hearing that Hunter had called Shephard.

Fear spawned by my imagination played on a loop in my mind more than once today until I heard the story Hunter's told everyone. I don't really know what I thought Calder would do.

But no part of me believes Hunter jumped off that cliff by himself—he was either thrown or ran off because possible death was a better option. Both scenarios scare me.

Although now that he's okay, I wish someone would've checked his pants because I'm confident he shit himself. Fucker.

"Are you sure you're okay?" my mother questions, smiling down at me from where I'm lying on my bed. She holds out a bottle of water for me to take.

I nod, wrapping my fingers around the cold plastic, tucking it in next to me.

"I'm fine, Mom. Swear. It's just two stitches. I can't believe I've made it this long without any considering how clumsy I am. It barely hurts anymore."

The lie tastes sour, especially since it's for Hunter.

"That's the pain pills, but I'm happy you're okay. You scared us, darling." She looks behind herself at the door, then back. "Your father would be up here too, but he had some work to attend to because of this little...situation." She gives me a smile as if to say *don't worry about being a bother.* "Get some rest. I already emailed the school, so you can stay home if you'd like."

"Okay. Thanks, Mom."

She leans down, kissing my forehead. "We'll see you in the morning."

I sigh, getting comfy as she walks away until she spins around.

"Silly me. I almost forgot." Her hand reaches into the pocket of her long cardigan, pulling out my cell. "Hunter dropped this off with the housekeeper. Shame he didn't stay. I bet he feels guilty for not being there when you hurt yourself. You should call him tomorrow. Make him feel better."

A tight smile is all I can manage as I accept it, plugging it into my charger. She pats my cheek before finally leaving, closing my door behind her.

My eyes hit the ceiling. The adrenaline is long gone, all my emotions finally settling into my bones. Today kind of felt like a blur, but there are two things that I am completely clear about.

One—Hunter is a dick.

And two—I choose Calder.

Fighting how I feel is futile. That much was obvious to me yesterday because it wasn't until Calder wrapped his arms around me that I took my first real breath. I don't understand why I feel this way. I just know I do, and it's too strong to fight off anymore.

My fingers run over the edges of the bandage stuck to my leg, dropping my eyes I look at it. What would've happened if Calder wasn't there today? My eyes close, recalling his promise.

"...no matter what, I'll come to you tonight."

Will you? How?

The idea is beyond unrealistic, but that doesn't stop me from slipping the blanket off my body and placing my water bottle on the dresser before standing. I make my way across the room to the double french doors that lead out to my balcony.

"This is stupid. He's not coming," I whisper to myself, but I turn the lock anyway.

A warm breeze billows through my short sheer white nightgown as I open the doors.

A bright full moon greets me as I step out to hold the rail. My eyes drift from star to star, then back to the first one I saw, remembering what I used to do with my grandmother when I was little.

My lids drift closed, seeing only Calder behind them.

"Star light, star bright, first star I see tonight. I wish I may, I wish I might, have this wish I wish tonight."

"I wish for you to keep your promise," I whisper, eyes reopening.

But it doesn't matter how hard I hope for wishes on stars to be real. I've outgrown them.

Another breeze causes goose bumps to rise over my legs, reminding me of my injury. I step back, turning around, and make my way back inside before closing the doors behind me and leaving them unlocked.

He promised, and my heart wants to believe him.

I walk over to my bed and get back in, pulling my plush cream blanket over me. Reaching for the lamp next to the bed, I turn it off, making the room dark, with only the light from the night's sky coming in.

I lie there staring at the door, head tucked onto my pillow.

Seconds turn to minutes, minutes to hours, as my eyes grow heavy. No matter how much I fight it, the events of today bury me. I'm exhausted in more ways than one, so without permission, my eyes close, and sleep takes over.

He'll come.

My shoulders jerk, breath sucked in as I shoot to sitting, eyes rapidly blinking open. I fell asleep. Shit. I reach for my charging phone, but sunshine beams through my window, giving way for disappointment to weigh heavily on my shoulders.

I groan, hating myself a little for believing in fairy tales. Did I really think Calder was going to crawl up my balcony? Past all the cameras—without even having my freaking address?

"Jesus," I say to myself, rubbing my face and stretching my arms. I throw back my blanket, but my movements are halted as a piece of paper glides up into the air, winding its way down toward the floor.

What the hell?

My eyes pop out of my head as I scramble to get it, a very sore leg protesting.

Pressing my palms on the floor, I sit down mermaid-style, staring at that folded cream paper lying on the throw rug.

There's a capitalized *S* on the front.

I run my forefinger over the scrawl, almost too nervous to open the letter. *What if it's from my mom or dad and this day goes back to sucking?*

Lifting my eyes toward the balcony doors, a smile that bests all smiles graces my face. No way. He was here. I fucking know it. Plucking it up, I unfold and begin reading.

I couldn't wake you. I'm sorry. You looked like an angel, and honestly, I was fucking scared. You scare the shit out of me. Everything you've heard about me is true. You saw as much with your own eyes. I'm all that bad shit people say and worse, but I want you to know my heart. Read this. I wrote it the day I kissed you.

If you feel the same way, meet me at the confessional tomorrow around noon.

–C

Sunday—

Fuck. She's beautiful. The first day I saw her, I couldn't stop watching, and I didn't even know her name, but it wasn't her fiery red hair or the way her eyes seem to shine when she smiles. It was more than that. I thought I was crazy, just horny and dumb, but then I caught her with that fucking cigarette.

I couldn't stop myself. I had to touch her, be close to her—so I took it, but she'd already taken more. I was hooked that very moment and reeled in on the beach, watching her yell at the moon and smelling like fucking grapefruit.

But today—my whole life flashed before me. Playing so fast that I couldn't really see it, only feel it down to the depths of me.

Her lips touched mine, but my soul recognized hers.

I never believed in soul mates. I don't think I even believed in love.

But Sutton—she makes me want to.

I silently scream with my eyes closed, the letter pressed to my chest, before hearing the handle of my door turn. Scooting quickly, I shove the note under the throw rug and turn over my shoulder with a smile, meeting my mother's face.

"Darling, why are you on the floor?"

I shrug. "It hurt to walk, so I took a break."

She scowls but walks toward me, helping me to my feet. My

eyes dart to the rug and back as she walks toward my balcony doors, opening them.

"It's stuffy in here. Let's leave these open."

I nod, holding my hands behind my back.

"I think I'll take you up on the offer to stay home today. It's not like there's anything to do the last week." *Because I kind of want to live in my head all day with this letter.*

She pauses, giving me a thoughtful look. "You could just be done."

"No," I blurt, scrunching my nose before I take it down a notch. "I'll go tomorrow. Just in case I want people to sign my yearbook. I just want a day to make sure my leg isn't sore anymore."

For fuck's sake, I'm a terrible liar.

She shrugs, accepting what I offer, pointing toward my closet.

"Do you need help dressing? If not, breakfast is ready downstairs—Rosie made a lovely quiche Lorraine. Come down soon."

I walk gingerly toward my closet to aid in my lie, smiling. "I'll manage. I'll be down in a bit."

My mother pats my shoulder as she leaves, closing the door behind her and letting my nerves relax as she does.

I scamper over to the rug as quickly as I can. Pulling it back, I grab the note before taking it to my closet, burying it in the back of my underwear drawer.

My cell rings, so I walk back out and grab my phone, seeing Aubrey's name flash. At the same time, a text comes through.

Piper: Do not ignore us. We're coming over.

What the hell? These two. I hit the call button.

"What are you talking about?"

Piper's voice blares over the speaker, making me turn my volume down. "I told you she was avoiding us."

"I'm not avoiding you." My eyes drop to the face of my phone, seeing that it's 10:00 a.m. "Shouldn't you be in class?"

"She's totally avoiding us," Aubrey snaps, talking to Piper like I can't hear her before adding, "but it doesn't matter, ho. We both skipped due to trauma."

"Trauma?" I snark. "From my leg? Are you serious?"

I hear Aubrey clap her hands together, yelling as Piper says, "Wheel," in the background.

"No, bitch—we're traumatized that our best friend keeps fucking lying to us. Your life has never been interesting. You're an open book, but now suddenly, you're shut tighter than a clam."

"Mmhmm. Unacceptable," Piper chimes in. "We ride together. We die together. Or have you forgotten?"

I laugh, running my hands through my hair.

"Isn't that what Vin Diesel says in *The Fast and the Furious*?"

Aubrey yells, "Don't change the subject," as Piper says, "Yeah, and it applies. Also, I just fucking love those movies. RIP Paul Walker. The man was fine."

I'm nodding. "Yeah, he really was taken too soon."

I come off speaker because Aubrey gets louder as she bitches at me. "Focus. We're on our way. Massage those lips, Sutton, because we expect them to be loose."

The line disconnects, and I roll my eyes. I knew that sooner or later, they'd figure me out, especially after the beach. But I was really hoping for later. What am I scared of? My brows draw together because I know—I'm scared they won't ride or die this one. I'm afraid I'll have to go it alone.

Crushed gravel under tires echoes through my open balcony doors, pulling me back to the present as I release a tiny growl.

Unbelievable.

On their way? They were literally around the corner. Assholes.

I walk to my closet, throwing on my favorite band T-shirt and a pair of comfortable lounge shorts. God. Where do I even start?

They're going to kill me when they find out I've told them nothing this whole time.

Leaving the closet, I head into my bathroom and grab my toothbrush just as I hear their voices bust through my door.

"Hello." ... "We're here."

"We're here," I mock in a shitty voice inside my head.

I walk out, giving a half-assed wave, toothbrush in mouth. Piper follows me back inside my bathroom, jumping up onto the counter to sit, glaring at me.

I spit, lifting my eyes to hers.

"What?"

"What? The nerve you have."

I roll my eyes as she wags her finger at me. "You've got some explaining to do. Start talking..." She's trying to be the bad cop, but she's terrible at it because she adds, "Also, I brought up some breakfast for you. And how's your leg, babe?"

I smile before rinsing my mouth and patting it dry with a hand towel.

"Thank you, and it's much better today. Barely sore to the touch."

She follows me back out. I sit on my bed, accepting the warm plate she hands me. I tap the fork against the edge, watching as they both stretch out on the soft blush-pink chaise across from me.

We're silently staring at each other as I take my first bite, chewing on more than just the eggs. *Fuck.*

Aubrey's head drops back dramatically. "Oh, come on, bitch. Speak. I can't with you. I'm dying here."

Piper's eyebrows raise, so I drop the fork and let out a heavy breath. "Where should I start?"

"Are you in love?" Piper shoots out.

Both sets of eyes lock on me as I hesitate before shaking my head.

"No, but it feels like it's happening—I don't know if that makes any sense."

Aubrey frowns. "But did you fuck him yet?"

Piper slaps Aubrey's arm, making me giggle before she says, "So what you're saying is that you're falling for him?"

"Yes."

I've never been more nervous. I keep searching their faces for any hint of what they may be thinking.

"How long has this been going on behind our backs?" Aubrey says it snarky, but for a brief second, I see the hurt flash in her eyes.

Crap.

My face drops to my plate as I put it to the side before looking her directly in the eyes, saying what I should've from the beginning.

"Aubs. I'm sorry. I'm sorry that I lied to you. You're my best friends, but I was scared you'd be so mad at me that you'd hate me for being so reckless. You have to believe me, at first I didn't think Calder and I were even possible, so I kept the first moment we had locked inside of me because—"

I lift my hands before letting them fall back to my knees, at a loss for words, but she finishes for me.

"Because then you could at least dream about it without your shitty friends being judgmental and ruining shit."

Her bottom lip pushes out, pouting before she says, "I'm sorry too."

Piper rubs her arm, looking at me. "What changed, though, to make you guys possible?"

"Nothing else other than he kissed me. That's really it." I run my fingers through my hair, biting my lip. "I know how this sounds. But the minute Calder kissed me, it's like we became destined to happen. The stars aligned—" I exhale, before adding, "And that shit's impossible to fight. I know. I tried."

Shrieks and squeals. That's what happens. All the heaviness of the moment instantly changes as Aubrey slides down the chaise, making us all laugh.

"Bitch. That fine-ass man put his mouth on yours. Oh, my Gawd. Details. Immediately."

My teeth find my bottom lip before I pick my plate back up, tucking into my food. I start from the beginning, telling them every delicious and insane moment I've shared with Calder Wolfe as they stare back at me.

Piper steals my plate when I'm done, finishing my food, both enraptured as I tell them about the beach. Lots of "holy shits" happen when I get to the part at the church steps and how my father despises his. Aubrey's face pales when I confirm the rumors about who Calder's family is and then grows red with rage as I tell the story from the cave, lobbing a "fuck that dick" toward Hunter.

They sit patiently through all of it, mostly listening until I tell them about the note from this morning.

"What! That's perfect. It's right during the last mass for school," Piper yells, smacking Aubrey's leg, who's bouncing up and down. "Oh my God. I'm dying over this. It's like fucking Romeo and Juliet."

Aubrey claps her hands, but I shake my head.

"Uh, no. They die in the end."

Piper waves me off.

"Just skip that part, but, like, it's so fucking romantic. Calder might be scary, but he has my vote." She turns to Aubrey. "Right? Because he protected our girl."

Aubrey nods. "Absolutely. I guess your Romeo comes with tattoos, guns, and a taste for blood."

My hand shoots to my mouth, laughter popping out before a pang of reality hits, and I stare back at them.

"Oh my God. Is this stupid? Am *I* fucking stupid? What am I doing? This could end so badly. What do I know about anything?

Especially falling in love."

Aubrey stands and comes to sit next to me, as does Piper. They each take one of my hands as my head volleys between them, but it's Aubs that speaks first.

"What's there to know? I would do anything for love. Anything for someone to love me so much they'd burn the world down. Do you think he'd do that for you?"

I answer without hesitation.

"Yes."

"And Sut," Piper interjects. "I'm going to say something hella controversial. I get that he's bad news, like a part of a criminal family or whatever, but that shouldn't define him. I think we can all understand how fucked-up that is—being judged by your name alone."

Aubrey snaps her fingers. Piper's right. It's a cross I understand bearing.

She kisses the top of my hand and smiles. "The way he looked at you when he had you in his arms—I've only seen that shit in movies. It's like everything we've all hoped could exist does in the way he stares at you."

I smile, understanding exactly what she means.

"I love you guys."

They hug me, sandwiching me between them, and whisper threats to my life if I ever lie to them again.

"Never again," I promise, knowing that I've already broken it because Calder going up to the top of the cliff with Hunter will die with me.

Chapter
Eighteen

Sutton

"Hail Mary, full of grace—" The familiar prayer rushes between my lips quietly from where I'm knelt reciting my contrition, but I'm barely able to concentrate.

Because during my entire day, there's been one singular thought commanding my full attention—Calder.

At least yesterday, I had Aubs and Piper. They hung out with me for most of it, overanalyzing, deconstructing, and plotting my escape upstairs today. It was perfect, but it didn't make me any more patient for this moment.

I look over my shoulder mid-prayer toward the front doors, hoping to see him sneaking in.

"Hey. Freckles. Psst."

My eyes spring back, prayer still on my lips, glaring at Hunter. He's such an asshole.

As if Wednesday wasn't enough of a reason to hate him. This morning he asked me questions about my leg during homeroom as if he didn't know anything. Then he let me look like a bitch when I ignored him.

"Hey. Will you please talk to me?"

Eww. Aubrey makes the sign of the cross, kissing her middle finger and blowing it at him as Piper leans forward, whispering, "Grudges, jerk. We keep them—forever. Don't talk to her."

Turned around in his place, he stares at me. "Can you call off the dogs? I want to talk."

"No," I whisper back.

"Freckles."

"Are something I have." I narrow my eyes. "My name is Sutton. And Hunter, I don't forgive you. At all. What you did—said in the water. You're gross. Don't talk to me."

He frowns, but I don't care, ignoring him.

"This is why men call women emotional. You're overreacting."

Three sets of pissed-off eyes dart to his face, effectively making his mouth snap shut.

Piper makes a blow job motion against her cheek before whispering, "Ferociously suck a dick, Hunter. How's that for emotional?"

A laugh, too loud, bursts out from me, garnering a harsh "shh" from Sister Agatha. But it's fine because it forces Hunter to turn around.

Asshole.

The music for the service begins, calling us off our knees and to sit. Aubrey taps my hip, motioning with her head for me to sneak out of the pew. We chose the row closest to the back to make my escape easier, but Hunter makes me nervous.

I don't trust him anymore. He might try and rat me out just to be a dick. I'm staring at the back of his head before I glance back to Aubs.

She pretends to punch his face and put him in a chokehold before mouthing, "I got it. Go."

I duck down, crawling over the lower benches we use for our knees before waiting at the end of the pew, looking back to Piper. She cranes her neck to make sure I'm clear before giving me a thumbs-up. The privacy of the hallway can't come soon enough as I keep my footsteps quiet, bent over as I dash away, sliding behind the wall.

Thumps reverberate in my chest. God, I could get so busted for this. I can't even think about how that conversation would go if my parents were called. My eyes close for a second as I cringe at the thought.

I check over my shoulder, walking down the short hallway, nerves growing as I sneak toward the stairs. *What am I doing?* My lips curl into a grin because even though I'm freaking out, the reward of seeing Calder insanely outweighs the risk of getting caught.

As my feet hit the stairs, each step is taken painfully slow, trying to ensure nobody hears. Not even a creak. Rote responses from the congregation rise to the ceiling in a chorus as I come to the top, making my way into the room, instantly not seeing him.

Shit.

I'm too scared to call his name or walk over by the organ—too close to being seen—so I stand in place, fingers finding the ends of my hair.

It's all romantic until nobody has a timeline. I check my phone, the time showing 12:45. *Shoot, what if he waited and then thought I didn't come?*

"Stop overthinking, dummy," I whisper to myself, leaning down and adjusting my knee-high socks.

As I stand, I shift my head, looking around the room, first to a dusty bookcase along the far wall and then to the stained glass, remembering the first time I saw Calder here. The colors from the windows aren't shining as brightly today, muted by the clouds outside.

The sound of Bibles opening and pages fluttering from below makes me feel exposed. If anyone were to come up, I'd be caught, so I turn, walk over to the confessional, and open the sculpted dark antique wooden door before slipping inside.

Darkness envelops me until my eyes quickly adjust.

"About time."

I jump, covering my gasp as Calder's face, shielded by the partition, comes into view. My eyes close, and I smile before I open them, teasing.

"You should've been more specific. You just said this room, not the exact time, so you only have yourself to blame."

He chuckles, "Fair," and I warm.

The silence stretches out as I sit, listening to him breathe, not really knowing what to say or where to begin. But I don't get a chance to try anything because he whispers, "Do you regret coming?"

Never.

"No. But I am scared. My father hates yours."

Damn. I should've only said the first part.

"Yeah, same…to all of it."

Oh. I lean forward.

"I'd do it all again though."

I hear him let out an exhale. His fingers touch the wooden screen. Tiny bits of his skin press through the cutouts, and on instinct, mine meet them.

"Every fucking time I see you, it's like this pull. I can't explain it—you pull me to you. Do you feel like that too?"

"It's like I've known you my whole life, except I haven't, but I like the way it feels. I feel safe…" I pause for a second, trying to figure out how to say the rest but Calder presses.

"But—"

I shake my head.

"No but. I was going to say that I never really feel safe. I keep all these thoughts locked up inside my head because I'm too scared of disappointing people or making them mad. But it's different with you. I just say things—all the embarrassing things. And the most honest ones."

He's quietly brushing his fingers over mine as words I think he means to keep inside fall out.

"How are you possible—real, even? This feels like life's cruel joke. Like I only get you because tomorrow I'll die or some shit like that."

There are so many things I want to say—like that I feel the same. That even though we seem impossible, the fact that a soul like Calder's even exists seems too good to be true.

But instead of any of that, I say the honest thought screaming in my head. Because I can't not—not with him.

"What if that were true? A relationship between us will most definitely come with conditions, lies, and deception. And it's still probably doomed to fail. So if you were dying tomorrow, would I still be worth the trouble?"

My heart drops into my stomach, terrified that he'll finally realize what I refuse to face—that we're a beautiful tragedy.

His forehead drops against the screen.

"I don't want to hurt you, Sutton, and I'm fucking terrified that's what I'll do. But I lay next to you the other night, watching you sleep, trying to think of every fucking way to save us from ourselves, and I came up empty. And that's crazy because we barely know each other, but I can't stop thinking about you and wanting to be near you."

He lifts his eyes to mine, only partially visible through the screen. But the emotion behind them bleeds outs, holding me hostage as he says, "So yeah. If I only get today, then I'll take it because being without you feels like hell anyway."

It's in this moment that the headiest feeling washes over me—so strong and clear.

I don't want to be saved from ourselves. Fuck everything. I want Calder, even if it damns us to hell. It's selfish and hateful, but I don't care. I can't just forget him or walk away.

This time around, it's me reaching for the door first. I don't say anything, rushing out and pulling his side open. His beautiful, broken face fixes to mine as my heart pours out onto him.

"I want you too, Calder. None of the rest matters."

Strong hands reach for me the minute I step inside. I'm hauled onto his lap, straddling him as our mouths meet. We're devouring each other, kissing like it's the air we need to breathe.

Because this is how we'll say our story begins—with me, him, and this damn kiss.

Calder growls into my mouth as his palms cradle my face.

"Is your leg okay?"

I seal my mouth over his, our tongues dipping and swirling as our heads tilt from one side to the other before I pull back, breathless.

"I'm fine. Thank you for protecting me."

He leans in, but my hands in his hair force his crystal-blue eyes to mine. I just need to look at him.

Fresh bruises and cuts surround his eye, and there's a cut on his lip. I lean down, feathering a kiss to his brow.

"It never hurts, baby."

Never. Hate swells inside me for whoever puts them there. And as I think it, I also feel the realization finally cementing inside of me.

"I'm not turning back, Calder. I'm yours. And you're mine."

The anger that's always lurking behind his eyes falls away, and for the first time since we met, Calder looks at peace. He looks like someone who could love, believe in soul mates, and live a life full of magic. He searches my eyes, brushing his hands up and down my cheeks before weaving them into my hair as our foreheads touch.

"I'll never give you up, Sutton. Ever."

The world falls away as our lips meet again and our hands begin to roam. Calder's warm breath slides over my neck as I sigh, peppering soft kisses over his bruised face.

"Nobody ever touches you again. Promise it, baby."

We don't owe each other apologies, yet everything outside of him feels like sin, so I give him the oath.

"I promise."

Calder's arms wrap around my waist, holding me flush as his lips drag up my neck. He buries his face against my skin, sucking on a tender spot by the nape of my neck, making my body quiver.

"Promise me you'll never touch another girl," I pant.

Capable hands splay over my back as he answers, "I swear to God I won't."

I draw back, slapping my hands against his chest.

"Don't you dare swear to someone you don't believe in."

He grins, leaning forward for my mouth, but I hold him back as his eyes narrow.

"I do believe in God, Sutton. I just don't think he's all good. But I promise on our lives that I will only ever touch you. Because I definitely believe in me and in you."

Calder leans in again, taking my bottom lip in his mouth, letting it slide out agonizingly slow.

We stare into each other's eyes, and the air begins to shift, feeling thick on my lungs, forcing me to take slower breaths.

His hands feel warm under my blazer against the thin button-up blouse as he closes around my rib cage, pressing his fingers into me. I trace his jawline with a finger over to his soft lips, licking mine as he presses a soft kiss to the tip.

We feel electric, raw, like chemistry that's attracting and

building the longer we stay connected. Eye contact is vulnerable. It's intimate. It touches you in places you don't expect. Rattles your emotions and fucks with your mind.

Ten seconds of staring at Calder feels like I'm floating in a starry sky—just us, surrounded by nothing and everything, as if we're the center of the universe.

There's no other sound than the beating of his heart and no other existence than the one inside this confessional. His hands drop to my hips, fingertips digging into the fabric of my skirt, silently desiring things we shouldn't.

But it doesn't matter that we're in a confessional or a church— *we* are the only sacrament that exists.

With his eyes on mine, he urges me forward, scooting me closer to him, my cotton panties catching on the roughness of his jeans. He guides my hips slowly, rocking them up and back, over his growing length as I weave my hands through his honeyed hair.

We say nothing, never breaking eye contact, leaving our bodies to speak for us.

My mouth falls open, wanting to taste his again, but he teases, coming close only to pull away before our lips touch.

The more I grind, the more I lose myself to the lust-filled heat that begins to soak through the folds of my pussy. My teeth find my bottom lip as I drag over his hard cock, shuddering, wanting more each time.

"Oh my God."

I just barely whisper it, almost unable to breathe past the pleasure. He's controlling me, leading me to heaven each time he urges me forward—the intensity of the feeling only matched by Calder's quiet growls.

"Mine," he grits out.

I clasp onto the back of his neck, shoulders lifting, losing myself to the sensation as I grind harder, staring into his ocean eyes. Short, quick breaths take over as I move, my words coming out in pants.

"I'm yours. Just yours."

"Fuck."

Calder rips a hand away, ardently bunching my skirt. There's no question or hesitation. He knows exactly what I want—I don't have to say a fucking word.

I dart down, helping him just as he slides underneath, straight to my center.

My lips press together, hiding the gasp from the exquisite bolt of need that racks my body as he pulls the cotton aside, running his finger through my wetness.

I'm pleading with my eyes as he rubs rhythmic circles over my swollen, begging clit. I'm lost, hips circling, as he stares at me with an intense smirk.

"You feel like silk on my fingers, baby. I'll never stop fucking touching you."

The old me would've never done something like this. But who I am with Calder overshadows my normal senses. I want Calder more than I understand, and not just sexually. I want to own every piece of him—no boundaries, living by only the rules we make.

"You wanna come like this?" He leans forward for my mouth, so I give it to him freely as he says, "Or like this," pushing his thick finger inside my warmth.

"Oh my God." I gasp as our eye contact finally falters.

My eyelids flutter as I squeeze against his finger, feeling it glide in and out—a welcomed intrusion making my heart race.

"God. You're so fucking beautiful."

He pulls out only to press back in slowly, letting my hips drive forward to meet him. Our mouths come together as his finger curves inside me again, touching just the right spot and pulling a soft mewl from my throat.

"More," he demands, kissing me with force as another finger

presses inside of me, stretching the delicate barrier of my virginity.

My body tenses, hands shooting to his shoulders, nails cutting into him through his shirt. But he doesn't stop, and I don't want him to. I'm stretched, full, and fucking aching for more.

"Jesus. You're fucking soaked. Do you like my fingers in that beautiful pussy?"

I nod as sensations build, rising and falling, tightening my stomach, spurred on by his filthy mouth. Calder finger fucks me faster and faster until I'm almost bouncing, my sock-covered shins sliding over the edge of the wooden seat.

"That's it. Show me how much you like it. Come on my fingers."

I spread my legs wider, head falling back, giving him room to fuck me harder, wanting to feel that explosion my body's greedy for.

"Fuck. Sutton. Take what you need."

Tightness coils in my stomach with every thrust as I squeeze my eyes shut.

"Yes."

Calder's fingers glide in and out through my cream with force, engulfing us in the filthy sounds of my slickness and the heady smell of sex. We're a goddamn abomination, but all I want at this moment is for him to make me dirty and never look back.

His thumb presses to my clit, and my eyes open, locking to his. I feel the crescendo possessing my body accompanied by a sharp sting that makes me gasp. I grab his head, sealing our mouths together as a deep moan rattles my chest.

Calder's hand replaces his mouth, silencing me as he continues to dip his fingers inside of me, wringing every drop of my orgasm from my body.

I come so hard that I tremble over and over, legs shaking as waves of pleasure crash down on me. I ride his fingers until my head falls back again and my shoulders go limp.

His lips press to my neck as he drags his fingers from me,

waiting until he's done to remove the hand over my mouth and grip the nape of my neck. I'm guided back to his face before he kisses me earnestly, whispering into my lips.

"I like the way dirty words sound on this mouth." A small peck wets my lips. "Are you okay?"

"Mmm. I am. And I guess I'll have to practice saying some really fucking dirty shit."

The smirk on Calder's face makes me want to do more than getting fingered in a confessional, but we can't have forever. Not yet.

"I don't want to leave."

His nose rubs over mine.

"I don't want you to leave."

"Take me somewhere tonight?" I rush out. "I'll meet you by my front gates after my parents fall asleep."

He nods, brushing soft kisses to my cheek.

"Gimme your phone."

I reach into my blazer pocket, pulling it out, still trying to slow my breath.

His face turns away from mine as he takes it from me. So I kiss his jaw, smiling as he groans when I rub over him again.

"Done," he says, bringing back his perfect smile and dropping my phone back into my pocket before he frowns again.

Neither of us wants to say goodbye, but we both know we have to. I hate this.

"Tonight?"

He nods, patting my hip with his hand.

"Go before you get caught."

I crawl off him, straightening my skirt, suddenly feeling the urge to pee. I reach behind myself and open the door, smiling shyly. It's stupid, but I can't help how I feel.

"Do I look okay?"

"You look like mine—so yeah. You look perfect."

He stands, crowding me, jerking his chin for my lips again. They're bee-stung, swollen but obedient as I lift to my tiptoes, pressing them to his.

"See ya tonight, baby."

I drop back down, opening the door, and walk out, glancing back over my shoulder at my beautiful villain until I'm too far down the stairs.

The chorus of song hides my steps as I walk quickly toward the bathroom, internally freaking out. This is where I'll hide until everyone files out so that I can blend back in. It was genius, really. I'm glad Aubrey thought of it. I push into the door, shutting it behind me, throwing my back against it.

"Holy shit." I quietly squeal before walking toward the toilet.

But the moment I pull down my underwear, I see a small spot of blood.

Oh my God. That's not my period. Calder tore my hymen.

Embarrassment burns through me, realizing that it might be on his fingers too.

"Oh, God." I shoot off the toilet, not even thinking as I right my clothes and pull open the door.

I only take three steps outside the bathroom when he catches my eye.

Calder's standing in the entry, next to the basin of holy water. The congregation room doors are shut behind him, but he doesn't seem to notice because he's staring down at his hand, gently rubbing his thumb over his first two fingers.

Compulsion takes over, my feet hurrying quickly toward him as heat spreads up my neck. His face swings toward me, stopping me in my tracks, the intensity behind his eyes almost leaving me breathless.

My mouth opens to apologize, but Calder reaches for me,

dragging me into him, snaking his other hand into my hair.

"Don't you dare fucking look at me like that. You will never feel shame or embarrassment. I demand all of you, Sutton."

My chest rises and falls so quickly as he stares down at me because I want to give him all of me, including my innocence.

"Calder. I—"

But nothing else comes out because Calder dips his tainted fingers into the holy water, never taking his eyes off me, bringing them to his forehead. I watch, feeling stripped, raw, and completely obliterated by him. His hand moves down to his chest, then to his left shoulder before finishing the sign of the cross.

"Now I'm baptized in you."

A heavy exhale leaves my mouth just before Calder's mouth meets mine, ravaging it. It's fitting because it feels like he's already done that to my fucking soul.

Chapter
Nineteen

Calder

Her: Why is your name Wesley in my phone?

Me: Because yours is Buttercup.

Buttercup: Again, I ask…Why?

Wesley: They're arguably the most iconic couple in film. How is this a question?

Buttercup: So in addition to being insanely attractive, intimidating, and exhibiting an overall lack of impulse control when it comes to punching people—you're a movie buff?

Wesley: Insanely, huh? I like it. And I'm a lot of things, baby. Wanna find out what else?

Buttercup: Yeah.

Wesley: Good. See ya tonight.

Buttercup: So, also a tease. Got it.

The sound of knuckles rapping against my door forces my eyes up. I've been lying on my bed, rereading my texts with Sutton on and off all day, imagining the faces she makes when she writes them.

"It's open."

West peeks his head inside the door, smiling like a goofy bastard.

"Dude. Guess what?"

I raise my brows, but he doesn't continue, so I say, "How long are you going to make me wait, West?"

He swings the door open, barreling in like I've given him an invitation, and plops down on the mattress. So I sit up, pocketing my phone and snapping the journal in my other hand closed.

"I'm coming with you and Roman tonight to the docks. We're leaving in twenty."

The excitement on his face makes me instantly sick. *Fuck no, you aren't.* My brows draw together.

"Says who?"

"Pops himself. It's my time, bitch. I'm coming up."

He's staring at me for a reaction, but I offer nothing as I wipe my hand over the stubble along my jaw. West grumbles, shoving my shoulder.

"Come on, dude. Don't look like that. This is huge for me."

But I keep quiet, sifting through my thoughts, tapping a finger against the leather cover of my journal.

The docks aren't a fucking joke or a playground.

Barrels of ecstasy divert here, never hitting the New York Port Authority. And thanks to the hundred-year-old railroad that served as the only land transportation in and out of this fucking town, we're able to sneak a shit ton of little white pills right back into the city.

Roman and I handle the docks with Pops' number two, Aiden, who always arrives with the ferry. It's always just the three of us because if shit doesn't add up or someone gets squirmy, we do what we need to.

West isn't ready for that.

Fuck.

He shakes the mattress. "Fine. Be a bitch, but you should still totally let me sit in the front seat of the car tonight."

Goddammit, West. This shit's not a game.

I reach out, smacking his cheek playfully. "You're never sitting in the fucking front. And you're not going." I push off the mattress, standing up. "Where's Roman?"

The heavy book in my hand lands with a thud on my nightstand as West stands up too.

"Garage. Same place he always is. And yes, I am. The decision's above you."

I turn, walking out of my room, hearing West yell my name as he follows behind, talking a mile a minute. He's trying and failing to convince me he's ready the whole way to the garage, but I'm not listening. I'm only interested in shutting this shit down.

How I plan to do that, I haven't figured out yet. I can't say shit to my Pops because it doesn't matter if I'm his son. I work for him. Saying "*fuck you*" to our hierarchy is the highest form of disrespect—and a death wish.

"Bro. What the fuck? Let it go. You aren't changing shit," West yells from behind me.

A smirk pulls at the corner of my mouth just as we hit the garage. I look over my shoulder, his feet stopping quickly.

"Nobody ever said you had to make it out of the car. I'll put you in the fucking trunk if I have to."

I swing open the door. The resounding thump of bass from the rap music playing greets us as we enter. Half of Roman's body is hidden under the GTO we've been tag-teaming.

"Romes," I bark, turning down the music.

He slides out, wiping his greasy hands on a rag as he looks up at me before darting his eyes to West.

"He must've told you about the docks."

I nod. "Then you already talked to Pops."

"Yeah, dawg, but he wasn't hearing it. West is coming tonight whether we like it or not. You wanna throw him in the trunk?"

I love that we're always on the same page. West throws his arms up in protest, making Roman chuckle as he sits up.

"You ain't ready for the docks, little bro. Just trust us. We ain't trying to have you get us killed. Or yourself clipped."

Maybe we're protecting him for good karma. God knows Roman and I could use all that we can get, but the way we grew up, the shit we've seen—that's not West's story. He's not ready for this chapter yet.

West grew up in an orphanage, picked up by my father at thirteen and shielded by Roman and me ever since. He's always been our little brother, following behind us, mimicking everything we do. I feel responsible for him, and I've done a lot of fucked-up shit in my life—helping West die before he's ready won't be one of them.

West crosses his arms, looking between us.

"This is bullshit. Both of you started younger than me. I'm fucking ready—stop treating me like a kid. I'm not going to fuck up. I'm gonna prove myself."

"Men don't have to prove themselves," I cut in, crossing my arms, irritated that Pops put us in this position.

Roman hops to his feet, shoving the rag in his pocket, looking at me as I shake my head, but before we can say any more, West hurls an empty motor oil can across the room.

The clang on the concrete is the only sound in the room as Roman mirrors my stance, our eyes locked to West. *What the fuck?*

West runs his unruly hair back under his loosened cap, not looking at us, nostrils flaring. He stabs a finger toward the ground as he paces, voice raised.

"Men do have to prove themselves, Calder. It's how we become them. If you two never let me dip more than a toe in this world, it'll be your fault when I get clipped."

I lift my hand, waving him off as I hurl, "Shut the fuck up with that. Don't say that shit. That's not happening."

Roman steps forward as West kicks the tire on the car, barking, "Settle down, dick."

West locks eyes with Roman's. "No. You settle down and fucking listen to me."

I've never seen him get this worked up before other than when he was hitting that kid on the ground with the bat—it's as if everything he's stored inside of him is about to explode.

Looks like West has shit to say to us.

A deep grumble rocks my chest as I catch his eyes. "You got something to say? Say it. But don't expect us to treat you like a grown man when you're having a fucking tantrum. This is real fucking life, West. With real motherfucking consequences."

"I know that."

"You don't know shit," I bark.

His face lifts to the ceiling as he shouts, "You two can't protect me forever."

I start forward, but Roman's hand on my chest stops me, pulling my eyes to him as he shakes his head.

"Let him speak, C."

West looks between us, spreading his arms as he speaks before letting them drop.

"I don't want you to protect me. I want to know what the fuck I'm doing so I can take care of you the way you do for me."

His eyes swing to mine. "You told me that men in this family never let anyone else fight their battles. So then, stop now."

Roman's face shifts to mine, eyebrows raised.

Fuck.

We stand in silence for more than a few seconds, their eyes on me. Roman would never give him the green light before me, but that's precisely what we have to do. My voice is deep and clipped as I hurl my words at him.

"You do what you're told. Or you go in the trunk."

He nods, shoulders relaxing, eyes darting to Roman as Roman says, "You listen. Don't speak."

"Or you go in the trunk," I add.

"Got it." West smiles, clapping his hands and rubbing them together.

But I frown. "West—" My eyes lock to his, a deep indent forming between my eyebrows, "I can't protect you out there. Do you understand that? The dock is real business, not the dime bags of weed we let you sling to rich assholes with money to burn." I motion to Roman. "We have a say over what happens to you right now. But once you cross this line, I can't—"

He's nodding, but what I'm trying to say won't come out—*stop you from dying.*

Roman's hand falls on my shoulder, patting it twice, but I can't shake the feeling I just signed off on my little brother's death warrant.

He closes the distance between us, patting my cheek the way I did to him earlier.

"I got me, Calder. Stop worrying. I'll be fine. You should worry about that little piece you can't stop texting."

I push his face away from me, and West laughs as Roman throws an arm over his neck, pulling him into a headlock, talking shit. But I turn and walk out past the garage door opening, not feeling as celebratory.

The hairs on the back of my neck stand on end as my head swings to the left, sensing eyes on me.

Pops.

He stares back at me, seated on the porch, an apple in one hand, knife in the other. I don't have to ask. He heard everything.

The knife spins round and round as we stand in silence.

His eyes search mine, questions I don't like behind them. He may be my Pops, but I don't want his attention—none of us do.

The sound of the knife piercing the apple is crisp, popping the skin as he takes the chunk straight from the blade before saying, "You boys don't be late," and that impenetrable wall falls back over his face.

If there was ever anything I've learned from my father, it's that you can always spot the Devil among demons.

Chapter
Twenty

Calder

I roll my Mustang to a stop a few houses down from Sutton's, engine killed, headlights off as I pull the hood of my sweatshirt over my head and lower my face to my cell.

Wesley: You comin' or what?

Buttercup: Shut up. You're early. Patience. I need to be cute.

Wesley: You're already fucking cute. Get out here.

Buttercup: And what are you going to do if I make you wait? Huh, tough guy?

Wesley: I'm gonna knock on your door and tell Baron that I'm the daddy now.

Buttercup: OMG! I'll kill you.

My eyes lift to the gate before dropping back to the screen. Fuck, this girl has me all twisted up. I want to text her again, even though I know she's on her way out, but now that I have a direct line to her, I'm a fucking addict.

There will never be enough Sutton.

My thumbs hover, about to say some more dumb shit, when something catches my eye, forcing my head up.

Red hair tucked inside a black hoodie paired with black leggings slips through the gate. Sutton ducks down as soon as she's clear of it, running toward my car. I chuckle, dropping my phone into my lap because she's fucking adorable.

It's midnight, on a street chock-full of old people. Who the fuck's watching?

I lean over, shoving the passenger-side door open, laughing as she throws herself in the car and scoots down super low in the seat.

My head is turned in her direction with a grin on my face as I stare.

"What are you doing?"

She blinks up at me through her thick lashes, smiling brightly, pulling the strings on her hoodie to make it tighter around her face.

"Go before someone sees us."

My hand slips under her arm, hauling her up as I shake my head, loosening her hood with my other hand and pushing it off her head.

"First, kiss me."

Her chin lifts immediately as I lean down, brushing a kiss onto her lips and breathing her in, feeling peace for the first time tonight.

"And second," I say against her mouth before I pull back, "how many people in this neighborhood do you think sit on their porches watching traffic after midnight?"

Her face relaxes as she thinks, embarrassment coloring her cheeks.

"Plus, I cut the wires to your cameras."

She slaps my arm, giggling, "Liar." But then her eyes grow wide. "Wait. Are you serious? What if someone tries to break into my house?"

I lean over again, wanting more of her mouth. "Baby, I'm the scariest thing on this island. I wouldn't worry about it, and you're right. I'm lying. Now gimme."

The vibration of her giggle gets lost between our lips as we kiss again. Fuck, her mouth is the worst kind of temptation. I could kiss her all day long, and it'd be worth every minute lost to everything else.

"That's better," I whisper, opening my eyes as I only just barely pull away.

She smiles, fingers coming to my stubble, her eyes on mine.

"Better?"

I take a deep breath, feeling what I always am around her— honest.

"I had a shit night that I can't tell you about. I'm worried about my younger brother, West, and I almost put him in my trunk twice tonight. Shit sucks with my Pops. And I feel like a pussy because I couldn't stop counting the fucking minutes until I got to see you. So yeah, now that I kissed you, I feel…better."

The smile on her face could only be rivaled by the feeling it gives me.

"I missed you too," she whispers like it's a secret as she crawls over the console.

She straddles my lap, wrapping her arms around my neck, tucking her face into the crook as my arms engulf her, sinking into her hug.

"Better?" she mumbles again against my flesh.

Fuck. So much.

I nod, not wanting to let go because I can't remember the last time someone hugged me. Although it's just *her* hugs I want. My face burrows in her hair, our chests rising and falling together in the silence.

After a few moments, she whispers, cheek on my shoulder, "Is it weird to feel this connected? To feel like I know you even though you're a stranger?"

I shrug, enjoying the smell of grapefruit on her hair.

"Fuck it. Let's just be weird."

I feel her smile as she snuggles in. "So, where are you taking me?"

"Nowhere if you're on my lap," I tease.

An arm leaves my neck, fumbling for the door as she says, "'Kay, it's been fun, see you later."

Aw, she thinks she's funny. I wiggle my fingers against her ribs, tickling her sides, making her squeal. Her body jerks as she tries to protest through her laughter until two small hands smack down onto my cheeks, garnering my attention as she brings her lips to mine.

I stop tickling her—full stop, because this kiss has heat behind it.

Her tongue slips inside my mouth as my hand slides up the nape of her neck, weaving into her hair. Our lips glide in between each other's, tongues teasing, becoming more and more fevered until I growl, reaching down, gripping her leggings at her hips. I raise her up a few inches as she squeaks out a sound.

"Unless you want your neighbors hearing you scream my name, your beautiful little ass better find the seat and buckle up, Buttercup."

She shakes her head as she plops down. "No. Don't make me leave." Her arms wrap back around my body, speaking her words back against my neck. "Drive with me like this because you make me feel better too. You're like the sun—I want to soak you up for as long as possible so that I can feel you lingering on my body later."

It takes me a second to answer because she's knocked the wind out of me.

There's an ache in my chest from this fucking feeling she gives me. It's that visceral. I don't even know how to label it, but that doesn't matter because she keeps serving it every damn time I see her.

My mouth opens to speak, but I don't even know what to say back. So, instead, I do what I can—give Sutton what she wants.

I kiss the side of her head, wrapping one arm around her as I turn the engine over.

"Only on the local streets, okay? Once we hit the highway, you sit."

She nods, somehow molding her body even closer to mine as I pull out, driving past her house with her in my arms, like a goddamn thief.

We drive down street after street, too slow, but I've got precious cargo, and I don't really want this to end either. All I feel are Sutton's contented sighs feathering my skin until we pull to a stop at the sign for the main highway.

"Ride's over, baby."

I smile as she lifts her head, looking like she's waking up from a dream.

"Better," she breathes before crawling back over to the passenger side.

She spins around, her ass landing on the seat, laughing as she brushes the hair from her face.

"Fuck, you're beautiful," I rush out, smiling as I catch myself saying shit I didn't mean to say out loud.

Her eyes drop, shy as ever, but lift back to mine. "Where are we going?"

I lean over, pulling the seat belt across her chest, buckling her in. My face is close to hers as I frown, teasing.

"I thought you had a plan?"

The tip of her tongue is caught between her teeth as she narrows her eyes on me.

"Liar."

I nod, slowly grinning before I wink, hitting the road with a quickness she doesn't expect.

"Holy shit," she screams as we barrel down the dark empty highway.

After a few miles, we turn down a dirt road with tall grass on either side and towering oak trees that block the view I've brought her here for.

I pull into a hidden turnoff, the kind that if you don't know it's here, you'll pass it. I'll never tell Sutton how I know it's here. The Mustang bounces over the bumpy path for a few minutes until the gigantic trees and grass give way to nothing but an empty clearing.

Her face turns to mine.

"Did you bring me out here to make out?"

I shake my head, stopping the car and reaching for the button to slide the top back.

"Nah, I brought you here to see stars, baby."

The top begins moving backward, her head lifting to look at a crystalline sky as I kill the engine.

"Whoa."

Chapter
Twenty-One

Sutton

A billion twinkly lights fill the blacks of my eyes as I stare up, a smile etched on my face. I unbuckle my belt, grabbing the windshield, and stand, keeping my neck craned toward the midnight blue overhead.

"This is amazing, Calder. Everything's so clear without the town's lights."

My hair falls forward, framing my face as I look down, the stars making him just bright enough to see.

"Hey."

He grins as our eyes lock.

"Hey, back."

"Thank you for the stars."

He draws his bottom lip between his teeth, releasing slowly before he says, "They're almost as pretty as you."

My cheeks heat, knowing he means what he says because I

don't think he's looked at the sky, just at me.

"False. How would you even know? You haven't looked at them yet."

He grabs my waist, hauling me into his lap, coaxing a giggle out of me. My head lies back against the top of the door, cradled in his arms.

Calder brushes a few errant strands of hair from my face, his eyes solemnly fixed to mine. Butterflies explode in my stomach.

"Why would I need to look? When to me, you look just like heaven."

My eyes close. I want to memorize this moment as he leans down and kisses me under the stars, an unsaid promise of forever on his lips.

I open my eyes, feeling lost in a haze. His eyes are so blue even in the dark, and the golden stubble over his face scrapes my fingertips as I sigh.

"Have you ever grown a beard? I mean, you are almost a man. I hear they do that sometimes."

"Almost?" He laughs. "Yeah, I do. Want me to grow it out?"

I nod, biting my lip, tipping my face to the sky. The idea of Calder with a beard does tingly things to my body. Who am I kidding? Just the idea of Calder makes me tingly.

We sit together, me cradled in his lap, looking up at the stars in comfortable silence. Oh my God, that's what he is—immediate comfort. The kind I usually feel when I'm all alone because I don't have to be "*on*" for anyone. I feel like I can just be with him.

His thumb brushes back and forth over my arm as I stare at the sky, lost in thought. I look at him, finger lifting, tracing the top of the inked constellation on his neck. It's peeking out from under his hoodie.

"What's this one?"

He grins with a sparkle in his eye before dragging the hoodie over his head to give me a better look. I smile as his motion crowds us, pressing us together, before he tosses the sweatshirt to the passenger side, tilting his head for me to get a better look.

"Wanna hear a cool story?"

"Yes," I rush out dramatically, lifting up to kiss his neck softly. "I thought you'd never ask."

He chuckles, and I swear I'm mesmerized. He's just so perfect—down to the tiny scar right under his jaw. Even his flaws are beautiful.

His eyes search the sky before he points to a cluster of stars.

"There. Right there—you see that?"

I nod, recognizing it as the same one on his neck.

"That's Draco—" he muses.

My head shifts to his. "As in Malfoy?"

He sneers playfully. "No, nerd. As in Latin for 'dragon.'"

"Oh." I giggle, mouthing, "Fancy," as he ignores me, looking up again.

"There's this story in Greek mythology—" He pauses as a look of surprise crosses my face. "What? I don't just throw people off cliffs."

My mouth drops open, trying not to laugh because I never thought he was stupid. But who just knows random stories about Greek mythology? Before I can say just that, he winks, continuing.

"A chick named Hera married a terrible dude named Zeus. As a wedding gift, he gave her a tree that had golden apples."

"Wow, setting the bar high, Zeus."

He grins, nodding. "But Hera was terrified someone would steal them. Because golden apples, right? So she placed a dragon at the base of the tree to breathe fucking fire on anyone that tried."

I'm staring up at him, waiting for the rest, but he doesn't say anything, staring back at me like he suddenly remembered something sad. I raise my eyebrows.

"But?" I rock my body, making us shake. "There's always a

but in these stories. What happened? The dragon got the apples and made off with Zeus? Because rumor has it, those gods fucked everything around."

Calder laughs, and I exhale at the sound, drawn into him.

"No. He was killed. With a poison dart, and the apples were stolen."

My bottom lip pops out.

"That's the saddest story. Why would you get that on your neck?"

He shrugs, the easiness of his laugh from before growing muted in tone again.

"Because before she died, my mom was into Greek mythology and all that kind of shit. She had this book, and in it, she had Draco circled. I don't know why…maybe she liked the name. But sometimes, I feel like I was that dragon, sent to protect my brothers and our family tree. So I got it to remind me of her."

My fingers follow the lines on his neck from dot to dot, lingering on each.

"I don't want you to be the dragon. Because that means you die in the end."

His face hardens, but his eyes are soft as he speaks to me. "We all die in the end, but at least I had purpose."

There's so much he's seen that I'll never experience. I can't even put myself in his shoes. *I wonder what baby Calder was like before life got a hold of him.*

"Was it strange growing up without a mother?"

He looks up at the sky.

"I wouldn't know the difference."

But something about the look in his eyes makes me think there's more sadness inside him than he realizes. He takes a deep breath. As I drop my hand, his face turns down to mine.

"Are you close with your family?"

I shrug, adjusting in his lap to sit up. I don't want to talk about my family because it makes me feel shitty. *Who am I to complain?*

"Close is a deceptive word. Because yes, we know each other, and I know they love me." My shoulders tense as I look down at my fingers. "But given a choice, I wouldn't choose my life—no."

An indent forms between his eyes as he huffs a breath. "Says the girl in the castle."

My face swings to his, fear imagined. He thinks I'm a bitch. My eyes narrow because I'm gutted.

"That's not fair. I know how it looks from the outside. But my mom and dad never ask me what I want or if I'm okay with their plan for me. They just tell me how to be for the cameras and the crowd. They discuss my future as if it's a press release, including who I should date or where I should attend school. They don't even really know me. So yes, I live in a castle, but the walls are cold, and the rooms are fucking empty. I'm alone."

Calder grips my jaw with his hand, making me look into his eyes. Why do I feel like I'm going to cry? Fuck. Because being with him feels like I'm stripped down and unprotected. The cut hurts more when he's holding the knife.

"Hey—" The way he says it is gruff, with all the gravel in his voice, but it doesn't scare me. "I didn't mean it like that."

I try and move his hand, but he doesn't let me.

"I said it like I agree—like 'even says the girl in the castle.' My world, your world. It's all fucked. Baby, we're the same, you and me. Damned by our last names. But don't you ever fucking think for a goddamn second that I'd believe anything less than perfection about you. Do you understand me?"

I nod against his fingers, re-seeing how he said it in my head. Feeling stupid. But Calder shakes his head.

"Do you want to know what I think about you?"

I blink because I didn't even realize that I do until now. He starts to speak, but I cover his mouth, needing to say my part first.

"I'm scared of how I feel. It's so intense. And it's like we got here, under these stars, at a lightning-fast speed." He frowns, but I grab his wrist. "I know what you said before about me being worth the trouble. But I'm scared now that we have time to get to know each other, you won't like me anymore." My voice raises. "Because maybe I am just some spoiled rich little princess. And you're all this real life that I don't know anything about." I drop my eyes and let out a half-laugh dipped in the rawest truth. "So you'll leave—and how can I blame you. But then I'll be left trying to figure out how to unfeel this."

"Look at me."

I do, not shying away from how I feel.

"Baby, I wouldn't know how to walk away if there was a gun to my head. You're mine. And I'm yours. That's the deal."

He tugs my face to him, pressing a messy kiss to my lips, melding our mouths as I shift in his lap straddling him, never breaking our kiss. This one isn't like the others.

We're all over each other, tongues, lips, hands—an inelegant mess of lust. Calder's hands run up and down my back as mine slide through his hair.

I'm breathless, dying more and more with every glide over his tongue, rocking my hips into his hardened length below me.

"Sutton," he growls as I rub my tits over him.

"Be my first," I whisper into his mouth.

The kiss deepens as he backs me up against the steering wheel. My head drops back as he molests my neck, sucking and biting at the flesh.

"Calder," I breathe. "Fuck me."

His breath whooshes over the dip at the base of my throat before his eyes lock on mine.

"I will be the only man that owns that pussy." My eyes roll back into my head over his words. Calder leans in, licking my fucking mouth, breathing quietly. "But tonight, baby, we walk before we run."

I'm still, staring back, burning for him.

"Teach me how to walk?"

His nose rubs over mine. "Mmm, the first lesson. You come first."

Chapter
Twenty-Two

Calder

I reach for the door, opening it and flipping on the headlights before taking her with me. She wraps her legs around my waist as I step out, my mouth still on hers as I carry her toward the front of the car.

"I've fucking dreamed of this—you on the hood of my car," I rush out as I pull away. Her chest rises and falls faster with each of my words. "All spread out for me to feast on."

Her hands grip my shoulders as I place her slowly on the hood, watching her tongue drag over that perfect mouth. She swallows, biting the inside of her cheek as she looks at me.

"Nervous?"

"No…"

I raise my brows because she's pretending there wasn't a question mark at the end of that.

She grins. "Maybe."

My hands trail down her legs to her sneakers, pulling them off her feet, letting each drop to the ground with a soft thud.

"Tell me what you're thinking."

She's watching me, taking it all in. And it's fucking sexy.

"What if it tastes weird?"

"Impossible. Baby, I want your cream all over my fucking face. Trust me. Everything you got is everything I want."

She sucks in a breath, biting her lip. I lean forward, palms against the metal, retaking her mouth, tugging that goddamn lip from her teeth to suck it before letting it go with a pop.

"What else?" I push inches from her face.

Her green eyes blink at me as she reaches for the bottom of her hair. My hands leave the hood of the car, fingers dipping into the top of her leggings. I motion with my chin for her to lift her ass.

She does, saying, "I don't know what I'm supposed to do. I don't want to be bad," as I strip off her pants.

But the minute I pull them off, my eyes drop to her pussy, and I growl, "Fuck," because she's not wearing any goddamn panties.

Her pussy is perfect, that small patch of hair calling for me to separate it with my tongue and tease her clit. Fuck me. *If she owns any fucking underwear, I'll burn them.* I'm staring down as I speak.

"Baby, your job is to lie back and let me lick you until you scream. Now spread your legs. I want a better look."

My head lifts to hers as she slowly lowers herself back onto her elbows. I take a step back, adjusting my hard cock in my pants, gritting out, "Open for me."

Hesitantly, she spreads her legs before gasping as the air hits her in delicate places. I smirk, enjoying every fucking minute. Sutton's head drops back as her legs open wide, giving me a full view of her wet pussy.

Something dark stirs inside of me as I look at her. Possession. More potent than anything I've ever felt. This fucking girl is mine, for better or for worse, and I'll kill any motherfucker that tries to take her away from me.

I step in closer, running my fingertips down her thighs, splaying my hands against her pelvis. Her head darts to mine just as I lick my lips and say, "Mine," taking what I want.

A deep inhale fills her body as I flatten my tongue, licking straight through her folds.

My tongue rolls over her clit as her thighs try and snap closed, overwhelmed by the sensations.

"Oh fuck. Calder. Oh my God," she gasps, ass scooting back, but I follow her up the hood, greedy for more, growling into her pussy like a fucking animal.

My hand slaps the top of her ass as I tear my face away, dragging her back down the warm metal hood.

"I knew you would taste like sugar. Sit still."

She's already convulsing as I dive back in, hands finding their way to my head.

"Fuck yes, baby." I hum against her clit, making her jump again.

"Holy shit. I can't take it."

I flick my tongue over her clit, pushing her thighs open, spreading her wide. High-pitched whimpers and mewls tumble out of her as I devour the sweetest fucking taste.

"It feels so good. Oh fuck. Don't stop. Please. Like ever."

I switch between flicking and rolling over her sweet fucking clit, teasing her as I hold her open. Sutton's body bucks, her moans growing louder as her hips begin to rock. The hand she has on my head grips my hair as she pushes me closer to her pussy, wanting more.

That's it, baby. Fuck my face.

She's unabandoned, all the worry she had gone. Lost to the fucking moment. My tongue moves faster and faster in time with her panting, until she's begging.

"Ohmygodohmygodohmygod."

Her thighs begin to shake as her entire body tenses before she screams, back arching off the car, sweet juices exploding into my mouth. The hand not in my hair slaps against the hood as she comes, wave after wave, each a little smaller than the first.

I lick her slower, laving my tongue in lazy swipes, listening to her gulp for air, her breath slowing.

Sutton lifts her face back to mine, jaw slack, watching as I lick her pussy slowly, letting her come down. My tongue dips to her entrance, sliding inside her slit, wanting more of her pleasure.

Her eyes roll back again, but she doesn't stop watching. I fuck her with my tongue, slowly and gently, as her hips begin to circle, the fire reignited. Goddamn, she was made for this—for all the filth and the luxury. *One day I'll give her both.*

My tongue glides out, running down toward the seam of her ass where she dripped her sugar. She tenses, breath hitching, but there won't be any fucking part of her that I don't taste or fuck.

I nip at the inside of her thigh, making her grin before she relaxes, opening her fucking legs even more. I make figure eights with my tongue over the skin, stopping just before her most innocent part, teasing until she's breathing hard again.

"All clean," I whisper against her skin before I raise up, pressing a kiss to her swollen mound.

"Oh, shit," she groans, stomach sucking in.

I crawl over her, lowering my face, and kiss her with cum-smeared lips. She wraps her arms around me, tongue diving into my mouth, letting out a moan before I pull away.

"You like the way you taste?"

She nods with a blush on her cheeks, my hand on her ass.

"Me too, baby."

Chapter
Twenty-Three

Sutton

C alder pulls me back up so that he's standing and I'm sitting again. Goose bumps prick my skin as he steps back from between my legs before looking to the ground, bending down to grab my stuff.

Holy hell. That just happened. All of that just fucking happened. The smile on my face feels permanent because it was amazing.

"Will it always be like that?" I breathe quietly.

He nods with a smirk, shaking off my pants and turning them right side in. My knees swing open and closed lazily as he steps back up to me. The way he's looking at me like we're not done, it makes my hips rock forward before I squeeze my legs shut.

He licks his bottom lip, taking my ankle in his hand, extending my leg. His eyes dart to my center as he does it. "I like you bare. Do that shit all the time. I want to know that if I were to reach my hand up your skirt or down your jeans…that all I'd feel is your wet kitty."

My lips purse, blowing out a breath because—fuck. The way he talks about my body makes me feel hot all over. I nod, biting my lip as he pulls the leggings over my bare feet, running them over my legs.

"Lift, again."

My palms press against the hood, raising my ass so he can tug my pants back into place, but not before he places a soft kiss to the Band-Aid on my leg. His body wedges itself closer between my thighs as he does it, and I swear my back arches, hoping to feel him against my center.

Jesus, I'm so horny that it's embarrassing. But he did say "the first lesson." So there has to be a second.

It's as if he can read me because he chuckles.

"Did I create a monster?"

Kinda.

He's putting my shoes on, not saying a damn word, and I'm freaking dying as I watch. Every single part of Calder's body is attractive. The way his shoulders move. The muscles that ripple under his T-shirt.

It all makes me shiver as I watch him.

He switches to my other foot, and his bicep flexes as he lifts my leg. My eyes run the length of his forearms, the veins on display as he wiggles my foot back into my sneaker.

He's making me weak.

"So what's—" *lesson number two*, I was going to ask, but I'm silenced because as Calder stands, he reaches down and adjusts himself. He's hard.

The length of his cock is strained against his pants, hypnotizing me because I *am* a monster. A lusting over Calder one.

God, I wonder what his dick looks like?

Calder's hand comes to my face, calling my eyes to his. He smirks, thumb brushing over my cheek.

"How do you feel, baby?"

I shrug. Amazing. Addicted. Ready for more. But I don't say that, opting for flirtation.

"Eh, I've had better. Maybe you should give it another shot?"

Calder laughs loudly, and it makes me join in before he attacks my neck, gently biting and sucking my skin in between breathing his words.

"If I didn't know it was a lie, someone might die tonight. I'm all fueled up on testosterone. High because I made my girl come so hard. I'm an animal. You don't know what I'm capable of."

I sag into his lips. Fuck. His voice touches me in all the right places. I wrap my legs around him, pressing myself as close as possible, wanting what he won't give.

"Oh, but I do know..." I purr, lifting the sleeve tucked over my hand, biting my lip to hide my smile. "Because you've got something...right...here—"

I wipe his whole mouth as he pushes my hand away, giggling again. He grabs the front of my hoodie, tugging my face to his. Enviable long lashes brush together as he blinks, hiding his blue eyes for milliseconds at a time from mine.

God, I can't get enough. I want more. Right fucking now. I want him to be my first. Screw walking. *One little french kiss south of France, and I've become a sexual beast.*

I rub my cheek against his hand that's gripping my sweatshirt, batting my damn eyelashes. He lets out a long exhale.

"Who taught you to flirt like this? Because baby, you can have anything you want if you keep looking at me like that."

I smile demurely, bringing my face closer, rubbing my nose to his.

"I want you...inside of me."

His eyes search mine as his hand runs up my chest to my neck, wrapping it around my throat, pushing me back gently. A rush of wetness coats my pussy as he holds me in place, staring, his chin lifted, looking down at me like I'm at his mercy.

He's right. I am at his mercy.

"Baby," he levels, bringing his other hand to cradle my face. His thumb drags over my bottom lip. "Tell me what you saw that night in the cabana."

I blink, sucking in a breath. Vivid memories flick through my mind as I stare back at him.

"Lesson number two. Be specific when you ask for what you want. I'm gonna be inside of you, but it's not your pussy I'm filling tonight."

He steps back as I begin speaking, sliding me off the hood with him so that I'm standing in front of him. Fuck, I'm so turned on. I don't even recognize my voice as I speak because it's husky, drenched in lust.

"I saw a girl on her knees. Her hands were on his hips."

Calder places my hands on his hips, eyes not leaving mine. I lick my lips, feeling overwhelmed with need.

"His hand was gripping her hair."

A quiet moan escapes my mouth as he grips the base of my hair, forcing my head back.

"Oh my God."

He winks. "Keep talking."

"Um." I swallow, already feeling weak in my knees. "She had his—" I hesitate, but he scowls. "—his dick in her mouth."

Two fingers, the same ones he had inside of me earlier today, push inside my mouth as my lips close around them. The taste from the salt on his skin bursts over my tongue as he slowly glides them in and out of my mouth.

"Did you watch her suck dick, Sutton? Did you watch her head bob?"

The deep voice is a bass of gravel, making my nipples harden under my hoodie. My eyes are on Calder's as he jerks his chin for me to show him, stopping his movement.

I do, circling my hand around his wrist as I lower my head, sucking on his goddamn fingers.

"That's my good girl."

My thighs squeeze together, shivering as he says that. Calder watches me before he reaches down, rubbing himself through his jeans.

Sweet Jesus.

"Hollow your cheeks. Suck them good," he directs, smiling as I listen.

My pussy aches as I grip his wrist harder.

"That's it, baby. Fold your lips over your teeth."

I'm obedient, sucking harder, making sure my teeth don't touch his fingers as my head bobs faster. I feel on fire. God, I want him so fucking bad. The sounds coming out of my wet mouth filter into the night, mixed with his groans as he watches.

"Fuck, you're gonna suck me so good."

Calder guides my head, holding tightly to my hair, as he pushes my head further down his fingers. My hand on his hip digs into his jeans as he says filthy words that make me feel like I'm going to explode.

"Did she gag on his cock, Sutton?" As he says it, his thick fingers press further toward the back of my throat, making tears spring to my eyes, but I don't gag…I moan.

His fingers leave my mouth, arms dropping to his sides. "Fuck. Baby. Suck me."

He looks drunk…on me.

I drop to my knees. Because I've never wanted anything more than to have him in my mouth. Fumbling with his belt, I unlatch it, but he moves my hand, pulling it from the belt loops, gazing down at me before he lets it drop to the ground.

He unbuttons his pants, lowering the zipper, his bulge immediately coming into view.

I reach up, rubbing over the protruding length behind his boxer briefs. It's so hard, and it pulses as I touch it. His head drops back to the sky as I look up, hearing a whoosh of breath releasing from his lips—*my god at my mercy.*

My impatient fingers brush over the elastic band, folding it back. The tip of his cock shines with cum that's beading at the top.

I don't know if I should. But I can't stop myself. I dart my tongue out, hungry to taste him, taking a lick.

"Fuck," grits from between his teeth. His fingers pinch my jaw, holding me in place. "Give me a second. You're fucking killing me, baby."

Not listening, I tug his pants down, face held still because I want to see all of him. Calder releases me, reaching down, gripping his shaft. My eyes are locked on the motion.

I'm mesmerized, watching how his thumb rubs over his smooth tip, smearing his juices over the head before gliding his palm over and down his thick cock.

His dick is beautiful.

I don't know if people think things like this, but his cock is the most beautiful thing I've ever seen.

I'm hungry to taste him as I look up from my knees. "Just like your fingers, right? With my hand like yours?"

He nods, jaw slack.

I look back to his dick, slowly leaning in, replacing his hand with mine. My palm drags down, but he stops me.

"Get your hand wet. Spit on it."

I let him go, bringing my hand to my mouth, looking up at him as I take a long stroke of my tongue over my palm.

"Oh fuck. You're a...very. Good. Girl."

A strangled groan bursts from his mouth as mine covers the tip of his cock. I wrap my wet hand around the base, moving in tandem.

"Fuck yes."

I suck down his thick shaft, jacking him off, again and again. Each time, I get braver, finding a rhythm and bobbing my head as I hollow my cheeks.

"Your mouth is pure fucking velvet." He groans, hand finding my head.

His fingers weave between my locks, and I can't help but remember how that girl looked when she was like this. I want that. I want Calder to fuck my mouth.

Whimpers vibrate between my lips as his grip tightens.

I take my hand away from his dick, holding on to his hips, letting him move my head faster. *Yes. Fuck my face.* His moans fill my ears as his dick slides in and out of my warm mouth. My thighs squeeze together, clit begging to be touched.

"Fuck. Sutton. You're sucking me so good."

Without thinking, spurred on by his dirty mouth, my hand drops from his jeans to my center, rubbing as I blow him.

"Oh shit. Baby."

My eyes lift to his like he called them. Calder's face is dark and animalistic. He's locked on me like a predator lost to its need. His hips rock toward my face, moving faster and harder into my mouth.

His words are spoken through gritted teeth, making my fingers move faster.

"Rub that greedy little clit. You like sucking my dick, huh?"

Need barrels through my body. Calder pulls my hair so tight that I feel stinging as he fucks my mouth.

"I want your throat. Trust me."

It's not a question. Because he doesn't need to ask. I want everything he gives.

His face is strained as he presses my head closer, filling my mouth with his cock. Back further until it feels almost like I can't breathe.

"Swallow."

Tears leak from my eyes as I do, making him growl before pulling back and looking down at me. *More.*

"Again."

My entire body starts to shake as he pushes back in, clit throbbing as I rub faster and faster until I'm humming on his cock. I swallow his dick back, launching into an orgasm, screaming around the thickness.

"Oh shit," he bellows, pulling back as warm cum shoots into my mouth, spilling onto my chin as he pulls out of my mouth.

"I'm sorry," he says in a ragged breath, milking his dick with his hand around his cock.

My head tilts up, fingers wiping over my chin, gathering his pleasure. I'm staring up at him as his chest rises and falls, his eyes barely open.

I'm yours, and you're mine.

His head lowers, eyes piercing mine. I lift my fingers to my mouth and run my tongue over them.

"You tasted me. It's only fair I taste you."

He blinks but says nothing before swallowing.

"I don't expect—" He shakes his head. "I wouldn't expect for you to do that. You just brought me to my fucking knees faster than I anticipated."

I smile, happy and proud.

"Well, now you know my answer. So, I guess there's always next time."

That smirk he wears so well peeks out. He reaches behind him, dragging off his T-shirt, showing off his flawless body before he hauls me to my feet.

"Another lesson?" I say, almost breathless, but he laughs, wiping his hand off before tossing the shirt on the hood.

"Pace yourself, killer."

Calder leans down, kissing me senseless until my lips feel raw and my body feels ready all over again before pulling back, locking eyes with me.

"When can I see you again?"

Chapter
Twenty-Four

Sutton

My eyelids flutter open, streaks of light filtering in as I yawn. I stretch my arms outside of the blanket, body still warm from sleeping as the sides of my lips tug up, remembering…last night was not a dream.

"When can I see you again?" His words lie over me like the naughtiest invitation.

"Holy shit," I whisper, covering my hands over my center before lifting my fingers to feel my swollen lips.

I draw the comforter over my head as squeals erupt, partnered with my kicking my feet.

Aubrey's ringtone blares from my nightstand, causing me to scramble out from under the blanket. The last text she and Piper got from me said I was sneaking out with Calder. So I know they're dying to know what happened, but first, I have to text him.

I sit up, brushing my hair from my face, hitting Decline as my fingers race through a text.

Buttercup: 🩶 I really wish I could see you rn. But I'll settle for tonight. I'll leave my balcony open. P.S. I'm playing hard to get… is it working?

Giggling, I throw myself back onto my bed, staring at the ceiling, just as my cell rings again, making me quickly hit Answer.

"Bitch. Did you decline me?"

"Aubs. I don't even know how to explain to you how amazing last night was."

"Well, you'd better figure it out because we need to debrief stat. While you were finding the Bonnie to Calder's Clyde, Piper got pipe laid by the one and only Shephard. Picking you up in ten, beotch."

"Oh my God."

The line disconnects, and I jump out of bed, rushing to my closet to get dressed. I reach for some overalls as a thought crosses my mind.

I have a boyfriend.

No, that's not the right word.

When Calder dropped me off last night, I almost never made it out of the car. We couldn't leave each other, coming back for more kisses each time we said goodbye. It's as if each time we're together, the stronger the impulse grows to never be apart.

"I won't make it a whole day. Tell me I can see you today."

"You can see me today and tomorrow and the day after that, and the day after that."

Calder's hands cradle my face as he stares into my eyes.

"Tell me I can have you forever."

Smiling at the memory, I toss the overalls and grab my cute jean cut-offs. I shimmy them on, catching sight of a cropped T-shirt I bought last month but haven't dared to wear. But today's the day. I slide it right over my head, turning to look in the mirror.

My lips are bruised. A blush only Calder gives shades my cheeks. My hair is wild. Sexy. I look like the hottest version of me. I'm different. Changed. He touched me and made it so.

I grab a hair tie off the center dresser, pulling all my hair into an on-purpose messy bun. I look at myself again, remembering all the most delicious parts of last night.

Until the signature sound of Aubrey driving too fast has me hustling to shove my feet into my high-top Converse. I run to the bathroom and brush my teeth, grab my bag, then jet out of my room.

My hand hovers over the rail as I take the stairs, hearing a singsongy "Hi, Mrs. Prescott."

I'm not even paying attention to what my mother says back as I bound down, buzzing with excitement.

"Hi, Mom."

Her eyes dart to me as I pass. I push Piper backward, hoping to leave quickly before speaking over my shoulder.

"We're going to get coffee and then maybe do some shopping. I'll be home later."

"Freeze."

Shit. I turn around slowly, smiling.

"Firstly. Good morning, Sutton. And no, you will be home in an hour. We have the fundraiser itinerary to discuss and a tasting to attend. Lastly—" She narrows her eyes. "—do we think this outfit is the best choice?"

I drop my head to the front of me, then back to her questioning face. Granted, I'm typically more conservative, mainly because her voice is always in my head, like, *"Darling, would we want someone to receive the impression being given? Probably not."* But this time, more than ever, the answer is *"Yes, we freaking would."*

If Calder sees me, I hope the impression I'm giving is *hot girlfriend.* My arms cross in front of me as my lips part to say something I shouldn't, but the girls chime in.

"I love it. It's so on trend." Aubrey smirks as Piper nods.

"Exactly. It's like Sutton has her pulse on today's youth. What an asset to have."

I try and hide my smile. Such conniving little geniuses. I give my mother's frowning face a wave. "My outfit's fine. I'm going for coffee, not a press conference. Bye, Mom."

Taking Aubrey's hand, I tug her away, Piper following. The minute we shut the front door behind us, laughter erupts, and Piper imitates my mother.

"Is this outfit the best choice?"

Aubrey answers, grabbing her car door. "Uh, yeah. Because Sutton isn't worried about what America will think, Elizabeth. She's hoping her outlaw thinks she's smoking hot."

I shove her shoulder as we all pile into the car, me in the back. My hands slap down on the soft camel-skinned leather in Aubrey's Range Rover, shifting between them.

"So, is Shephard's staff as big as expected?"

Piper screams. I laugh. The car starts, and music blares.

Aubrey tears out of my driveway as Piper sticks her arm out the window. I can't remember the last time I felt this free or this happy.

And it's all because of him.

The closer we get to downtown, the more my eyes start to wander. First to the basketball courts, not seeing anyone, then to every possible place he might be. I can't help myself.

"Did you text him? Or are you doing that Sutton thing and waiting for serendipity to strike?" Aubrey snarks.

I smile, pulling my cell from my bag and rolling my eyes because my messages are always silent to avoid my mother's glare. So I should check to see if he texted back yet.

"Yes, I texted him. But he's probably still sleeping."

But when I open my messages, I suddenly realize there was one waiting...above the one I sent. "Oh my God. You guys. There was a message waiting from last night. I typed mine so quickly that I didn't even check the one above. Why am I so embarrassing?"

They laugh as I read it.

Wesley: You're probably already sleeping. But I wanted to say something fucking poetic for you to wake up to. All I could come up with is—Better.

My heart straight up leaps out of my chest. It's one simple word, but to us, it has the biggest meaning in the world. Calder's right. Last night made everything better in the most dramatic freaking way. Jesus, even the sun seems to shine brighter today.

The music fades when I don't say anything, so I look up before I type back. Piper turns to look at me.

"Either read that text or start talking because that goofy smile on your face is too much. We're dying over here. Tell us everything."

I giggle, dropping my phone into my lap.

"Last night was…earth-shattering. Life-changing."

"You fucked him," Aubrey yells, making me look around because I'm sure people outside the car just heard.

"No," I blurt as I shush her. "But—" My hands cover my reddening face before I peek through my fingers. "—he went down on me."

Our bodies bounce as Aubrey hits the parking space curb.

"Shit." She laughs before killing the car and turning back to stare at me.

"Where? Like where were you?"

Piper grabs Aubrey's shoulder, eyes fixed on me as I drag my hands down my face.

"On the hood of his car."

Aubrey's eyes get wide. "Holy fucking shit. That's so hot. You bitch."

I nod bigger as Piper cuts in. "Did you…go down too?"

The high-pitched and somewhat inappropriate words fly from

their mouths when I say, "Yes," until we're all laughing.

I'm the first one out of the car, making them follow me into the coffee shop as our laughter dies out. Piper goes to the front to put in our orders as Aubrey and I grab a table. As soon as our coffees arrive, we hold court at our small table, taking turns telling each other war stories from our nights.

"So," Aubrey cuts in, "when are you seeing him again?"

I close my eyes for a second, thinking about the text again. "I don't know. It's funny because that's what he asked me last night. I basically played hard to get and said every day."

My mother's demand filters back into my head as they both giggle. Shit. She'll monopolize my time for most of today, so only tonight works, but maybe I can sneak out again this week…unless my father starts doing late-night meetings like he usually does before these events. *Shoot.*

Piper raises her brows. "I know that look. Where'd you go? What are you suddenly thinking?"

"Just about how to see him. My mother's going to have me bogged down all week with errands. And it's not as if he can just come over and hang out. I have to think of something covert."

Aubrey giggles, licking whipped cream off the top of her Frappuccino.

"You're like sexy secret agents. Strangers in public and freaks in private."

"More like vampire secret agents because it's the same with his dad. He can't know about me either. Midday meet-ups are looking impossible right about now."

"Right. Edward and Bella cannot sneak over to his side of town either."

She nods along with her words, voicing the "shit that complicates Sutton's life" checklist. *Thanks, Aubs.*

"Exactly. We can't be seen here, there, or any-fucking-where—

it's like my life just became a maudlin Dr. Seuss poem."

I laugh, but it isn't genuine because I'm feeling a little doomed right now. Piper puts her chin on her hand, staring at me.

"Do you have a plan? Because before you start really investing in that frown...put me in coach. I'm ready. I have all kinds of calculating shit saved up. I've been waiting for you to become a badass." She pretends to cry as she adds, "Welcome, friend."

This time my laugh is genuine, and so is my smile.

"You're insane. I feel unprepared for badassness, but I'm all in. I know that I'm punching above my weight. You guys know sneaking out last night was a first for me. And the only reason I could relax is because I knew my mother had taken a sleeping pill. But I did it. And it was more than worth the risk. He is worth all the risks."

Aubrey leans, giving Piper a discreet high five.

"Sutton, there's a reason the Lord introduced us. We're terrible influences. He knew you'd need us, eventually. My parents are gone again Fourth of July weekend. I know it's like a month away, but you can totally use my house to satisfy your lady boner. But...make your boy bring his friends. I can't be the only bitch without a fun story."

Piper claps her hands together before almost bouncing in her seat. "And...you said your mom will have you tied down this week, right? That's perfect. Give me your list for Tuesday. I'll do everything for you. You can sneak away. I refuse to believe Calder won't know how to hide in broad daylight."

I press my hands to my cheeks, feeling grateful for these two.

"Really? Be serious. Are you sure?"

"Yes," they say in unison until Piper adds, "Dibs on West for the Fourth."

Aubrey and I swing our heads in Piper's direction. But she shrugs, taking a sip of her coffee.

"Shephard and I said we weren't official. We're just summertime fun. I feel no guilt."

"Piper Jean," Aubrey teases, bringing a full smile to my face. "I'm shocked. Such a little whore."

"Shut up." She laughs. "And my middle name is not Jean... What the hell?"

Aubrey smirks. "I know, but it should be because you're as trashy as Miss Britney Jean Spears circa barefoot at a gas station bathroom. And I'm here for it."

Laughter erupts as I pick up my coffee and take a sip, but Piper turns her head toward me.

"I'm proud of you, Sut. It's about time you went for what *you* want."

Agreed. I chew on the brim of my cup, staring at them talking because I hope for the rest of my life, I never forget who these people are to me right now. There are no better friends.

Aubrey lifts her cup. "Here's to a summer full of bad ideas."

Piper joins. "With good times."

I raise mine, tapping theirs. "And a badass destiny."

Chapter
Twenty-Five

Calder

Buttercup: 🩶 I really wish I could see you rn. But I'll settle for tonight. I'll leave my balcony open. P.S. I'm playing hard to get… is it working?

F uck. I run my hand over my morning wood, pushing it into my hand. Damn, if I don't know exactly how she's feeling today. She was my first thought when I woke up twenty seconds ago.

Last night was the kind of perfect I never wanted to end.

I sit up, cracking my neck, before leaning over to grab my journal. My fingers brush past all the filled pages as the pencil tucked between them falls out, but I swipe it up, writing the truest thought in my head.

She tastes like the kind of temptation I'm never fucking coming back from.

The pages snap together as I close it, tossing it back on my dresser before grabbing my phone.

Wesley: Did you just booty call me?

Buttercup: Don't be offended. You're at the top of my rotation.

I hit Dial. Sutton's laugh answers the phone for her.

"Keep laughing, punk."

There's background noise I can't make out, but her voice dominates the line the way a phone that isn't on speaker does.

"Shut up. Did you just wake up? Your voice is all—"

"Mmm," I rumble, interrupting her, "I did. This wild chick had me up late last night. She smelled like grapefruit and tasted like bourbon, and after I ate her pussy, I felt drunk on her."

Silence. Just the sound of her breathing.

"I hate you." Her voice drops to a whisper. "I'm literally standing in a room full of event planners with my mother, preparing for a cake tasting."

Now it's my turn to laugh before I make my voice huskier.

"Lemme eat your cake."

The sweet sound of her giggle makes my eyes close. I could get used to this.

"Sneak away."

"I can't." Her voice becomes hushed. "I have a thousand dumb errands. And I'll be with my mom for most of them. But Piper said she'd cover me for Tuesday. And I'll leave the door unlocked tonight."

My eyes open, chin lifting to stare at the ceiling as a growl leaves my throat as I think.

"Oh, God. Quit it," she rasps.

"Tuesday's too far, and tonight's not good." I smirk as an idea pops into my head. "Share your location with me. I'll find the perfect time to steal a kiss from those lips. Nobody will see me. I promise. I'll just take what I want and go."

"Done," she breathes out before adding, "Coming," to someone in the background. "I've got to go."

"See you later, baby."

The call ends, and I lie back, eyes only lifting as the ping comes through my phone to accept the invitation to see her location.

I'm staring at my phone as my door swings open and Roman pops his head in.

"Dude, get up. We got business with Pops."

I nod, pushing off the bed, but as I turn my back to him, he adds, "Where'd you go last night?"

My face swings over my shoulder to Roman's stare. He's guessing correctly, telling by the look on his face. But I'm not listening to a fucking lecture. West's face comes into view behind him, a grin from ear to ear.

"Yeah, Calder, where'd you go?"

"If I wanted you to know, I'd have taken you with me."

West looks at Roman, who seems less amused by the answer, saying, "Oh shit. I think our boy got laid. Was it that stripper from the beach?"

Fucking West. I almost laugh. Instead, I walk toward the door, slamming it closed just as he says, "Can I hit it too?"

"Tyler. Please sit," Michael offers from his patio table chair, backdropped by his pool.

Roman, West, and I stand behind my father as he sits. That's our job. To watch, listen, and ensure nothing happens that Pops doesn't want to happen.

As we rode over, he gave us the warning to behave today, wholly aimed at me, but he also gave me a gun.

Michael wipes his mouth on his napkin before giving my father his attention.

"Connor wants a date for the product."

Michael doesn't answer. Instead, he shifts his face to look at me. "I see you brought your sons." Michael's eyes flick over the bruises on my face. "I'm sorry to see it came to that, Calder. Lessons can be hard learned sometimes."

Was that a flex? He better be fucking joking talking to me like that. I motion to step forward, but my father holds up a finger, halting me in my place. Even with his back to me, he knew that I'd react.

I stand in my place, eyes on Michael, as Pops lowers his hand.

"Mr. Kelly, lessons *can* be hard learned. I suggest you answer my question, or I'll arrange for Calder to show you how we teach them. Maybe he can recreate your son's."

Michael blanches, stuttering, "This is no way to treat a business partner. It's not as easy as a date…I own a whole company that produces more than just your street drugs. I have to be careful. My reputation is on the line if I'm caught. My family's name is a founder of this country."

Pops chuckles, reaching out and grabbing Michael by the collar before slapping his face, fucking hard. *Damn. Shit just got real for you, Mikey.*

"Please," he cries out, lifting a hand in front of his face.

I don't even need to look at my brothers to know they're grinning the same way I am. Michael sounds a whole lot like his bitch-ass son. Pops lowers his voice as he leans in.

"This isn't a partnership, Michael. We don't give a fuck about your family name. You're just the whore we use to get what we need. You let us fuck you for a few dollars because you don't have a choice. That's why you sought us out—desperation. Imagine what the world would think if they knew the kind of trouble you're running from."

Pops lets go of Michael's collar, straightening it out for him.

"Now, Connor gave a little with our sons' beef, but if we don't get our product, there will be no fucking grace for your family."

We take a step back as Pops pushes from his chair to stand.

"You have one week to get us our shit, or one of your little prick sons won't just be tossed off a fucking cliff."

My eyes meet with Michael's, and I give a wink before my father turns, and we follow. The moment we're clear of the house, Pops turns to look at me.

"Change of plans. I'll take West to the docks tonight. You and Roman keep eyes on Kelly. He's scared. And fear makes people do very dumb things."

Chapter
Twenty-Six

Sutton

"**S**utton, make sure a sample of the lemon cake is brought to the table," my mother directs curtly, turning back to the event planners sitting around the table.

I nod as I make my way past the glass cases of desserts and pies all stacked neatly, making my mouth water. The man behind the counter smiles, already pulling out the cake, having heard her.

"Thank you," I mouth as I walk by.

We've been at this bakery for the last hour and a half, debating desserts for my father's fundraiser. And what could've been fun was introduced to my mother. She scrutinizes everything as if people are more generous after cherry pie versus lemon meringue.

I get it. Securing election funds is a year-round hustle, and my mother knows how to do it best. And I've already heard the lecture about this re-election being key in my father's political career. But it's cake.

She's just exhausting, and because of that fact, I just lied and said I had to go to the ladies' room so that I could escape, scroll Instagram, and text my friends.

Or just text Calder.

I pull my phone out of my mini crossbody bag as I walk down the short hallway. There are a ton of texts in my group chat, so I open the chain as I reach the bathroom door. But a swishing noise pulls my eyes to the right just as the kitchen door of the bakery swings open.

Crystal-blue eyes arrest my heart.

A smile breaks out over my face as I'm pushed—no, shoved— into the ladies' room, barely in time to hide his lips meeting mine.

"What are you doing here?" I rush out, pushing him away only a little.

"Exactly what I said. Now shut up and kiss me back."

My arms wrap around his neck, and I press my lips to his, letting him lift me off my feet. He reaches back as our tongues taste and locks the door before winding his arm around me, the other hand in my hair as we kiss and kiss until I start to lose track of how many seconds have ticked by.

I pull back, breathless and happy, but his eyes are hooded as he stares down at me.

"Baby. You're gonna need to be very quiet for what I'm about to do."

The way he says that makes my heart start to beat faster, as does the smirk on his face. I nod as Calder sets me to the ground, turning me around, gently pushing my back against the door.

My eyes stay on him as he lowers down to one knee, running his hand up my skirt before hooking my leg over his shoulder. He raises it, revealing my bare pussy, smiling before he lifts his eyes up to mine. *I remembered.*

"Oh fuck. Such a good girl. Now give me the kiss I really came for."

That's the last thing I hear before I'm forced to clamp a hand down over my mouth. Because Calder's eating me like it's his fucking mission, and my muted gasps are the only sound filling my ears.

His fingers grip my thigh as my eyes roll back. God, it's like the first time all over again. My body is instantly overwhelmed, every nerve ending short-circuiting. Without thinking, I push down on his head with my free hand because it feels like I can't take it.

"It's too much. Oh my God," I mumble.

But he growls, gripping my leg hard, flicking his tongue faster over my clit.

Fuck.

Calder's holding me in place, up against the bathroom door as my body begins to quiver. His finger pushes inside my pussy, rough and fast as his tongue works me over.

I'm being thoroughly fucked. A second finger pushes in, and I bite down on my hand to stop from moaning. He's pushing in and out, faster and faster, touching me in just the right spot as he kisses my swollen bud.

My hand curls into his hair as the divine feeling begins to take over, building and building, until my thighs shake uncontrollably. I moan into my hand, rolling my hips into his face, hearing him hum his appreciation until I explode, squeezing my eyes shut as the waves of my orgasm feel like they're drowning me.

Calder licks me, drinking me in as I drop my hand, panting with a smile on my face.

"I can't believe you just did that."

He smiles up at me, kissing the inside of my thigh, before standing and licking his lips.

"Baby, that was as much for me as it was for you."

He straightens my skirt before turning me back toward the door and whispering in my ear, "Go be a good daughter. Until you can be my bad girl later."

"When?" I rush out, but he's already turning the doorknob, pushing me back out.

I run my hands over my hair as I walk back down the hall to the table, fighting the urge to look over my shoulder.

"There you are," my mother calls, standing alone, the others having clearly left.

Jesus, how long was I in there?

"Sorry, I'm not feeling well. I thought I was going to throw up. I hope no one was offended."

My mother's discerning eyes rake over me. "You do look flush." She feels my forehead. "We're heading home now anyway. You can lie down before dinner."

I nod, smiling weakly before glancing over my shoulder, only catching a glimpse of tattoos as Calder ducks back through the kitchen.

Chapter
Twenty-Seven

Sutton

Wesley: Did you dream about me last night?
Buttercup: Yes
Wesley: Was it dirty?
Buttercup: Is there any other kind?
Wesley: Then you should spend some extra time in confession today.

"You look chipper this morning," my father muses, staring at me.

I shrug. "It's a nice day."

But all I'm thinking about is yesterday in the bathroom and how Calder better be at our spot today. I think that's what his text meant. Either way, I can't stop smiling.

"There doesn't seem to be any press today. I'm surprised since we're so close to the fundraiser. They usually turn into vultures around this time," my mother snarks, ripping me from my daydream.

"Huh? What?"

My parents stare at me like I've lost my mind. I have—completely and totally over Calder Wolfe.

"Are you okay, darling?"

I nod, feeling heat crawl up my neck. *I'm fine, Mom. Just a brazen hussy embarrassed by my wet daydream. Jesus.* My head swings toward the window just as the cross on the steeple comes into view. *Call, and he comes.*

As the car slows, I reach for the door with my smile firmly in place.

"Do you mind if I sit with Piper and Aubrey today? I mean, since there isn't any press."

My mother raises her brows, dropping her eyes to my bouncing knee—the one I stop bouncing immediately.

"I suppose that's fine," my father offers as his door is opened by the driver before he adds, "This wouldn't have to do with a young man? Would it?"

My heart stops beating for a moment before I kick it back into gear.

"Dad. Seriously?" I roll my eyes like a typical teenager, hoping to quell any further questions.

Because I know exactly who he's talking about. At least Hunter's good for something.

He holds up his hands, eyeing my mother, who's smirking.

"Go. But model behavior, Sutton."

I don't wait for further conversation, nodding as I duck out of the other side, immediately spotting my friends. My legs go as fast as they'll take me, all but running toward Aubrey and Piper as their smiles grow.

Aubrey appraises me, shaking her head as I come to a stop in front of her.

"He's here. Isn't he? You are all shiny and happy. Like a puppy."

I nod, quickly answering, "Yep," as she grabs my hand, turning and pulling me up the steps as Piper chuckles behind me.

We walk inside the mostly still-empty church as Aubs spins around.

"You have ten minutes, ya whore. We'll cover for you until the service starts."

I smack a kiss to her cheek and sneak into the hall, rushing up the stairs, looking back to see them take a seat at the bottom. Best friends ever.

The minute I get to the top of our hiding spot, Calder's eyes lift to mine from where he's sitting, flipping a Bible in his hand. He stands, tossing it on the table next to him before closing the distance.

"Hi," he breathes, wrapping an arm around my waist, lifting me up as we instantly kiss.

His lips break from mine again, dragging down over my jaw as I hold him tighter.

"Hi. I only have ten minutes before someone notices I'm gone. The girls are covering for me."

He pulls back for a moment, breath warm against my neck. "Why does it always feel like it's been a hundred years since the last time I saw you?"

God, he's right. We've been apart for half a day. And it feels like forever.

Blue eyes connect to mine as my feet touch the ground, but I wrap my arms around his waist, refusing to break away.

"I wish you could just steal me away. Is that dumb to say? But I just want to be with you without an expiration date."

Calder sweeps my hair behind my ears, forcing me to step back as he looks down at me. And I know he feels the same. I can't get enough of him to last me. It's impossible.

"I would, baby—if I thought I'd get away with it."

My smile blooms at his teasing as I weave my fingers through his. "We have Tuesday. And the fundraiser is Saturday, and I'll say I'm sleeping at Aubrey's. So we only have to make it a week before we can sneak away for a whole night. Can you find a place for us?"

"Only a week, says the girl that owns my fucking thoughts. But beggars can't be choosers. I'll find a place. But if shit doesn't work out, I'll just have to burn your fucking house down...because I'm gonna see you."

He bends down, tucking his head into the crook of my neck as he growls. My hands find his hair, and I let out a giggle as his face rubs against my shoulder.

"Fuck, I just want to bathe in your smell so that I can keep you with me. How am I supposed to watch you walk away? When all I wanna do is pin you the fuck down."

I blink, pushing his head back, as a deliciously bad idea comes to mind. Oh my God, what am I doing? Licking my lips, I slowly begin gathering my long maxi skirt.

Calder takes a few steps back, his eyes locked on the movement, watching, narrowed, as his lips part.

"Mmm. If you're doing what I think you're doing, then I'm absolutely gonna lose my mind this week."

I pull the fabric all the way up to my waist, revealing my white satin panties. Calder raises his brows, but I shrug, looking up at him innocently.

"I'm in a church. I have to wear them here."

His eyes half blink as he steps toward me again, voice lowering.

"I am gonna steal you. I've decided. And I'll never give you back. Because you are mine, Sutton. Do you understand how deep I mean that shit, baby? I will never fucking give you back. Ever."

Right now, no matter if what he's saying started as teasing, it's my every wish that his promise is true.

"Swear it," I whisper.

He grips the back of my neck, pulling my lips to his roughly before he says, "On my life."

I'm released, eyes on his as I shimmy off my panties. We stand silent before I take his hand, flipping it over, palm up. The silk folds over itself as it drops over his greedy fingers.

"Now, you can take a piece of me with you until you take all of me. And I hope you don't mind, but all I've thought about is you—so they're wet."

Church bells sound like the clock striking ten, making him scowl as I lift to my toes, kissing his lips quickly before turning and running back the way I came.

But before I take the stairs, I look over my shoulder as Calder raises the white satin to his face and smells my goddamn panties.

Chapter
Twenty-Eight

Calder

"Hi," she answers, and I can tell she's smiling.

"Hi, back. I missed you all damn day, baby."

She sighs into the phone. "How are my panties doing? Are they helping your cravings?"

"Not at all. Monday usually sucks, but this one's been the fucking worst. I want you on me. Now."

"Today is almost over, and tomorrow Piper will cover for me— so we have four whole hours in the afternoon."

I groan because patience is not a virtue I possess when it comes to Sutton. She giggles, but my smile fades because I'm staring out the window, watching Michael Kelly help his wife into the back of their town car. Pops told us to follow him and make our presence known tonight.

"You got quiet. What are you doing right now?"

My head shakes as I answer. "Just stuff."

"Ah. Stuff. Stuff you can't tell me."

"Stuff you don't want to know."

Roman taps the hood from where's he sitting outside, grabbing my attention. My arm dangles out the window, and I give a wave as Roman and I stare down Michael's car as he passes. *We're watching, motherfucker.*

I turn my attention back to my call as Roman pulls out his cell to let Pops know we said *hello.*

"Okay then, tell me this," she muses. "What would you do if you weren't born into the life you're in?"

My head tilts, a smile returning to my face.

"We're getting deep. All right." She giggles again. "I'd probably work on cars. Like maybe restore old cars. I like taking something that somebody overlooked and seeing what's beautiful in it."

She laughs but not as if what I said was funny, and I don't like it. I can feel her mood change.

"What's that laugh? What's wrong?"

The sound of her sheets rustling fills the phone before she says, "Nothing. Just what you said kind of hit me hard. Today was a shitty day with my mom, and as you were talking, it felt like you were describing me."

My brows pull in. "Bullshit. How?"

I'm gruff. I don't mean to be, but it pisses me off that anyone would make her feel like that.

"No, seriously." She half-laughs. "I've always felt kind of overlooked, obviously by my parents. But even by my best friends. Don't get me wrong, they love me so much. I know that. And they're amazing friends, but they've always been closer, the two of them. I've never really been special to anyone until you."

Until me. My eyes drop to my lap because she just fucking guts me when she says shit like this. I swear to God, our feelings double in intensity because they're the same. Nobody's ever truly seen me until her.

I draw my bottom lip between my teeth before I let it slide out.

"You're not just special to me. You're the one on every level." My hand runs through my hair as I lift my eyes. "Nothing compares or competes. It's just you that I think about...that I want. And a really shitty part of me is happy those people don't see your worth because then I'd have to share you. And I want you all to myself, for as long as I can have you."

She's so quiet that I push my face closer against the phone, trying to listen to her breathe before saying, "I wanna kiss you right now."

"I wish that too," she whispers back.

Another beat of silence goes by, and then she says, "I have to go. My parents have donors coming for dinner, so I need to change... But...I don't ever want you to share me either. I like being yours, Calder."

I say nothing as the line dies, trying to internally catch my breath. She feeds the darkest parts of me. The possession, the selfish adoration I have for her. I'm falling for her, more and more with each breath she takes, and it feels like euphoric doom. A death I'd welcome.

Roman pulls the car door open, sliding inside as he looks at me. "You good?"

I ignore him, staring ahead, deep in thought. *I want to fucking kiss her.*

My eyes narrow as I think. I bet I could sneak right the fuck in, and nobody would be the wiser. Doesn't matter that it's still light out. Her house is enormous. It's not like they could hear us from where her bedroom is tucked away.

And her security system is a fucking joke. I always thought senators had fancy bodyguards until I learned that's only for when they're in Washington. If I wasn't here on this island, I'd tell her to make her father get a better system because he's making it too easy for Connor.

All my bad ideas must be evident because Roman laughs as he stares at me.

"Dude. Whatever it is you're thinking right now looks like fucking trouble. You don't even have to tell me. The answer is hell no."

I grin, lighting a cigarette.

"I just need to make a quick off-the-books stop before we visit Tag."

Roman scowls. "I fucking knew it. This is about the redhead."

I shrug, sucking in a drag, "So? It's nothing."

"What the fuck, C? You got your ass beat because of her. Did you forget that?"

The cigarette spins to the ground as I flick it before shifting to face him.

"Careful. I said it's nothing."

Roman stares back, stubborn as fuck. This is how everything goes down between us. We always make it back on the same page, but sometimes it has bloodstains.

"You should take your own advice and be careful. Business before pussy. Or have you forgotten?"

My hand darts out for his throat before I stop myself, wiping it down my face instead.

"Watch your fucking mouth, Roman. I won't warn you again. You won't ever call her that. Am I understood?"

He's staring at me, doing that fucking thing he does, trying to read me before he settles back against his seat.

"Roman." I barely contain my anger. "Say you understand. Because if I have to bash your fucking head into that steering wheel to make sure you get it, I will."

He nods his head, jaw tensed.

"Yeah. I get it."

"But?" I toss out.

His fist thrusts forward into the dash, and he raises his voice.

"But… 'It's nothing?' That's your answer. Even though you're ready to fucking kill me?"

"That's what the fuck I said, isn't it?"

My blood is boiling. Roman needs to fucking leave this alone.

"Fuck you. You can't be into her like this. It can't ever work. What the fuck are you doing, C? You're not *for* this girl. She doesn't even fucking know who you are."

My voice is thunderous, filled with rage.

"Nobody tells me I'm not for her. Or that she's not for me. Nobody, Roman. Not even you." I stab my finger at him. "What I'm doing is none of your fucking business. So, you will leave it alone. Because just like I remember my place, you need to fucking remember yours."

I should've just hit him. Because that blow was worse.

Roman kicks the fucking door open before the keys hit me square in the chest. "Fuck off, asshole. Drive yourself, then, boss."

I smack the dash, then shove open the car door, stepping out into the street.

"Roman."

He stops, turning around to look at me. I can't tell him how I feel because then I put him at risk. Doing this, sneaking around, being with her, without anyone knowing, keeps him safe.

"This is on me. All on me. You have to trust me. I take this on the chin alone."

I know he knows what I mean, but he shakes his head anyway.

"No. Nothing is ever all on you. We're brothers, Calder. I don't fucking work for you. I stand next to you. No matter what. And I'm telling you to cut her loose. Trust *me*."

Trust him? Even if I did, there's no going back now. Maybe there never was.

"She's not some stray I picked up off the street, Romes. This girl means something. She knows exactly who I am—better than anyone. I don't hide from her. That's the truth."

Anger sets on his jaw again. "Tell me you're joking. You're a fucking fool. She doesn't love you—"

"She will," I bark back, but he doesn't stop.

"You're just fun. This bullshit could get you hurt, man. What happens when Connor wants Prescott six feet under? Huh? You gonna kill him or Connor?"

My head is shaking as my hands ball into fists, ready to crack his fucking jaw.

"C, I'm sure she's great. One in a fucking million, but she ain't my family. How am I supposed to protect you when you're fucking sleeping with the enemy? I watch your back. Not hers."

"There's no difference." I spit it out so fast that his head draws back. "If you protect me, you protect her."

Roman stands ten feet away, staring back at me. The gravity of what I've just said imprisons us in our places.

I could argue how wrong he is, tell him that I know everything she feels because it's as if we share the same goddamn heart. Tell him that loving her isn't an *if*. It's a *when* ...maybe even an *already*. But this world doesn't afford men love. We only get violence and allegiance. So, I'm claiming her as mine—if he protects me, then he protects Sutton.

"You've known this girl for—"

My hand raises to stop him. "How long doesn't matter, Roman. You heard me, and I mean it. You will carry my truth as your burden. Forever. She is mine, forever, Roman."

What I just said will change everything. Our whole story. Because I've condemned her to a family she may not want.

But I don't care.

Sutton belongs to me. Now she belongs to us.

My eyes haven't left my brother's, but I don't have to say shit because he gives me a nod.

"You got my word."

Chapter
Twenty-Nine

Sutton

I pull my hair into a messy bun as I walk into my bathroom and turn on the faucet, letting the water run into the tub. As I make my way out, I open my balcony doors, letting in the ocean breeze. It's still light out but already cooler than the afternoon.

My eyes close as I stand there, thinking about his words, enjoying the breeze that's feathering my face.

He said I was the one.

Taking a deep breath as my shoulders shrug, I open my eyes and walk outside, looking up. God, it's so clear, not a cloud in the sky. A perfect blue canvas.

Still, it's nothing like the night Calder took me to the field. That was magical.

I rest my forearms on the banister, staring up as I close my eyes, dreaming about that moment again. It used to be that I'd shut my eyes and dream about all the things I'd hoped would happen, but now my real life trumps the imaginary one.

My tongue darts across my bottom lip, wetting it as I remember him kissing me. And the way his lips are always so soft against mine. The memory is so visceral that I can almost feel the warmth of his breath.

Oh my God. My eyes spring open, a squeal erupting from my throat as I push away from lips pressed to mine. But I'm halted by a hand in my hair and the scent of the man I was just dreaming about.

I smile big and wide as Calder kisses me. Our faces are so close that he's blurry for a second as he pulls back.

"What are you doing?" I say, hushed, looking down over his shoulder to see him standing on a small ledge against the façade of my house.

"Climbing up your balcony. What does it look like?"

His grin makes my heart want to jump out of my chest.

"You can't be here. We'll for sure get caught." I glance over my shoulder, suddenly scared someone might just walk in before I look up at the cameras on the house. "It's not dark enough. You'll be seen."

He shakes his head. "In case you didn't realize, baby, there isn't a risk I wouldn't take for those lips. And don't worry, that camera is pointing toward the tree. But if you want to play it safe…"

I bite my bottom lip, watching him descend back down, peeking over the rail.

"Wait. Just one kiss?"

He smiles, gripping the rail again, launching himself back up. "I like you bad. Kiss me a hundred more."

I lean forward without hesitation as he cradles my cheek. My arms wrap around his neck, pulling me even closer.

"You're crazy," I say, practically breathless.

"About you."

He's smirking as he rubs our noses together, but the sound of my door makes me spin around, almost knocking him down the wall. A faint "Oh fuck" is all I hear as my mother walks inside, eyeing me on my balcony.

"Sutton. Come inside. You'll let bugs in."

"Okay." I nod, desperately wanting to look behind me.

Instead, I close the doors, just as my mother extends a typed piece of paper toward me.

"What's this?"

"Your father wants you to look over these talking points for Saturday, especially the one about his 'Clean the Streets Initiative.'"

My face drops to the paper, brows pulling together. "Why would I need talking points?"

She smiles wide. "He'd like *you* to head a youth anti-drug and alcohol platform. We'll handle the day-to-day, so it won't conflict with school, but PR thinks it will be very successful in making a statement. And your father is going to use it to spearhead a push on the Hill for stricter regulations. They won't even see it coming, because 'from the mouths of babes.'"

My eyes lift to hers. "What does that mean?"

She huffs. "I thought you'd be pleased to help your father. Why don't I feel any excitement from you? Sutton, now is not the time to argue the benefits of marijuana or whatever cool statement drug Aubrey likes to partake in, pretending she's backing a cause."

Her judgment of my friends is unwelcome.

I shake my head. "First off, I don't do drugs. Neither does Aubrey. Second, I just don't understand why anyone would be interested in what I have to say. Why me? You've never needed me before."

Suddenly her demeanor shifts, her smile dropped, the ease in her stature lost. Now she's all hard jawline and crossed arms. Gone is the mother that's selling me on the virtue of good deeds, and in walks my real mother—the woman with strategy and a purpose.

"Because you are a beacon of good values and upbringing. That's what we're selling. You make him look good. Perfect daughter equals perfect candidate. And that all lends to people wanting to back his cause. It checks all the boxes. Don't be dense." She tips a smile in my direction. "He's asking Hunter too. Does that give you more of an interest?"

I cross my arms.

"No. I'm less interested. Also, he does drugs."

I think. Probably. Who cares?

She narrows her eyes. "Does anyone know?"

My head tilts, eyes opening wider.

"Mother. Seriously?"

She snaps her fingers at me when I don't answer, making me blink before I let out a whoosh of breath.

"No. Nobody knows that would tell. And I'm not sure he does them. I just hate him."

Her hands find her hips, the way they do when I've clearly made her angry.

"Then keep your mouth shut, Sutton. That is exactly the kind of unhealthy gossip that should stay dead. The two of you, together in a campaign like this—you could be the next Caroline and John-John."

I frown. "Who?" She waves me off, but I press. "I can handle it alone. Whatever it is."

She snatches the paper back from me to set it on my desk.

"We'll circle back to this later. In the meantime, you'll be speaking about this Saturday night. I expect you to be fluent."

I nod as she walks back to me and puts her hand on my shoulder.

"This is a wonderful message for our community, Sutton, while being helpful to your father. The trash that's washed ashore, living among us, needs to be thrown out. You'll be proud knowing that you're responsible for ensuring that happens because once he gets you on the air, all eyes will be ready to watch those filthy Wolfes."

My head swings to her. "Dad's targeting the Wolfe family?"

"Of course, Sutton, and you could really spur the cause. We know they've tried selling drugs at the park. A park where you and your friends hang out."

I shake my head. "No, they haven't."

She walks toward me. "Listen to me. That family is scum. Together, you and your father will rid us of the Wolfe family and that goddamn O'Bannion curse that hangs over his head. Remember what you just demonstrated. Facts don't always have to be true. They just need to appear that way. I'm sure you've seen a thing or two that was suspicious, right? And if you haven't, you've always excelled in the field of imagination."

Oh my God. No. Is she fucking serious? I hate her.

I swallow, feeling panicked and angry.

"I can't…I don't know…I'm—"

What are the words? I can't seem to find the right words. Because what I won't say is that I'm falling for the boy I shouldn't and that hurting him feels physically impossible.

But I also don't know how to say no to her.

And that's the gut punch that's left me silent.

She rubs my arms, smiling at me. "People listen to today's youth. Especially when they're personally affected."

My mouth drops open. *Just fucking say something, Sutton.*

She shakes her head. "And between us, mother to daughter, I think it's time you found a place in this family—brought something to the table, so to speak." She pats my cheek, pointing to my bathroom. "Don't let the bath run for too long. Dinner is at seven sharp, darling."

The moment she walks out, I remain imprisoned in place. Of all the shitty things just said to me, it's the last that's making it hardest to breathe.

"I think it's time you found a place in this family…"

It almost knocks me to the floor—that familiar feeling. The one that reminds me that I'm just a cog in the wheel.

That words like *daughter* are for sound bites, not proud moments in private. That hugs are relegated for the cameras, not to console or display love.

I just fucking work here.

And if that wasn't bad enough, apparently my new job is to ruin my boyfriend.

The lump in my throat grows thick, but I suck in a breath, pushing it all down, suddenly remembering Calder. I turn around, walking quickly to open my balcony doors.

As they sweep open, Calder's eyes lock to mine from where he's seated just inside, ass on the floor, hidden from view.

He heard everything.

It's evident by the way he refuses to let me look away, head tilting, catching my eyes as I try and look everywhere but at him.

But I'm embarrassed and ashamed. It's one thing to tell someone the secrets about your life. Having them witness the tragedy is a whole other kind of evil.

When he frowns, I smile and shrug. "Remember when your face was full of bruises? You said it never hurts. Same. I guess my bruises are just on the inside."

He doesn't say a word as he stands. But the way he's staring at me, cataloging my body, makes everything I just said feel like a lie. Because it's as if he can see all the cuts and scars below the surface, on my heart.

The bluest eyes fix to mine, with only the promise of the truth behind them.

"Do you want me to hurt her back?"

My lips part, but I shake my head. Every damn part of me is sickly comforted by his words but also equally afraid of how easily he said them.

Even still, I'm undeserving of his brutal kindness. Because I hate myself for my silence. He heard everything—my cowardice and humiliation. And he's still protecting me.

Calder walks inside my room, straight to the bathroom, before I can say any more. I turn, heart already pounding as I follow, shutting the door, then twisting around to lock it.

He can't leave before I say what I should. Except, everything I want to express is all jumbled inside, refusing to come out.

Pressing my back against the door, I start with the easy part, but it's the wrong order, even though I mean it.

"I'm sorry. I'm so sorry you heard that."

"No," he whispers. "You don't say that to me."

He turns off the bath before grabbing my waist and hauling me forward, unlocking the door behind me. My hands coming to my chest, feeling like I can't catch my breath.

"Please don't leave me," I whisper.

Calder reopens the door as he looks down at me.

"Wait here."

I nod, numb and confused as he moves past me, walking out into my bedroom. It's almost like I'm feeling too many things all at once, and I can't focus.

God, why didn't you make them love me the way other parents love their kids? Or make me not care? Because this feels cruel. She'll make Calder hate me. Because he'll see what a coward I am. I just want him to know that I'm sorry. And I need him to stay because—

I suck in a shaky breath as my forefinger picks at the polish on my thumb, trying to keep everything bubbling inside of me down. But I just as quickly stop, remembering I must be presentable for tonight.

"Perfect daughter equals perfect candidate."

Perfect daughter. Be the perfect daughter…but how would they know if I was? They look right through me. Calder's the only person that sees me.

I peek around the doorjamb, hearing a click before seeing him returning. My head swings back inside, waiting and trying to breathe, but as soon as he's in the room, all my words rush out, spilling over onto him with urgency.

"Calder, I won't do what she's asking. I swear. I'm sorry. Please believe—"

He cuts me off, brows pulled together, his finger pressed to my cupid's bow. "Shh. You don't ever fucking apologize to me for them."

He reaches behind him, dragging off his shirt, then stares down at me. But I'm not moving.

My eyes drop to the floor, but his fingers gently press under my chin, lifting them back to his.

"Let me make it better, baby."

He steps in closer, lifting my arms, pulling my T-shirt over my head before he kisses my forehead. My breath hitches as I stand silently, watching him undress both of us.

There's nothing sexual about what he's doing. It's care. And it feels so good that I almost break.

Calder takes his time, kneeling, helping me off with my shorts before pressing a kiss to my hip bone just above the rim of my panties.

He doesn't even say anything about me wearing them, leaving them on as he stands.

A drip of water plinks into the tub, and I blink as he toes off his shoes before undoing his belt.

My chin lifts, trying to keep everything I'm feeling at bay.

I hear the zipper sliding down on his Dickies before he pushes them to the ground.

"Look at me, baby."

I do. We're standing in our underwear, vulnerable and half-bare. But I've never felt safer in my life. I shut my eyes, unable to stop the wave of emotions crashing in on me, but my mouth keeps opening and closing, wishing I could just speak. But nothing comes out.

There are no words. No apologies. Nothing.

He didn't just strip me of my clothes. He's stripped me of every barrier. All that's left is to feel it—all of it.

His fingers brush down my face as he looks at me with so much care behind his eyes that it nearly splits me in two.

"We're alike, Sutton—bound to our names. Held down by our obligations. Robbed of love. Until we found each other. That's why we're so connected, because I am you, and you are me."

A ragged breath shakes my chest as I throw myself at him, arms hooking around his neck. He lifts me off the floor, whispering into my ear as tears fall from my eyes.

"She doesn't have to be dead for you to know what it's like to be without her."

There have never been truer words. I've lived without a mother for so long, grieving the loss of something I never really had.

"Shh. It's okay. I got you. Everything's okay now."

Calder steps into the tub, taking me with him, arranging us so that we're sitting face-to-face. Our legs are entwined, mine over the top of his. The water's hot, stinging my skin, but I don't care if it burns. I'm not leaving him.

His hands come up to my cheeks, wiping wet thumbs over them as he cradles my face.

"Don't cry. Not over her. She doesn't deserve your tears."

That's not wholly why I'm crying. I shake my head, tilting my head to press my cheek into his palm as I speak.

"How can I do something that hurts you? Even if it's supposedly what's right."

He says nothing as I stare up at him. "Do you think you can

care for someone so much that right and wrong stop existing? Like what's right for them is wrong for you. Because I think I feel that. I don't care what you do. What you've done. I won't hurt you."

He leans in, feathering kisses over my cheeks, then my eyes, traveling over my nose before he locks eyes with me again.

"You should care, Sutton. Run us off. It's okay. I'm not going anywhere. My place is with you…not them. Be the dutiful daughter. As long as you're with me, nothing matters."

My chin trembles as I climb onto him, sloshing water outside the tub, our bodies flush.

"I hate them. I'm sorry. I'm sorry for both of us," I whisper into his ear.

I cling to Calder, feeling crushed by everything stacked against us as his hands run over my back, in soft strokes up and down, comforting me, holding me.

"We don't get forever, do we?" I breathe out onto his shoulder because it all suddenly feels impossible.

His stubble scratches my cheek as his head moves.

"I don't know, but I know we get right now, and that's what matters. Because if we only had today, it would be worth it."

It's the answer to the question I asked him in the confessional that day. I pull back, looking at his beautiful face, staring at him.

I love you.

"Better?" he whispers.

I lean in, speaking my answer into his lips before I kiss him. "Better."

Chapter Thirty

Sutton

"Taste," Calder growls, smearing my juices across my lips with his middle finger before pushing it into my mouth.

His lips find mine, sharing the sweetness as his two fingers thrust back inside me. It's only his breath I inhale because our mouths are sealed, desperate for one another.

After last night, the way he held me, bathed me, before we were forced to say goodbye—Jesus, we felt like live wires the moment we snuck away today.

My back arches off the leather, from where I'm lying on the back seat of his Mustang. We're hidden under a carport, a tarp used as curtains to keep our dirty doings a secret.

"That's it. Come all over my fucking hand."

Fuck. Me. He's relentless, pushing in over and over as my eyes begin to roll into the back of my head, gripped by the sensations pooling in my center.

The build starts to compound as his rough hand covers my breast, rolling my nipple through my shirt between his fingers.

"Oh fuck."

My hand smacks against the window above me, leaving finger marks on the fogged-up glass. Calder's lips drag over my neck before he stops just below my ear.

"I wanted to fuck you last night in that tub. Bury my dick in that tight pussy until you screamed my name to heaven and left your blood on my cock."

My fingers curl into the fabric of his T-shirt, gripping him as he hovers over me, spreading my legs wider, carried higher into ecstasy by his dirty mouth.

"Fuck me, Calder. Please. Right here."

I'm begging. I want him inside of me so badly.

"Back seats are for bad girls," he growls low and quiet. "Is that what you are, baby? My bad girl?"

The wet slaps of his fingers thrusting inside of me, mixed with his wicked question, tips me right over the edge.

"Oh God. I'm…fuck. I feel it."

His eyes meet mine as he grips my jaw, holding me in place.

"Look at me. I wanna watch you come."

Oh my God.

"Yes," I scream, tightening around his fingers as I explode.

His eyes bore into mine, watching in exaltation as I quiver. My mouth hangs open as the long, drawn-out mewl echoes inside the car.

A smirk forms on his lips, and my thighs shake before he covers my mouth, thrusting his tongue inside as I happily accept.

We kiss slowly, savoring each other until my breathing finally matches the pace. Calder pulls away, eyes on mine.

"This is the best date, down at the docks, I've ever had."

I giggle. "Nobody has dates at the docks."

But as he smiles, the words I thought last night come back to me. *Is this what love is?* I've never felt it, but if it's despising being apart from someone and only really feeling alive when you're with them, then I love him.

"How long has it been since we met?" I ask, staring at his grin.

Calder leans down again, chastely kissing my lips before dragging his fingers slowly out of my pussy as he answers.

But I barely hear because of the gasp I've sucked in.

"Three weeks or so. Why?"

"Oh my God. Why does that feel so good?"

He chuckles as he reaches into the middle console and pulls out the panties I gave him. I bite my lip, watching as he wipes his fingers on them.

Fuck. He's so sexy. Everything he does drives me insane.

My legs drop off the seat as I push to sit, giving him room to do the same. But his eyes drop to my bare center, and I can't help but spread my legs just a bit.

"It feels so good because you were made for my fingers." He leans forward, kissing my mouth again, breathing, "And my lips," before he cups my pussy, groaning, "and me."

I sigh as he pulls away, letting my head drop back against the seat as he speaks.

"Is that why you're asking how long we've been together? Is my baby ready for another lesson?"

"When?" I say breathlessly, perking up, making him laugh.

He sits back, grabbing my shorts off the floorboard before he smiles at me, placing them in my lap.

"Do you remember the night we met?"

I nod.

"That girl deserved magic. So I'm gonna give it to her. And that's not the back seat of a car." His eyes drop from mine down to his hands.

Oh my God. He looks scared. And it seems as unnatural on him as I think it feels.

His eyes lift to mine again. "There are things I want to say, Sutton…shit that I need to say before—"

I cut him off, crawling over onto his lap, pressing my lips to his.

He's afraid of me. Because I feel it—Calder loves me too.

A few weeks ago, sex was a transaction. It was something to check off my list. But it's different with him. He's made me different. So, if he wants to give me magic, I want to believe in it. It's that simple.

His fingers weave into my hair, forcing me back as his eyes search mine. "I'm gonna give you the stars, and the moon, and—"

"Love. You're going to give me love."

It's not a demand. Just a statement of fact. One we both feel.

His lips part to speak, but instead, he nods before touching his forehead to mine, whispering, "Yes, baby. All I have to give."

"Where have you been all afternoon?"

I stare innocently at my mother before placing the bags in my hands down on the foyer floor.

"Running errands. Where else?"

My head tips toward the bags to stress my point. She rolls her eyes.

"Forgive me, but I didn't think the dry cleaning and a few other measly items would take hours. You missed Hunter. He came by with Michael…to speak with your father about the initiative."

I swear to God. She's never going to stop hoping we happen.

I shrug. "Shame."

Her eyes narrow because I definitely didn't pull off anything close to genuine, so I quickly segue.

"I was stuck forever waiting at the cleaners because they hired someone new. And you know how that can be."

Thank you, Piper, for that little detail.

She eyes me suspiciously, or maybe I just think that because I'm a big fat liar. I almost smile. Best lie for the best reason.

"Well, leave all the bags there. I'll get Rosie to put everything away." She turns toward her office. "I've set out some dress options for the fundraiser on your bed. Remind me never to plan another garden party again. Everything appropriate is bound to burn us alive. Take a look-see so I can approve."

I'm nodding with a smile on my face like I care about what she's saying. Because I need her happy for what I'm about to ask.

My mouth opens, but she dismisses me by ignoring me to speak to the housekeeper. Shit. The window of opportunity is lost.

I start up the stairs but pause. Fuck it. With my back to her, I squeeze my eyes shut, asking, "Hey, Mom, would it be okay if I slept over at Aubrey's after the main part of the fundraiser is over?"

She hums in acknowledgment that I've spoken but doesn't answer, so I turn around, pressing the issue.

"We wanted to brainstorm more ideas for the initiative Dad asked me to head. I'm actually pretty excited about it. And I figured I'd get out of your hair so you guys could mingle and not have to worry about me."

Her head pops up from where she was looking, eyes on mine. Now I have her attention. I watch all the pros and cons pass over her features until she smiles.

"I'll need to speak to her mother, but yes. And make sure you let your father know. I like the team playing, Sutton."

"Thank you," I rush out. "I will."

My grin is almost too wide. Not because she's happy but because I got my way. Saturday night, I get Calder and magic for a whole damn night. I pull out my phone as I trot up the stairs, immediately texting Calder, letting him know I pulled it off, giggling as he responds.

Wesley: Goddamn, I like you bad.

Chapter
Thirty-One

Calder

Buttercup: Everything is set for tonight. I'll be at Aubrey's at 6:30 sharp.

A smile tugs at my lips. Fuck, I think I'm already feeling the adrenaline pumping through me. I can't fucking wait to get my goddamn hands on her. The last four days have been torture, even though I snuck in another kiss on Thursday while she was in town.

I type out a quick text, letting my tongue drag over my bottom lip.

Wesley: I'll be there. If I don't fucking die waiting first.

She's giggling. I can hear it in my mind.

I push off my bed, cracking my neck, thinking about all the dirty shit I'm gonna do to her as a warm-up when my phone pings again. There's a smile already in place as I look down. But it fades quickly as I read what's on the screen.

Roman: Trouble's coming. He knows. Delete this.

What the fuck?

I don't hesitate, swiping to erase his message before scrolling quickly and deleting my entire chain with Sutton. Because there's only one thing to know. One damn secret.

Her.

Looking around, I grab a pair of jeans slung over a chair, pulling them on and throwing on a black T-shirt just as the front door slams. Fuck. I slip on my boots before sliding a hand under my pillow, pulling out my Glock.

That message meant one of two things: my father or Connor.

Neither option means anything fucking good. I've never lived inside a fairy tale that either man wouldn't kill me in cold fucking blood if I crossed them.

Sutton crosses every line.

My mind races, looking for any mistake I've made over the last few weeks, flipping through moment after moment.

Goddammit. I've been fucking methodical. Her name's not in my phone. I've made sure I wasn't followed. I know I've never been caught on camera sneaking out. And there's no fucking way Roman or West said shit. So how?

I tuck my phone into my back pocket as a steady breath leaves me. *Get your shit together.* My mind settles, forcing my entire body to calm as I listen, waiting, with my eyes on the door, but there's nothing but fucking silence.

Whoever's out there is waiting for me to come to them.

I've never killed a man. But today might be that day.

"Hey, West?" I holler to cover the sound of my doorknob twisting. "I got the greatest story to tell you about last night."

Silence.

I slowly open the door, peering into the empty hallway before slipping out quietly.

"Dude, there was this chick…" I throw out quietly, taking the safety off my gun. "She did things you've never seen."

I creep down the hall, stopping before I enter the great room. With my back against the wall, I stare across at the thermostat. No way Pops is around the corner. He'd have answered me. Someone wants me off guard.

I close my eyes, heart pounding because there's a chance that when I turn this corner, I may not come back. But nobody's gonna hurt Sutton. Even if that means I put a bullet between their eyes.

So, I step, gun raised. Locked right onto my father.

"Good mornin', boy."

Pops is leaned against the back of the couch, alone and unnerved. There's no doubt he's seen the end of a gun before, but the way he's looking at me—like he expected this—is throwing me off.

What the fuck is going on? And why the hell did Roman say "trouble"? Because there are no goons in sight.

I hesitate to lower my gun, staring back at him as he waves a hand for me to drop it. Because what did I just fall into? There's nothing right about this. My gut and my head are at war. Is this about Sutton?

My arm drops, suspicion on my brow. "What the fuck are you doing? I could've killed you."

He uncrosses his arms, narrowing his eyes before a smile spills out over his face. I shove my gun into the small of my back as he stands, walking toward me, grinning like the devil. He grabs the back of my neck hard, pulling me forward, locking his eyes to mine.

Air sucked between his teeth before he speaks.

"I needed to see what you're capable of…in *her* name."

The feeling of ice pollutes my veins. In an instant, all my fear is confirmed. He knows about Sutton. This *is* trouble. So much fucking trouble.

"You know, I wondered how you'd take Roman's message.

But killing me…" He lets out a hard whoosh. "There's more of me inside of you than I expected."

My jaw hardens, realizing I was set the fuck up.

"Ah, Calder." He sighs, letting me go, stepping backward toward the couch.

I wipe a hand over my jaw as he does, itching to pull my gun. But he's right. I am like him, even if I hate it. Because at this moment, I know exactly what I have to do.

In the back of my mind, I've always known. Since the moment I laid eyes on her. There was always only one end. A destiny we could never return from.

Our fall is destined.

Tyler wags his finger at me. "Love makes men act like fools and poets, Calder. But it's the villain I needed to see."

"How the fuck did you find out?"

He eyes me suspiciously before smirking, as if he likes the game he's playing. "Calder."

The look on his face is fucking sinister as he reaches down to the couch seat. My eyes follow, a hollow feeling growing in my chest as he says, "From you, boy."

In his hand, waved like a Bible from a preacher on a pulpit, is my fucking journal. His Irish lilt coats the words I wrote about her as he spits them back at me.

"Her lips touched mine, but my soul recognized hers. I never believed in soul mates. I don't think I even believed in love. But Sutton—she makes me want to."

Her name is spoken through gritted teeth before he snaps the leather closed.

Only she had that paper. I ripped it the fuck out of my journal because I wrote it for her. To give to her because it's the only time I ever mentioned her by name or in a way she could be discovered.

Has he been in her room?

My mind splinters.

Did he send someone?

They say before you die that your life flashes before your eyes. All the moments you've collected play like a movie until *bang.* You're gone.

It's still only her I see.

The wild way her red hair flies in the wind. And the smiles that feel like a gift. All the seamless curves of her body and the pattern of her freckles. The way she melts in my arms so that there's no me or her—we're always one.

She is my life.

Everything begins in slow motion.

Me reaching for my gun. Tensions exploding. Tyler lunging. Our voices bellowing.

I swing my arm around, aiming for him, but he crushes the leather journal against my hand, forcing the gun to the floor as he rumbles, "Ya' fucking little prick."

The sound of metal scrapes the floor, moving everything into fast-forward until we're hurling ourselves onto each other.

Tyler drives his shoulder into my ribs as I bring an elbow down on his back. But he grips my throat, throwing me against the wall, pinning me to it.

His nostrils flare, face red as spit flies from his mouth.

"You want me to kill you? Is that what you fucking want?"

My airway's cut off, but I try and choke out my answer. Fuck him. But my head is already feeling dizzy.

"Shh. Shh. The more you fight, the faster you die."

He's staring at me, watching me choke. My eyes begin to sting from the force of the pressure, but I stare back, feeding into his anger before his hand finally gives, and I suck in life.

"What am I supposed to do here? Kill my only son?"

He's laughing to himself like a lunatic as I tip my head back, letting more oxygen in.

Tyler sidesteps, checking how far away the gun is before he looks at me again. He moves toward me, and I flinch as he grabs my cheeks, cradling them. He's unhinged. And that makes him capable of anything.

"No. No. Don't be scared. I won't hurt you. Unless you make me again. You listen to me, boy. That filthy bitch will ruin you. Do you understand? She'll tear down everything we've built. Her family looks to destroy everything we stand for. There's no loyalty. No allegiance. They discard what they can't use."

I'm silent, trying to control my rage as he nudges my head back against the wall with more force than necessary.

"Do you know the evils I've committed? The unforgivable sins in your name? It's all for you. My only son. For you to be king, Calder."

I can't look at him, so I stare to the side.

"Look at me," he rumbles.

My eyes lock to his, chest heaving as we stare at each other.

"It's like looking in a mirror," he breathes out. "Except one of us is more dangerous than the other. I still don't know which."

He narrows his eyes like he just decided.

"You walk away and this dies. Not even Connor has to know. Do you understand?"

When I don't nod, he leans in, fingers gripping my hair so hard it stings.

"But if you don't do as you're told, your lass will be found in the river, filled with so much cum that the police won't even be able to match it to anyone."

I will kill him. Now I'll make sure he suffers.

I swallow, feeling my chest crack wide open because this is the end.

"I'm seeing her tonight. I'll end it. But give me tonight."

His eyes search mine, so I say it more forcefully.

"I'll fucking end it. Okay. Just give me tonight."

I'm released, but the weight on my shoulders remains. Tyler steps away, straightening his shirt as he turns toward the door, barking, "Come in."

The meatheads he's usually with stalk inside, dragging Roman and West in with them. My fists ball at my sides, seeing West's lip fucking busted.

"Boss, this one tried to get by." The dick motions to West. "Things got a little rough."

They shove them down on the couch as Tyler chuckles.

"My boys are handfuls." He shrugs, running his hand through his hair. "Clean the place. Take the guns. Wouldn't want anyone getting any more bad ideas."

Tyler looks at Roman, who seems almost as angry as me. He should be. Tyler's a cocksucker.

"You and West will go with Calder tonight. As insurance. If he fails, then you all fail." Tyler's eyes drift to West. "It would be a shame for West not to see eighteen."

Chapter
Thirty-Two

Sutton

"**W**e loved hearing what you said tonight. I wish more young people had their heads on their shoulders like you."

I smile as the shapely woman sips her martini. I don't know why my mother worried so much about the desserts and food. All anyone wants at these events is the booze.

She smiles, turning toward her husband, giving me a moment to reach into the pocket of my dress to eye the time on my phone. *5:30. Jesus, I'm going to combust.*

Time is slithering by so slowly that I'm losing my mind. God, I can't wait to see him. My mother calls me from across the room, beckoning me with her perfectly manicured fingers.

"Please excuse me. My mother's calling," I offer to the woman before I step away.

My eyes drop to the ground for a moment as I cut between two groups before lifting them, connecting right on Hunter's face.

For fuck's sake.

"I'm so pleased Hunter agreed to help Sutton," my mother gushes as she and Marianne air-kiss.

Everyone is pretending to be the very best of friends. My father and Michael Kelly pat each other on the back while my mother and Marianne throw around compliments like confetti.

And I try not to puke.

But no matter how disgusted I am, I stand with my eyes up and a polite smile fixed to my face in an elegantly appropriate knee-length sleeveless black halter dress.

I'm the embodiment of a good upbringing. Their perfect daughter. Because I have a half hour until bliss, and not even a deal with the devil, aka my mother, is stopping me from escaping.

"Sutton, darling. Let me introduce you to Hunter's mother."

Marianne's eyes drop to me.

"Hello, Mrs. Kelly, so nice to see you again," I say in response.

Marianne runs her hands up my arms before cradling my face. "Well, I can see the appeal. Your daughter is gorgeous, Elizabeth."

I'm right here. Marianne drops her hands as my mother beams.

"Thank you, but I think she's the lucky one here. Hunter is quite the catch."

My skin crawls. *Oh my God. I've thrown him away. Over and over. Get a clue.*

Hunter's arrogant face comes into view as he walks around Tag, beelining straight for me. His hand slides against my lower back as he leans down, kissing my cheek, making our mothers swoon.

I almost scream.

"Freckles. I was sad to have missed you the other day."

Oh my fucking God.

I stare into the void before I snap back and lift my chin to look at him.

"Yeah. Such a shame."

He smiles charmingly toward our mothers, shrugging. "But who cares about that? When Sutton looks so incredible today."

I hate you so much. *Dear Kellys, your son is a complete dick, and I hope that my boyfriend throws him off a higher cliff.*

Our mothers turn away, probably planning our wedding, so I take the opportunity to lean in and whisper, "Thanks for the compliment. I wore black because I thought it best to prepare for your funeral. I'll kill you if you touch me again."

A pinch to my back makes me jump before I glare at him, but he gives nothing away as he leans down toward my ear, whispering in it.

"Play nice. Or I'll tell your parents who you're really dating."

I turn my body toward him, putting my back to everyone else.

"Then I'll tell them you're a small-dicked rapey douchebag with a giant ego."

He chuckles, trying to brush my hair from my face with his middle finger, but I slap it away. We both immediately look around to ensure nobody saw.

"Easy. Don't act like they'd actually believe you." He licks his lips. "It's better to have me as a friend than an enemy, Sutton."

"Eww. No, thanks. You're a psycho."

Hunter grins. "And you're a rich little slut that likes to slum it across the tracks. We're all a lot of unlikely things."

"Oh my God. Just get out of my life," I spit quietly.

From behind me, my mother calls my name, but we don't move.

"I'm out, you narcissist. But my mother stays off my back because she thinks I'm breaking yours. Go along for the ride, Freckles."

My face distorts in disgust. "My name is Sutton."

He rolls his eyes. "Whatever. I'll stay quiet if you do, Sutton. Because if I had to guess, you've been eyeing the time on your phone because a certain greasy scumbag is waiting for you."

Hunter raises his eyebrows in challenge. And I wish I could punch him.

Instead, I take a deep breath, turning around to whisper my contempt.

"Let's just get this over with."

His hand slips onto my back again, just like the smile on my face. He leads me to follow our families outside to the garden deck, where a smaller group is mingling.

As we make our way closer, the conversation between our fathers seems to have everyone's attention. My father points his finger at Hunter and me.

"These two are a great example of why I'm so passionate about reforming New York."

Great. He's found a launch for another podium speech.

"St. Simeon is a perfect example of the values I'm hoping to spread across this entire state. Trust me. I've seen the evils that these crime families commit in the streets of our fine communities."

Michael Kelly postures, wrapping his arm around my father's shoulder.

"You have our support. There's nothing we want more."

My father nods as he continues, putting his hand in his pocket. Oh geez. He's going for the *"every" man* angle. My hand slips into my pocket, but Hunter taps my back, forcing my attention to my father's face but not before I cut my eyes to Hunter.

He raises his brows, but I know I can't say anything, so I turn my attention back to my father.

"I wasn't always a senator. Or a wealthy man."

Lies. His father cutting him off until he inherited a fortune isn't exactly the American dream.

"I started my career on the streets." *In an office.*

"Working for the FBI, on the organized crime task force."

Funny, Mom's always said his official title should've been barista because he was sent for coffee so often. I look around the small crowd of people, watching them eat it up.

"I've seen firsthand the horrors committed by families like the Wolfes." My eyes dart back to my father as he continues, "and the O'Bannions. This is why I pledge to run them out of this town. And then the state."

Michael Kelly begins clapping, the crowd joining in, making my chest rise and fall faster. I hate this, but I don't let on, joining in with the applause.

My mother looks at me, giving me a wink because she thinks I'm smiling over my father's speech. But I'm not.

I'm just playing the role. Something she's taught me how to do far too well.

Chapter
Thirty-Three

Calder

I'm staring down at the small box in my hand as I wipe my fingers over the top, dusting it off. It's been years since I've looked inside, but today feels like a good day to do it.

"Hey."

I look up at Roman standing in the doorway as he steps just inside.

"I didn't send that text. He snatched my phone and then me."

I'm already nodding, because I don't have to grill my brother to know he's telling the truth. I trust him with my life.

"Those assholes still out there?"

He nods.

When Tyler left, the guards stayed to make sure I did what I said I'd do.

"What are you gonna do, man?"

I half-laugh, as if there was ever a question.

"What I have to."

My eyes drop back to the wooden box, and I flip the lid. The wood top creaks as I open it, half smiling as I take in my mother's possessions.

"This was all I got...after my mom died. This stupid shit is all I have to feel connected to her."

I pick up the book about Greek myths, handing it to Roman as he sits next to me.

"I don't know. I know I'm doing the right thing by walking away. But I can't help it...I just want to keep her fucking connected to me. Ya know? Letting her go—it feels impossible. So I'm sitting here trying to find something to give her so she'll remember me."

West leans into my room, hands on the doorjamb. "Then we'll make tonight epic. At least you guys will have the memory."

"Hey," Tyler's goon barks. "I said, hey. What the fuck is that in your hand?"

The ugliest of the two guards is yapping at me as I turn a tarnished gold coin over my knuckles.

"I'm talking to you, dick."

I still don't answer as Tyler walks into our place, raising his hand to quiet his bitch.

"It's fine. It was Calder's mother's." Tyler holds out his hand, so I hand over the St. Michael coin. "She loved the saints. I've never met a woman that prayed more." He hands it back to me, walking past to look at Roman and West.

"Help your brother make the right decision tonight. This family is counting on your loyalty."

They nod, saying, "Okay, Pops" and "Yeah" simultaneously.

I stand, tired of his fucking bravado, but he calls my name, forcing me to turn around.

"She loved you." His eyes drop to the coin between my fingers. "Remember whose family you belong to, Calder."

My cold eyes meet his soulless ones.

"I never forgot, Pops."

Chapter
Thirty-Four

Sutton

Piper squeezes my hand as the Mustang pulls up into Aubrey's driveway.

"I know you wanted him all to yourself, but I'm so fucking excited to go into the city."

I smile because I'm excited too. Calder never ceases to amaze me. The only thing better than just me and him is to not be a secret.

Tonight, he's giving me a carnival in Bensonhurst, the unofficial Little Italy of Brooklyn. All the way in the city. We couldn't be more anonymous.

He's giving me all the magic he promised, and I honestly couldn't love him more.

I push my phone into the back of my cut-off shorts, feeling the breeze blow my midriff T-shirt up just as Calder pushes out of the car.

God. He should have his own personal soundtrack. That's how

hot he is.

Maybe it's knowing I get him all night or knowing what's going to happen at the end of it, but my body is already on fire. He saunters over, flicking the cigarette from his fingers as he lets his eyes rake over my body.

Goose bumps fucking explode as he licks his lips, coming to a stop in front of me, hovering. Calder always stands just a little too close, and I love it. There are no boundaries between us.

"You ready, baby?"

I nod, biting my lip, feeling all eyes on us. I don't know if he's even noticed though, because he hasn't looked at anyone but me. His hand lifts, fingers brushing my hair behind my ear.

"I fucking missed you. Ride with me. The girls can take West so they don't get lost."

Aubrey clears her throat, pulling a smirk from Calder's lips, but he doesn't stop staring down at me.

"Um. What if we don't want West?"

My head snaps to hers, but she's grinning. *Fucking Aubrey.* Before saying anything, Calder leans down, kissing my cheek, and then asks, "Which one's Piper?"

Piper's eyes become saucers as I turn to look at her. She stares back at me, cheeks turning red as I giggle. Because she knows I told him what she said about West.

Calder looks at her as she gives an embarrassed wave, but he offers nothing, taking my hand. Before he starts tugging me back toward the car, he gives her a wink.

"Yeah. You look like his type. Have fun."

I'm laughing as Piper shoots daggers at me. She's not really mad because West is already giving her an abundance of charm, circling her like she's prey.

Oh shit.

We load into the cars, Calder guiding me into the back seat, next to him, as Roman turns the key. This feels surreal. *All of us together.*

"Roman, Sutton. Sutton, Roman," Calder offers, tucking me under his arm.

I stare at Calder for a second because he's gruffer than I've seen him. Maybe he's trying to be cool in front of his brothers.

Roman stares back at me through the rearview. *Just as unfriendly as I remember.*

"Hi," I rush out, feeling nervous. "Calder's told me almost nothing about you." I can't help but giggle because it's the truth before I shrug. "I mean, understandably so. But it's nice to meet someone so important to him."

Roman says nothing, just stares before dropping his eyes. "She always like this?"

Calder chuckles, but it's empty. "Yeah. It's kinda fucking amazing."

My face swings to Calder's, watching him as he stares at nothing out the window. Something's not right. I feel it.

Roman looks over his shoulder with a frown, backing up. "I get it now."

I don't know what's happening, but my mouth drops open to say, "Stop the car" because my heart is screaming. As if it feels the sword coming near.

"Calder," I whisper as he turns his face toward mine, sorrow behind his eyes. "What's happening?"

His brows pull together as he tugs me closer, leaning down to my ear, whispering, "If we only had tonight, would it all be worth it?"

My heart begins racing in my chest. Because for the first time since we said that to each other, I don't want to say yes.

I don't just want tonight. I want forever.

My body shifts so I can wrap my arms around his neck, hugging him close to me.

"Promise me you'll ask me again tomorrow."

Chapter Thirty-Five

Calder

Watching her stare up at the Ferris wheel, the kaleidoscope of colors in her eyes, makes me want to kiss her and never stop.

But we have to.

That's why tonight is so important. I can give Sutton one night of magic. One epic fucking night so she'll always have it to carry with her.

Then it won't feel like a loss—that's what I keep telling myself.

I reach into my pocket, rubbing my finger over the gold coin before looking at her.

"You wanna go on?"

She shakes her head. "No. I've always been too scared."

"Come on." I grin, tickling her side. "I'll protect you."

She pushes my hand away, giggling before weaving her fingers between mine and following me to the platform. I hand over some tickets to a guy whose eyes dart to Sutton, then to mine before he turns around.

Good idea, dick. She curls in next to me, head leaned against my arm.

"I can't believe I'm holding your hand in public. I know I keep saying that, but it's—" My eyes drop to hers as she speaks. "It feels like a miracle…something sacred and spectacular. You know?"

I nod, giving her a half-smile as the Ferris wheel comes to a stop. The door is opened as another dude waves us on. She scrunches her nose at me before moving because she's nervous. But I shake my head, pushing her forward with a laugh.

She's fucking spectacular. So beautiful as she walks ahead, all that hair of hers flipping over her shoulder as she looks back at me. As I follow her on, my attention is pulled, hearing a quiet whistle come from that slimy-dicked fucking carnie.

Motherfucker. His eyes are glued to her ass as she steps in.

"Hey," I bark, gripping his chin and jerking it to my face. I lean in close, but everyone can still hear. "You put your eyes on her again and I'll rip them the fuck out of your head. You get me, dickhead?"

Sutton steps back toward me, eyes open wide. But I pat his cheek.

"We good?"

"Yeah, man." He breathes out shakily. "We're good."

I feel her hand on my back, so I spin around, hooking my arm around her waist, and pick her up.

"You ready, baby?"

The worry on her face is replaced with a smile before my lips press to hers. She wraps her legs around my waist, giggling as I walk us into the red-and-silver bucket.

"You're kind of different in the daytime."

It's eight o'clock at night, but I laugh because I know what she's saying. This night feels like we're seeing each other for the first time.

"I don't like people looking at what's mine. That hasn't changed since the beach, baby."

The minute I drop her into the bucket and the door closes, she taps her feet on the metal floor, gripping my hand again.

"Oh my God. It goes so high. I don't want to look. What if we fall out?"

I laugh. "We're not falling out. C'mere. You need another lesson."

She grins, shifting to face me.

My thumb runs across her bottom lip. "Nobody looks…the whole point of a Ferris wheel is the making out."

She blinks, a blush peppering her skin. "But everyone can see us."

I shrug, grabbing her bottom lip between my fingers and pulling her mouth to mine. "Then we should put on a good show, baby."

She sighs into my mouth as we lock into a kiss, not breaking once as we circle the sky, lost in each other.

Sutton

"Does the beautiful young lady want the kitten or an angel?"

Calder's grinning down at me as I clap my hands together because he's won me a prize. At a carnival. Everything feels perfect. His brothers, my best friends—it's been nothing but West making jokes and Roman being quietly intimidating, even though I caught him grinning from time to time.

I'm like the main character in a movie right now.

Calder leans in, taking my lips before answering for me. "Angel. Because she is one."

I'm forced backward as he snatches the prize, growling into my mouth as we kiss.

"Get a room." Aubrey laughs as we break away.

My head tips back as Calder lays his arm across my shoulder. I stare up at the sky, closing my eyes to make a wish on the brightest star, but Piper grabs my attention.

"Is that Tiffany Astor?"

"Who's that?" West questions as my head pops up, panic taking over.

Why would she be in this neighborhood? That was the whole point in coming here. I swing my head around as Piper laughs. "Never mind. False alarm." She turns to West. "She's just some random chick we know."

He shrugs as Aubrey snarks, "Jesus, Piper. Sut's having a heart attack."

But she's quieted as Roman stares down at her. My eyes cut between Aubrey and Roman because you can feel the tension. What's surprising, though, are the glances exchanged between Aubrey and West. Not that Piper seems to notice. Her interest fizzled quickly. I think she's more into Shepard than she wants to admit.

"So, what's next?" I breathe out, looking around as we walk.

Calder's playing with my hair as he says, "The night is yours. Whatever you want."

People are in line everywhere for the different rides. Some I'm all in for, but others there's no way in hell I'm going on. A group of guys walks by, catching Aubrey's and Piper's attention, making Roman playfully put his hands over Aubs's face.

She laughs as my eyes drift from one bright-colored ride to the next, all the neon lights illuminating the dark sky.

I'm just taking it all in, never wanting it to end. My eyes close just like that very first day I saw him on the basketball courts. I let myself get lost in the smell of popcorn and powdered sugar from the zeppole because it feels like I'm making a memory—of what being in love feels like.

My eyes open, compelled to say what I've been holding back. I turn my head, staring up at Calder's profile—his strong jaw and growing beard, and the way his lips part as he licks the bottom one before the words just tumble out.

"I love you."

Calder's eyes shoot to mine. Everything around us, the lights and sound, it all swirls around and around, turning into streaks encircling us into a bubble.

The arm over my shoulder slips off just enough for him to grab the back of my neck, pulling my lips to his. They press to mine, forcefully, as if he can't control the emotions inside him.

My mouth opens as his tongue slips inside, circling over mine as our heads tilt one way, then the other before he pulls back, crystal-blue eyes not leaving mine.

"Promise me you'll never forget this moment, Sutton."

My head draws back, but he stands quietly. Calder's eyes are filled with so much regret and sadness that I feel it too.

Every fear I felt in the car earlier pulls forward so fast it feels like I've been punched in the stomach. Tears threaten to spring to my eyes.

We're staring at each other, all the words unsaid killing us.

Because it feels like he's at the end of our story while I'm still in the middle.

"Calder."

He leans down, softly kissing my lips before saying, "It's time to go home."

My head shakes. "I don't want the night to end yet. Please. Just a little more time."

Oh God. I can feel my hands shaking.

"I love you," I whisper again.

Aubrey's voice cuts in as she grabs my hand, popping our

bubble. "Holy shit, Sut. It's that witch. Remember? From the tea shop. We have to do another reading."

I gasp, blinking quickly as she begins tugging me away. I'm pulled away faster, feet stumbling as I look over my shoulder. Calder takes a deep inhale before shoving his hands into his pockets, following behind me and the others.

As we near, my gaze roams over the black tent. It's tucked away from the crowds of people, back next to dark shadows and a dead end.

"What's that smell?" Aubrey giggles, but I don't answer.

It smells like patchouli oil, incense, and unease if that had a smell.

Roman and West joke about Aubrey finding out her future, and Piper laughs along, but I'm staring at the lady.

She stands in front, with those same dark eyes that feel like she's hiding the secrets of others. Her long, curly salt-and-pepper hair trails down her back, and she's wearing the same kind of long flowy skirt she wore before. She picks her hair up, fluffing it, making her bangles clink as she eyes Aubrey.

"Back so soon? Hoping for love again? Or just trying to choose between them?"

Her wrinkled, frail finger motions between Roman and West, making Piper tuck her lips under her teeth, trying not to laugh. Aubrey smiles as West and Roman glance at each other.

"Is it still ten dollars?" Aubs rushes out, letting go of my hand.

Piper eyes me, but I barely smile back because the heaviest sense of déjà vu takes hold of me. And I'm scared. It's ridiculous, but I am. I'm suddenly chilled all the way down to my bones.

The woman's dark eyes shoot to mine before she steps back, shaking her head.

"No more readings tonight. I'm closed."

She then looks over my shoulder and back to me as her face

grows cold.

"Come on. I'm a returning client," Aubrey whines, making Piper laugh, but I want out of here.

"Let's just go," I offer, pulling Aubrey's shirt to force her to come with me, but I run into a rigid body as I turn.

Calder's behind me, looking down as his hands find my waist. I let go of Aubs, spinning around so that my back is to Calder's front.

Aubrey's still trying to negotiate, offering more money. But the old woman brushes open the fabric hung as a door, stepping inside her tent before looking over her shoulder at Calder and me.

"You share an aura. That's very rare. It means your destinies are intertwined."

As West tries to make a joke, I lean back into Calder's arms, brows drawn together.

"Ooo, spooky. Auras."

Aubrey giggles unconvincingly, accepting West's arm over her shoulder because we're all kind of weirded out as the woman simply stares without reaction.

I turn my head to the side against Calder's chest. "I want to go."

He nods, but as my head turns back, the old woman walks toward me quickly, making my pulse quicken. A faint "What the fuck?" is whispered from beside me as she reaches down to take my hand. But Calder darts out, grabbing her hand before she does, sliding me just behind him.

"Careful, old woman. You don't touch her."

She's staring at him, pupils so dilated they look like saucers in her eyes. She twists her wrist, grabbing his hand, holding on tight as she tugs him close.

"Whoa, lady," Roman calls, stepping in closer as Piper says, "Oh my God."

But she's staring into his eyes as he stares back, neither breaking before she shivers.

"Ah. You're the end of her story. I told this girl once that you can't save her but that she could save you. She's your fate, you know? But *death* is your destiny."

My eyes lift to his profile, tugging his shirt, urging him backward. But he looks angry, full of rage.

He tries to pull his hand away, growling, "That's enough lookin', old woman. Go back to your tent."

But she digs her nails in deeper, laughing. "The devil already knows your name, Calder Wolfe. And one day, even he'll be afraid of the king."

What the fuck? How does she know his name?

She lets him go, laughing, making the hairs on the back of my neck stand on end.

I hook my finger through his belt loop, pulling him backward as everyone looks at each other. Her voice rises as she stares, a lump forming in my throat.

"Tragedy awaits you. Death is knocking. And it's on her doorstep."

Calder turns around, grabbing my waist and spinning me to take me with him. His face is dark as he guides me away.

Everyone follows behind us, mixing back among the crowd of people. Each of us glances over our shoulders the further away we get, our silent discomfort accompanied only by carousel music.

Piper crosses her arms, rubbing the top of them. "Maybe it's time to go? The freaks are definitely coming out now. How'd she know your name?"

Calder shakes his head but then nods. "Yeah, okay. Let's go."

I grip onto Calder's hand as we walk back toward the exit.

"What the fuck was that?" West levels, hitting Roman's shoulder, who shrugs as West continues. "Well, it was fucking creepy. Like some voodoo kind of shit."

Roman looks at Calder. "You good, C?"

But he doesn't answer. He just walks, staring straight ahead.

Piper nudges my shoulder. "Are you okay? Obviously, she's crazy, but man, does she like to pick on you. It's so weird. I bet she's high."

West glances back. "Maybe she's got extra?"

He's trying to lighten the mood, but nobody really laughs.

My eyes raise to Calder's face, feeling afraid because he seems lost in thought. I've never seen him look so worried.

"Hey," I whisper, tugging his hand. "Don't listen to that kooky old woman."

His head shakes as his eyes meet mine. "I'm good, baby. I'm good." But he's not. I can feel it. *And he just lied to me.*

I start to push, but my shoulder is bumped. I jerk my head over my shoulder, saying, "Rude," under my breath.

Calder pulls me to a stop, looking back before turning around.

"Watch where the fuck you're going, asshole," he rumbles, garnering interest from passersby.

A guy, maybe in his mid-twenties, turns around, facing Calder as the rest of us stare between them. *Fuck.*

Calder kisses the top of my hand before he lets it go, stepping in front of me. I want to protest, but it's Roman's reaction that makes me silent. He's shaking his head, speaking under his breath.

"C. You know better than to fuck with him. Cool it."

Aubrey grabs my hand as Piper squeezes in next to me. "Oh my God, Sut. What's happening?"

I don't answer, keeping my eyes on Calder.

"Fuck that," Calder growls to Roman before facing the guy again. "I don't give a fuck about him. Apologize to my girl. You don't fucking get to bump into her and not say shit. I'll break your fucking jaw."

West looks panicked as Roman tries to step between the guy and Calder, but Calder doesn't care, pushing Roman back. *Oh shit.*

"Calder. Stop," I rush out, reaching for him, but he jerks his arm away, throwing me back as his head darts over his shoulder with nothing but anger on his face.

"Know your fucking place, Sutton."

I blink, shaken to my core as I lower my hand. My eyes drop to the ground, hating everything about this moment as he turns back around.

"Oh my God. Did he just do that to you? What the fuck?" Aubrey hisses, staring at my face, but I can't look at her.

The guy steps in closer to Calder's face. He doesn't seem to be intimidated.

"What the fuck are you little Irish pricks doing in my neighborhood? You know better." He looks around Calder. "And with these little high-society bitches to boot."

I shriek as Calder lunges forward.

Aubrey rushes out, "Oh my God," pulling me back as Roman wraps Calder in a bear hug, forcing him backward. West steps in between them, holding his hands out. "Hey, Matteo. We're cool. Just a misunderstanding. No harm, no foul. Why don't you tell Antonio we say hello."

The guy gives a tight nod before looking right at me.

"Sorry for bumping into you, kid. Let your boyfriend know I said it."

I don't answer as he turns around and walks away. Because my head has already swung in the direction that Roman carried a belligerent Calder, just a few feet away. My mouth falls open, not knowing what to say before Calder stares back at me.

"What?" he barks, making my shoulders jump. "That guy was an asshole. Stop looking at me like that."

I feel embarrassed, looking around at people staring as they pass, as I remove myself from my friends.

"No, you're the asshole," I say quietly, closing the distance between us. "Why are you acting like an animal?"

Calder shakes his head, running a hand through his hair. "Because I am an animal. You just conveniently forgot."

My eyes glance again at the random people paying attention, snapping back to his as he says, "What's wrong, Sutton? Are you afraid people might see? Know that you're slumming it. Daddy's little princess likes it dirty."

"Stop it," I snap, brows furrowing, "What are you doing? Is this because of what that old lady just said? Is that why you're acting like a lunatic?"

I reach for him, but he steps back, shrugging.

"Does it matter? Does any of it fucking matter? We're too different, Sutton. It just took me until now to see it."

My eyes search his, swallowing before I answer.

"Quit acting like this. This isn't who you are."

His eyes are so cold as he looks at me before wiping his hands down his face, walking away. My heart begins racing as Aubrey reaches for my hand, saying, "Sut, let him go. He's a dick." But I don't, glancing at her before following behind him.

"Calder."

He doesn't turn around, walking deeper into the crowd as our friends follow us, so I call his name louder with more force.

"Calder."

He spins, locking eyes with me. There's so much anger behind his eyes that it makes my hands ball into fists, bracing myself for what he's going to say.

"Take it back."

My lips part in confusion before I say, "Take what back?"

He grabs my face, bringing it close to his. "That you love me. Un-say it. It makes me fucking sick to hear it."

I grasp his wrists, trying to pull them from my face, feeling the burn behind my eyes.

"Let me go," I rush out, my voice barely above a whisper.

He releases me as my feet carry me backward, putting a few feet between us. God, the way he's staring at me. It splits me in two. My chest begins shaking as ragged breaths leave me.

Because I already know what he's going to say.

He steps forward, eyes dropping to the ground. Oh my God, he can't even fucking look at me.

"How can you love me when you'll only ever get half of me?"

I shake my head as his eyes lift, wishing I could cover my ears. Because it doesn't matter that people talk as they walk past us or that the music grows louder in between screams from the rides.

All I hear are the words that break my heart.

"There will always be a whole side of me that you don't know. That old witch was right, Sutton. My destiny is death and destruction. Are you sure you can love that? Can you really?" His face grows cold again. "Because any chick that's with me would always know her fucking place."

Pieces of me break off like I'm slowly dissolving into nothing instead of crumbling all at once. Because that's how much I love him—I'll take his anything just to have him, if only for a moment longer.

"Why are you saying this?" I yell, tears beginning to stream down my face, eyes pleading with him. "You said I was the one."

His hand grips the back of his neck as he hurls his words at me. "Goddammit, you're so fucking desperate to be special to someone, anyone, you'd lay down with the devil. Wake the fuck up, princess. You don't belong in my world. Not because of cursed moons or fortunes from some fucked-up old woman—"

I'm sobbing, fat tears blanketing my cheeks as he stops mid-sentence, just staring at me. He sneers before letting out a vicious growl toward the sky.

My friends yell my name, arguing with his brothers to make him stop, but I'm numb. My heart is dying.

He takes a step away, and I suck in a breath because it feels like a piece of me is being ripped away.

"Tell me you don't love me back."

It's all I can think to say.

Calder looks me dead in the eyes, and suddenly he's someone I don't recognize. Seconds that feel like minutes pass as we stand in silence before a V forms between his brows.

"I never believed in love before you."

My heart waits, hoping to beat again until he pushes a sword directly through it.

"And you weren't enough to change that."

I scream inside of me, wild and angry, scratching the walls of my heart before my entire body gives out. I collapse to sitting on the dirty asphalt as my hands cover my eyes. I can't look at him. I can't see his face as he walks away.

My friends race to be at my side as sobs rip from my chest. Aubrey screams at Calder, calling him a fucking lowlife asshole as Piper wraps her arms around me, whispering that they're going to take me home.

"Everything's going to be okay. We're here," she keeps saying.

But I don't stop crying. Sitting on the ground, in the middle of a fucking carnival. Not until there aren't any more tears left. Because that's how I know he's gone.

I feel empty.

"Are you sure you want to be alone?"

I nod weakly, standing in the entry of Aubrey's house. "Yes. I just want to sleep. I'll be okay. I just…" The tears start up again as I wipe my cheeks. "I want to cry without anyone seeing. You know. In my own bed."

Aubrey hugs me, kissing my cheek. "I get it. We'll conspire on revenge strategies when you're ready."

Piper nods, sticking out her bottom lip. "Love you, Sut. If you need us, we're here. No matter what time."

I squeeze her hand before walking back out with my keys in hand. I click my lock, pulling open the door of my Mercedes SUV, and slide in. The moon roof draws my eyes up to that full globe in the sky. Tonight, it has a yellow ring around it—like a halo.

But it doesn't feel benevolent. It just feels like the moon.

The key slides in, and the car starts to life as I whisper to myself. "Time to go home."

Chapter
Thirty-Six

Calder

My father's standing on the porch, watching as I stumble out of the car, a bottle of Jack in my hand.

Roman and West get out, trying to help me walk, but I shove them off.

"Fuck you. Get off me." I spread my arms, liquor sloshing everywhere. "Are you happy, Pops? The prodigal son has returned. I did what you asked. It's done." I bring the bottle to my lips, throwing back the amber liquid before letting it drop as my voice grows quieter.

"I did what you asked. We're done."

He says nothing, looking at Roman and West, who nod before he taps the railing in front of him. "Let him sleep it off. He's earned that much."

My brothers follow me back to our house and all the way to my room in silence. None of this is their fault, even though I can feel how they wish shit were different for me. I fall on my bed, face-first, keeping the Jack upright.

West clears his throat. "Nothing's gonna be the same now. Is it? He's not coming back, is he?"

"He'll be fine, West," Roman levels. "We'll all be fine."

I listen as they make their way out of my room, closing the door before I roll over and stare at the ceiling. West is right. Nothing will ever be the same.

My mind spins in circles, looping back around to that old woman and her dark words.

"Death is knocking, and it's on her doorstep."

My eyes are fixed to the ceiling as I take a deep breath, dropping the bottle onto the floor as my eyes close.

Not anymore, baby. You're safe now.

Sutton

THE HEAT FROM THE HOOD OF MY CAR warms my palms as I scoot myself back onto it and stare up. It really is beautiful out here—this place. *Our place.*

My palms rub up and down my thighs as tears well in my eyes. I haven't stopped thinking about what Calder said to me in the back of his Mustang.

"If we only had tonight, would it all be worth it?"

"Promise me you'll ask me again tomorrow."

How can I be without him? It doesn't matter how much anyone tried to cheer me up. Nobody could ever understand the emptiness I feel when he isn't around.

Thankful that I found a hoodie in my car, I tuck the sleeve over my hand and wipe my cheeks, looking back to the stars, and whisper to myself.

"I love you, Calder."

The tiny white dots in the sky blur as more tears fill my eyes, distorting my vision. I drop my head between my arms, pull my knees up, and rest my head on them, wishing for the hurt to stop.

But how can it? He's not here to make it better.

My shoulders start to shake, the devastation of tonight taking over again until I hear it. *Hear him.*

"Don't cry, baby."

My head pops up, swinging over my shoulder to Calder's face. He pushes back his hood, smiling as he quickly closes the distance. I launch myself at him from the hood as more tears erupt, wrapping myself around him as he catches me.

"I got you. Fuck. Baby, I got you. Don't cry."

I draw my head back, my hands planting on the sides of his face.

"I was so scared nobody would believe us. Or that you wouldn't come."

His lips find mine before saying, "Nothing could've kept me from you."

Calder pulls back, frowning as he stares at my face…at my tears. "I hated how convincing it all felt. I hated saying all that shit to you. You knew I was lying—" I'm nodding, feathering kisses over his face as he speaks. "—that I didn't mean a fucking word. But, still, watching you cry like that. It felt too true, too real. Fuck. Telling you to take back what you said. I'll never stop seeing the look on your face."

I wrap my arms around his neck, whispering into his ear.

"Shh. No. Forget it all. I'm not just crying to mourn the people we're saying goodbye to. Calder, I'm also crying because I'm happy—now, we get forever."

He grips my hair, tugging me back, eyes locked to mine. I've never felt loved more than in this moment.

"I love you, Sutton. And I hated that I couldn't say it back. But if I had, there was no fucking way I would've been able to walk away like I did. So, I'm saying it now, baby."

My chin trembles as his free hand cradles my cheek. "I love you. I've always loved you—my whole damned existence, even before. And I'll love you after I die. The world will have to dedicate stars to us. Because you will always be the only fucking one for me."

Our mouths crash into one another, whispering *I love yous* as his fingers weave through my hair, pulling me in closer, needing more of me. My head tilts, tasting Calder mixed with my tears as we kiss until we're breathless. Until there's nothing left but the love we feel.

He pulls back, eyes so blue they're like the ocean, touching our foreheads together and asking me the same question he did earlier.

"Tell me you're sure? Because there's no turning back."

Our conversation floods my mind because I'm doing what he's asking of me—being sure.

"Calder," I whisper as he turns his face toward mine, sorrow behind his eyes. "What's happening?"

His brows pull together as he pulls me closer, leaning down to my ear, whispering, "If we only had tonight. Would it all be worth it?"

My heart begins racing in my chest. Because for the first time since we said that to each other, I don't want to say yes.

I don't just want tonight. I want forever.

My body shifts so I can wrap my arms around his neck, hugging him close to me.

"Promise me you'll ask me again tomorrow."

"I can't."

My eyes shoot to his, but he leans back in his seat, pulling me close, whispering in my ear.

"Stay here. We're in Roman's blind spot. The things I'm going to say next are going to be hard to hear, baby. You're gonna want

to cry. But you can't, Sutton. You have to act like everything is chill. Tap my hand if you understand."

I do, feeling like I can't breathe, but nobody would ever know. If anyone can detach, play a role, it's this girl. I guess I have the senator and Mommy Dearest to thank for something after all.

"My father knows about us. About you. He's told me to end it. He threatened you and my brothers if I don't walk away."

My eyes search the empty space ahead, soaked in fear. Don't scream, don't cry. Be cool. He's trusting you to handle this, Sutton. Don't let him down.

"Everything's going to be okay. I'm gonna take care of us. But we're gonna break up. Tonight. And we're gonna make sure people see. You'll know it when it happens, so just go with it. It's better that you're in the dark so it feels real. Just remember I'm lying. No matter what I fucking say—it's a lie, baby. But I'm gonna make it hurt. That's the only way Tyler will believe it."

I tap his hand, letting him know I understand, even though I'm already shaking on the inside.

"When your friends come in for the rescue, say you need to be alone and pretend to go home. Lift up your shirt."

I swallow as I do, exposing my bra. Calder begins writing on my breast, so I glance down, seeing he's writing directions.

"Drive to our field. I'll meet you there."

He lowers my top, kissing my temple.

"First thing tomorrow, you tell the senator that you think someone's tried to break in through your balcony doors. Take a screwdriver or a butter knife and dig into the wood to make it look like someone tried. Because no matter what my father says, I don't trust him. Then you cry. Cry a lot so your friends talk about how sad you are. So everyone knows something's up. But we don't know each other, Sutton. Erase my number. Erase me."

I tap his hand, feeling like I'm going to break.

"Here's the but..."

Thank God.

"On the Fourth of July, this town will be packed with families in for the holiday weekend. You meet me at the church when the fireworks start, and we'll never look back. This is the only way I keep you and my brothers safe. I have to keep them in the dark and give enough time for my father to believe that I'm loyal. He'll be comfortable enough to not see this coming. That means you can't tell your friends either. Do you understand? Listen to me—I had to let Tyler almost kill me tonight to make him believe he holds power over me because if I didn't, we might not be here. This is the only way, but I don't want you to do anything that you—"

He doesn't finish because I turn around, sealing my mouth over his, whispering, "Yes. Forever, yes."

My hands brush over his beautiful face, giving his lips another peck before I smile as the memory washes away.

"You are the only thing I'm the surest of. I love you, Calder, and if running away is the only way for us to be together, I'll say goodbye to everyone. I can't live without you."

The smile on his face could power my heart forever. He bites his bottom lip before his voice drops lower.

"I have a surprise. I know it's a lot after tonight, but—"

I cut him off, saying, "Show me."

I'm set to my feet before Calder walks a few steps back, grabbing a duffle bag I hadn't noticed before. He motions with his head for me to follow as he walks out into the empty field, squatting and unzipping the bag.

A small camping lantern is pulled out, along with a yellow blanket. It billows as he throws it open, spreading it out onto the ground before he turns the tiny lamp on, illuminating the space in a soft amber hue.

I see his entire face as he turns back to me, looking up.

"This is our real night. Under the stars."

I sigh before taking quick steps back into his arms. Exactly where I've always belonged.

"Baby." He says it so tenderly that I suddenly feel fragile.

Calder's hands skim down my arms, stopping at the bottom of my hoodie. His eyes connect with mine before he slowly bunches it. My arms lift as the cotton sweeps over my face, my hair falling onto my back when he pulls it off.

We don't speak as my fingers tuck under the bottom of his sweatshirt, mimicking his actions. He bends down to help me as I tug it off, letting it fall to the ground.

Our eyes lock as we breathe in tandem. God, I'm already overwhelmed, and nothing's happened, but it's still everything I'd wished for.

He reaches for my crop top, letting his fingers skim the underside of my breasts, making goose bumps tickle my skin. The moment it's off, his eyes drag over my body, making me arch my back under his stare. Because I want him to look at me.

I lick my lips, reaching for his T-shirt, but instead of letting me take it off, he reaches over his shoulder, gripping the fabric and dragging it over his head.

It makes his hair messy and tousled, so I smile as he does the same.

Calder's finger traces the length of my arm, up to my shoulder, hooking a finger under my bra strap before he tugs it down. He lets it hang as he leans down to press a kiss where it once lay.

"I cherish the feel of your skin on my lips. There won't be any space on you that I'll leave unkissed tonight, baby."

I sigh into the feeling, reaching out to touch him, but Calder drops to his knees, fingers skimming my calves as my hands fall to his shoulders. He takes off my shoes one by one, pressing a kiss to my thighs before his head lifts, looking up at me.

I brush my fingers through his hair, staring down. He makes me feel so loved. So fucking worshipped. I watch as he unzips my shorts, pulling them off.

The moment I step out, I'm doubled over, hands slapping his back as his mouth connects with my clit through my panties.

"Oh my God."

"Mmm. Fuck, I love the way you taste."

Calder groans before standing, running his hand over my breast as he smiles.

"I want to defile your body. Teach you how good it can all feel. So, we're gonna start slow until we've done everything. Until I've broken you in and ruined you for anyone else. Because you're mine. And I'm forever fucking yours."

My lips part, drawing in a breath as he massages my tit, making the lace scratch as my nipple hardens under his palm. His other hand slides over my sternum, up to my neck, fingers closing around it.

Fuck. My body's exploding. I'm already wet, painted in goose bumps and want, staring up at him.

"I *am* yours, Calder. I want everything you are. All you have to give." Fuck. I feel high. Entirely owned by him. "I love you."

His head dips, tongue pushing into my mouth, kissing me like the first time. Except instead of prayers chanted in the eaves of a church, we have the heavens looking down on us.

The kiss is rough and demanding. We're desperate for each other. So completely fucking magnetized that I don't know where I begin and he ends.

I reach for his belt, wanting it off, along with his pants as he kicks off his shoes. His hand wraps around my waist, walking us toward the blanket. The feel of the soft fabric tickles my feet as he pulls me onto it further.

"I love you."

It doesn't matter who's saying it because we're both repeating it over and over as he lays me down. Calder's lips run over my jaw as his heavy thigh lies between my legs.

My chin lifts, giving him more room as my eyes open, looking up at the bright speckled sky. His hands roam my body, leaving a trail of heat behind as I suck in a breath. He's igniting my entire body with every touch.

"Goddamn, I just want to fuck you and lick you…and then die next to you. Do you know what I mean?" he says, almost breathless as his lips devour my neck.

I nod, running my hands over his back, feeling a tingle in my center each time his leg moves. My hips press up, rubbing my clit against his thigh, seeking the delicious friction again.

"I never want to be apart from you, Calder. I won't ever fucking leave your side. Not even in death."

A moan escapes as his hand dips between my legs, rubbing my clit from the outside of my panties. His fingers press lightly in a circle as his dick grows harder against my hip. I'm panting, gripping his shoulder, feeling hungry for him.

"I want you inside of me. Please."

His tongue runs across my clavicle, and I feel his growl against my skin.

"Not yet, baby. You're gonna come first because then when I fuck you, it won't hurt as bad."

My hips rock forward into his hand, but his face comes to mine, locking eyes with me.

"Not like this."

He pulls his hand away, running it up to my stomach, stopping at my nipple. It's rolled between his fingers as he stares down at me.

Oh God. He's watching me writhe under him, back arched off the ground as he pinches the hard bud.

"Calder," I gasp before biting my lip.

"Those lips. Fuck me. Those damn lips make me think the

dirtiest shit."

He reaches up, tugging it from my teeth, before he leans down and draws the plumpest part of my pout between his lips, sucking and letting it go with a pop.

"Take off your panties, baby. Let me watch."

He moves his leg from between mine, sitting up and shifting his body so he's facing me as I roll onto my back, doing as I'm told.

I hook my fingers into the band, sliding them off my body, looking down at him. He's watching, eyes on my pussy as I draw my knees up, pulling them off.

Calder scoots closer to me, leaning in.

"Open your legs."

The leg closest to him lies flat as I leave the other bent, but he's impatient. His palm presses to the inside of my knee, dropping it open, holding me spread wide.

"Fuck, that's so pretty."

My eyes roll back because the air hits all the most sensitive places.

His lips part before he leans in, fingers spreading my soaked lips apart. I squirm, but he doesn't move. He just stares.

God, he's so close that it makes me want his mouth on me so badly that I could die.

"Ah, Calder. Please," I practically whine, undulating beneath his touch.

My head drops to the side, racked with need, as I'm immediately fixed to what's in front of me.

Calder's cock is growing harder behind his briefs as he rubs himself. His hand moves inside his briefs, making them ripple and shift with the motion.

There's something so dirty and sexy about watching him do what he's doing inches from my face while he's staring at my pussy.

"Oh fuck. You just got so wet, baby."

He lets go of my leg, letting his finger slide through the slickness before he dives down, tasting me. I suck in a breath, mouth opened.

"Oh my God."

I reach for his cock, brushing my hand over where he's rubbing himself, itching to touch him. Jesus, I'm on fire.

"I want…" I breathe out. "I want to—"

Calder growls, making me gasp before I finish what I'm saying as he eats me. He's rude and animalistic, pressing my leg to the ground harder, devouring me. The sounds of him sucking and licking my clit sends shivers over my body. He's possessed with need, attacking my pussy with his desire.

"Fuck. That feels so good. Don't stop."

Calder licks and kisses me everywhere. Between my folds, the inside of my thighs, up the ridges of my clit until he drags his tongue back down, pushing it inside of me.

He draws back briefly before sucking my clit and speaking into it.

"I can't wait to feel your cream all over my cock."

I want to fucking taste him so bad. Moving closer, I grip the band of his briefs, tugging them down to his thighs. I lick my lips, stopping his hand with mine before darting my eyes down to his because I feel him staring at me.

His eyes are hooded, lips parted as he looks at me. One of his fingers makes decadently teasing brushstrokes over my clit as he licks the wetness off his lips.

He draws his bottom one between his teeth, then lets it out slowly.

"Are you my bad girl, baby?"

My words are raspy, almost ragged, because I feel like I'm going to explode.

"Yes."

Calder's stroking his cock in front of my face. He slides his hand up his shaft slowly, before running it down.

"Lemme get it wet."

I part my lips as he guides the tip of his cock into my mouth. A bead of saltiness explodes against my tongue as I swirl it over the head.

Calder lets out a deep exhale.

"Oh, baby. I love you bad."

His hand drops from his dick, coming to my head. I moan, gripping the side of his ass, pulling him into my mouth.

"Fuck," he growls. "Don't make me come, baby."

I don't listen. I want to swallow him down, so I suck, remembering everything he's taught me from all the times I've done this to him. My cheeks hollow as his hips rock forward, going deeper each time.

He groans. "Baby, I'm gonna make you come, hard, so I can bury my dick inside of you."

His arm hooks around my thigh, tilting me toward him, so that I'm on my side, as he seals his mouth over my clit. It's so intense that I almost scream in pleasure, but the sound is muffled by his dick, deep in my mouth, and that pushes me closer to the edge.

Calder fucks my mouth, eating me at the same time.

We're all need. Filthy fucking need. Wanting more, chasing our ecstasy. His hand pushes against my thigh again, opening me wider as he relentlessly licks my pussy. And I pull him closer, wanting to deep-throat him, begging to gag on his cock.

Breathless, lips glistening, he breaks away, pumping his hips into my face.

"Fuck, yes. Take that cock deep."

I moan, choking on his dick, before his tongue connects with my clit again. But I can't get enough. I want to taste him, swallow his salty cum as he fucks my face.

He's gripping my hair, bobbing my head faster, making messy slurps mix with quiet moans. But I can't concentrate because my stomach begins to tighten, wanting, needing, begging for more until I'm quivering.

Coming on his face.

"Oh my God," I scream.

He buries his face in my pussy, holding my shaking body as I keep coming. Calder doesn't release me, coaxing my body into another wave as my head drops back.

I'm breathless, entirely spent as he kisses my pussy softly, laving his tongue over all of me, chasing my cream down to my slit.

"Calder," I breathe out because it's so sensitive. "I can't take it."

"Shh," he whispers against me, making me shiver before his tongue runs lower, gently brushing over my tight hole.

I gasp, but he growls. "All of you. I'll kiss all of you."

Nothing comes out of my mouth except for pants as I'm enveloped by the sensation of Calder licking cum off my most forbidden place.

Because I'm a slave to my body and to Calder.

"Every part of you is mine," he breathes against my thigh before nipping at it.

I jump, but I hear him chuckle as he presses his rough hand to my hip, rolling me onto my back. My tongue darts over my lips, watching him shift around, stroking his dick again as he kneels between my legs.

His knees push my legs apart as my chest rises and falls faster because this is it.

This is the moment I've always wanted. Calder's face, like a damn bruised angel, stares down at me with the stars at his back. Like he was cast out of heaven.

"I love you," I whisper, bringing my hands to his face.

He swallows, suddenly looking scared. "I love you too." The way he says it, as if he can barely speak, makes a lump form in my throat. "You're my everything, Sutton. And I've never felt like this… You're my purpose. My only reason for breathing. There's nothing I won't give you. But it could never match what you're giving me."

My beautiful monster. His eyes are so crystal blue as he stares down at me with such reverence.

"You're not just giving me your body—" He can't finish, overwhelmed with emotion because I'm giving him my soul, and he feels it.

I lift my hand, placing it over his heart, staring up.

"Forever, Calder. We're forever."

His head lowers, lips pressed to mine, staying there as a tear leaks from my closed eyes. I feel him reach down between us just before the pressure springs my eyes open.

"Oh, God."

Calder's face doesn't leave mine, his words whispered so gently.

"We'll go slow, baby. If you want me to stop, all you have to do is say stop."

I'm nodding, but I don't want him to stop. He pushes inside of me a little more, and the sting makes me gasp as I dig my fingers into his shoulders.

"Breathe, baby."

I inhale through my nose, blowing out a shaky breath, locked to his eyes.

"It hurts, Calder."

He stops, jaw tensing. But his eyes are filled with love. Calder's forearms are anchored by my head, but his hand strokes my hair.

"I love you, baby."

We wait there as I take a deep breath before saying, "More."

I bite my lip as he pushes inside again, stretching me as wide as the girth of his cock. Seconds feel like minutes as we stay locked onto each other, me letting out stuttered breaths and him groaning as he forces himself inside of my tight pussy.

He lets out a whoosh of breath, dropping his cheek next to mine.

"Baby. Fuck. I'm all the way in."

It feels heavy and full, but mostly I feel something else. A tingling. My hips want to move.

"Move a little. Rock your hips and let my cock drag in and out. It'll start to feel good."

I listen, doing what I'm told. The stinging makes me suck in a quick breath, but I feel my cream coating us as I push him back in.

So I keep going, rocking my hips as he lets me take over.

Calder's face looks pained. He closes his eyes, and the hand in my hair tightens.

"Are you okay?" I whisper.

He nods, blinking his eyes open, lowering his head to brush his nose over mine.

"You feel like fucking silk. Your pussy's so tight. I'm gonna fucking come if I don't concentrate."

I lick my bottom lip, turned on by the idea of Calder coming. What does that look like? My words rush out without thought or consideration. Because I want him.

"I want to see you come. I want to feel it inside of me."

His eyes close again as a deep rumble vibrates in his chest.

"Baby. Unless you want me to fuck you so hard that you forget your name, I'd keep those fucking thoughts to yourself."

I half-laugh, but Calder drags his dick from my sore pussy and pushes back inside, making me gasp.

"There we go. Behave."

I nod, a smile tugging at my lips because the pain is subsiding. My arms drape over his shoulders. He pulls out and pushes back in again as I meet his movement.

Fuck, this feels good.

"Kiss me."

His head lowers as my lips part. The taste of me is still on his tongue as it pushes inside my mouth, making me feel naughty. I run a hand up the back of his neck, fingers weaving into his hair, feverishly kissing until we grow sloppy. He growls, pushing deeper inside of me making me moan into his mouth. But I want it. My legs wrap around his waist, feeling him move faster.

"Oh my God," I whimper.

"You okay?" Calder whispers just as I add, "It feels so good. Fuck me, Calder."

Calder presses his palm on the ground, pulling away, breathing hard as he looks down at me. My lips try and follow him, but his eyes drop between us, making mine follow.

"Move your legs off me. Open them wide."

As I do, all I see is Calder's huge cock nestled inside of me. It's glistening with my juices, moving in and out.

"Look at us. Me, inside of you. You're mine, Sutton. I took your blood. Made your pussy my home. And I'm gonna fill you with my cum. I swear to God, if anyone ever fucking touches you, I'll kill them. Do you understand that? That's how fucking deep I love you. You are always and forever fucking mine."

My jaw is slack as Calder fucks me slowly. His face lifts toward the sky as he yells, "Not even you can have her."

He's speaking to God.

I lift my body, wrapping my arms around his neck, and press a kiss to his jaw.

"Not even He can have me," I whisper back.

Calder begins pumping into me as I cling to him. It hurts, but the pleasure outweighs the pain. His face buries into my neck as he fucks me harder and harder. Until I almost can't take it.

"Touch yourself," he rushes out.

Without hesitation, I reach down, rubbing my clit.

"Fuck, baby. Fuck," he grunts, lowering to his forearms.

I dig my nails into his back, feeling my body tightening around his cock because I'm coming. Racked by a wave of my orgasm, stealing the breath from me.

"Oh fuck, you're so tight."

His muscles are tense as we fall back onto the ground. Calder grinds inside me two more times until he's deep, curled around my body, hand gripping my hair as a guttural moan leaves his body.

I'm filled with warmth. His cum.

Goose bumps explode over my body, feeling his lips against my neck as I try and catch my breath.

His eyes lift to mine.

"Are you okay?"

"I'm better than okay."

Our smiles match before he kisses me again. I giggle, feeling his dick twitch inside of me.

"Mmm. I don't want to pull out."

"Then don't."

We lie there, staring into each other's eyes, not moving even when he grows soft and eventually slips from my body, leaving me feeling empty. Something I never realized I'd hate until now.

Calder pulls me into his arms, dragging the blanket folded over us. We're face-to-face, noses almost touching, saying nothing until my eyes begin to close.

"I love you," he whispers.

"And I love you back."

Chapter
Thirty-Seven

Calder

"Two weeks."

"Two weeks," she whispers back before kissing me again.

My fingers press into her waist before I push her back, "Get the fuck out of here, or this plan is going to hell."

She giggles, taking a step, as I mouth, "I love you." The early morning makes her eyes impossibly green as she says it back, holding up the gold coin I gave her last night so she could keep me close to her over the next two weeks. She almost cried when I told her it was my mom's.

She turns around, walking away. My eyes stay locked on my girl as she slips into her car and drives away.

Last night was so much more than I thought my heart could ever carry, but Sutton makes everything possible.

I squint, looking up at the dawning sun before I hustle my way back through the fields, letting her scent fade from my clothes but not from my memory before sneaking back into my house.

"Connor was pleased you were able to find a resolution to our problem."

Michael nods weakly, handing Tyler a small bag full of pills with a shaky hand.

"Here's the sample. The entire haul is already on the ship, scheduled to arrive next Friday."

Roman's staring at me. He's been doing it all morning. I think he's waiting for me to erupt. It makes sense. He thinks I'm on the brink of losing my shit. If I could tell him, I would, but ignorance and time will be his savior. It's all I can give him before Sutton and I cause a shitstorm. I drift back to last night, holding Sutton in my arms under the stars.

"Do you think your brothers will hate you for what we're doing?"

"No. But I think Roman will be pissed that I left him behind. We've lived our whole lives making all the same decisions, living the same life—"

"If he loves you, he'll forgive you, Calder."

The sound of pills spilling out onto the table brings me back to the present. Powder-white little round pills scatter, all with a red heart stamped on the front.

Tyler holds one up, looking at it closer.

"Your idea?" he levels, staring across at Michael, who hasn't stopped looking nervous.

"Yeah," he responds, clearing his throat. "Designer drugs are making a comeback, so it seemed smart to be a niche player."

"Niche," Tyler repeats, looking back at me. "You believe this guy?"

I give half a shake of my head, not saying anything. Tyler only has me here to make a point. Which is why I'm the only one without a gun.

Tyler pushes from the table, nodding. "You made good. Your sons are safe. Let's not make a habit of being late." He looks over his shoulder. "West, bag these up. You boys take these out this week for a test drive."

Michael huffs, staring up at Tyler.

"You're going to sell these in our community?"

Tyler smiles. "No, your sons are. Tag's gonna throw a party. My boys will sell to him, and he'll sell to whomever he wants. Business as usual."

The look on Michael's face is priceless. Guess he didn't know what his oldest has been doing. Tyler's accompanied by his fucking goons as he leaves without saying another word.

West goes about doing as he's told as Roman and I stare down Michael Kelly, staying to do the grunt work of babysitting him until West is done.

"Make it quick, West," I mutter, crossing my arms as I hear the front door close.

Michael is fidgeting with his collar, and I can't help but notice the sweat line on it. Fuck. But I can't blame him. Until a few minutes ago, he didn't know if he would be left with sons or just a son.

Roman glances down at his pocket before putting his eyes back on Michael. A few seconds later, he looks again.

What is he doing? I watch him look down a third time as he cracks his neck.

"What the fuck?" I level, turning my head to stare at him.

His jaw tenses before he reaches into his pocket and pulls out his cell. It's vibrating in his hand, but he doesn't do anything, just frowns.

"Are you gonna fucking answer it?"

He doesn't though. Instead, he extends it over to me, eyes narrowed as he tilts his head to face me. "Maybe you should answer it, C."

I glance down at the screen, seeing "Aubrey" flashing. *Shit.* I shake my head, looking away, but as soon as the call stops, it starts again. *What the fuck? Why is she calling?* Sutton knows not to tell her friends.

"She's calling again," Roman pushes, glaring at me.

"Why the fuck would I answer it? That's your bitch. Your bad for giving some crazy stalker your number."

My nerves are fraying, worry beginning to take over. I stare down at Michael, watching as he tries to make conversation with West, who ignores him, but there's something off.

Roman clears his throat, so I swing my face back to his. "What?"

The phone starts buzzing again.

"Seriously? We're doing this?"

The look on Roman's face is pissing me off because he's too curious. He can smell the lies I'm telling. Goddammit.

We're just staring at each other as the call stops and starts again. *Fuck.*

"Calder," he barks, but I don't move until he says, "You'll never forgive yourself if something happened."

I snatch the cell from his hand, pushing past him, stalking out to the backyard, and shutting the door behind me before I hit Answer.

"Why the fuck are you calling?" I growl, slipping back into the asshole I was last night.

Aubrey's voice rushes out, biting back just as hard.

"Fuck you too. I don't even want to do this, but something's happening. I need to talk to Calder."

"You've got him."

"She called me, maybe by accident, I don't know. But I heard

296   JUST *like* HEAVEN

her mother and father screaming, then her mother was yelling at just her, and I think she slapped Sutton. And after that, all I could hear was her begging not to be taken away. Saying that she wouldn't leave you. I've never heard her sound like that. Whatever the fuck happened last night isn't important because she needs you. And Calder…fuck, I hate even saying this, but I think I heard Hunter's voice—"

I hit End, turning back toward the house, breathing heavily. Rage courses through me.

Why the fuck is Hunter at her house? Is that why Michael's so nervous? I knew something felt off the minute we walked in today.

Goddammit, I tried to do this clean—so nobody got hurt. I wanted to save her, not condemn her to my world. We were going to start fresh, just live for each other.

I'm a fool.

Dark words said by that old woman lay themselves out like some kind of fucking prophecy in my mind.

"You can't save her, but she could save you."

She already has. Sutton's the reason I live because she showed me how to love. But that doesn't mean I've forgotten how to kill. So fuck what that old bitch says, I'm going to save my baby.

Because I'm not afraid of death. I'll take that motherfucker back with me if I have to keep her safe.

Michael's bringing a glass of water to his lips as the back door slams behind me.

"Where's Hunter?" I rumble, walking toward him.

His eyes grow to saucers as he drops the glass on the floor, trying to stand from his chair. That's what I thought. Motherfucker.

Glass shatters, water spilling out everywhere as he begins to stutter. My voice booms through the house as I repeat myself, closing the distance.

"Where the fuck is your son?" I look at Roman. "They've done some shit to Sutton."

Michael scrambles to his feet, stumbling backward, face shifting between Roman and West for help. But they don't try to stop me. West quickly clears the pills as Roman closes around the other side, grabbing Michael by the arm.

"Calder asked you a fucking question. Answer him before he tells me to make you. Don't think I won't enjoy that, you motherfucker."

Michael's shaking his head, holding up his hands as I stand in front of him. I can hear the ragged fury my breath makes, scraping in and out of my lungs. I'm a fucking animal.

If he's hurt her… I slam the palm of my hand against his face, gripping it, taking his body back against the fucking wall with a thud.

My mouth comes close to his ear, gritting the words from between my teeth as I press against his skull as hard as I can.

"I'll gut you. And leave you for your sons to find. Don't fuck with me. Answer my question."

"What about your father?" he mumbles under my palm. "I'm protected."

"The devil already knows your name, Calder Wolfe. And one day, even he'll be afraid of the King."

Today's that day.

I squeeze his face harder, digging my fingertips into his temple, listening to him scream like a little pig before I let him go.

"Look at my face, Michael. If you think there's anyone that I'm afraid of, then you haven't been paying attention. I'll kill everyone if she's hurt. Including my fucking father."

He's still blubbering, not fucking answering me, so I turn, swiping a ballpoint pen off the table, and stab it into his goddamn stomach.

I slap my hand over his mouth to force him to swallow his scream, throwing the rest of the broken pen to the ground.

"Michael. It's important to trust me. I'll never lie to you. If you hurt my precious girl, I won't just kill you. I'll dig up the fucking roots of your family tree and make it so you never existed."

His tears spill over my hand as I stare at him before peeling it off his mouth.

"Please," he mutters, covering his stomach as crimson bleeds out on his shirt. "He's at Sutton Prescott's house. None of this was my idea. You have to believe me. It was my wife's. She thought of all of it. Please don't kill me."

My head swings to Roman's. We're thinking the same thing. He's setting us up. Roman snaps to West and motions around. This motherfucker tried to run a game on us. Twenty says he recorded everything with Tyler and us.

"All of what, Michael?" The tone of my voice alone is a goddamn threat. I barely contain my rage enough to ask the questions I need to.

Michael coughs, so I slap him so hard his teeth rattle.

"All of what?" I thunder,

"Found it," West announces, holding up a small lipstick-sized video recorder. I fucking knew it.

Michael's crying, fucking blubbering like the bitch he is. "We just wanted out. The camera's just for protection. The plan is really Sutton, as a means to an end. A way to deliver Baron to Connor. We thought you'd be forced to walk away…because your father had that note and then—"

I almost black out.

"It was you…you gave my father that letter? You went into her room?"

My head shifts around, looking for something to crack his head open with. He's dead.

"Hunter…Hunter did it. My wife made him do it. And he's setting her up with drugs too—they're going to send her away."

Roman reaches into his pocket, handing me his keys. "Go. We got this."

My hand closes over his, taking them from him as I stare back at him. I'm never coming back. This is it. I don't have to say anything because he already knows. So, I give a nod as his eyes search mine.

"We'll be fine, brother. I'll look after West. Just get your girl."

I back away, jaw tense, as West comes up in my place before I turn my back on my brothers.

The last thing I hear is Roman speaking.

"Here's what's happening. First, we're calling Connor, and you get to confess. And then, if I had to guess, we're gonna have some fun."

Chapter Thirty-Eight

Sutton

"No," I scream. "Let me go."

Two security guards grab my arms, throwing me to the ground. Shock reverberates through my body, leaving me momentarily breathless. But I don't stop fighting, forcing breath into my lungs, making my feet kick and body flail.

I can't believe this is happening.

"This is in your best interest," my father hisses, standing behind my mother like the coward he is.

This isn't in my best interest. It's in theirs. I hate them.

"Fuck you," I spit. "I'm not doing drugs. Hunter's a liar."

My eyes dart to Hunter, who's watching, transfixed. He looks pleased and like he's sickly enjoying this.

Tears spill over my cheeks as I'm dragged. Literally dragged toward the front door.

"Stop fighting, Sutton," my mother yells.

The grip from one of the assholes holding me loosens, so I squirm harder, jerking my arm from him.

"Fuck. Grab her," he yells to the other guy as I pull away, kicking at them before standing up and running.

Footsteps and yells follow me as I tear through the foyer. I'm running barefoot and aimlessly because I don't know what to do. But I'm scared. I'm getting fucking shipped away.

I won't leave him. Not without a fight.

"Sutton," my mother screeches, followed by my father yelling, "Stop right there."

My feet carry me quickly up the stairs as I look over my shoulder. The two guards stand at the bottom, looking at my parents for direction.

It's my mother that nods her head. Fucking bitch. But I don't see them follow me up because I'm already bursting into my room, locking the door behind me.

I swing around, eyes landing on my desk.

Fuck. Everything on top gets hurled to the ground before I grit my teeth, pushing it in front of the door. My face stains red with the pressure as I use all my strength to barricade myself in my room.

Bangs erupt against the door as I get it in place, making me jump backward.

"Open the door, Sutton." … "Don't make us break it down." … "It doesn't have to be this way."

All the yelling mixes together, crashing down on me. I slap my hands over my ears, trying to escape. I won't go.

"Calder," I whisper, hearing my own voice. "Please come."

Please, Aubrey. Please have called him. I need him.

"Open the door, Sutton."

It's Hunter's voice.

"I hate you," I scream back, dropping to my knees as I sob.

A half hour prior

I'm jolted from sleep as my bedroom door hits the wall, my mother busting in.

"Oh my God." I blink, the light hurting my eyes. "Mom? What's going on?"

My mother begins opening the drawers on my desk. Papers fly everywhere as I try to catch up.

"Mom. What are you doing?"

She looks over my shoulder just as my father walks inside with two men dressed in black.

"What's going on? Who are these people?"

"We know everything, Sutton," he levels as I draw my brows together.

How can they know about Calder? Oh my God. Lie, Sutton.

"Know what?" I snap back, but my heart is pounding as I see my mother walk into my closet. *She'll find the letter from Calder.*

I jump out of bed in nothing but a tank top and underwear as my father snaps at me.

"Cover yourself. Have some decency. Or is that long gone by now?"

I ignore him, grabbing my phone and rushing toward the closet. As I get to the doorway, my mother walks out.

The look on her face can only be described as hate.

If ever I wondered if this woman loved me, the answer is no. No person could ever look at another one the way she's staring at me right now.

Her words are delivered with an eerie calm, punctuated with hostility.

"You. Little. Bitch."

My eyes drop, not because it hurts but because my mind screams at me to call Calder, but I erased it. *Aubrey. Call Aubs.* I know she exchanged numbers with Roman before our fake breakup went down, so I hope she understands what I need her to do.

I hit the number, keeping it at my side so that mother doesn't know.

"How could you?" my mother spits, holding up a clear bag of white pills.

What the hell?

I shake my head, but she shrieks, her palm slapping my face. My head shoots sideways as my hand covers my cheek. Tears well in my eyes as the sting smarts my skin.

"I should've had an abortion."

My eyes dart to hers, mouth fallen open as I stand holding my face.

"I didn't do anything," I whisper, trying not to cry.

I'm grabbed by my arms from behind, causing me to drop my phone. Everyone's talking at once.

"You'll get the help you need." … "I can't believe you've done this to your father." … "How could you fall so far from grace? I'm ashamed of you."

My head is shaking as I plead. "I didn't do anything. Where are you taking me?"

But as I'm turned around, Hunter stands in the doorway. He walks toward me, and I can feel anger—no, hate—fill my body.

"Freckles, one day, you'll thank all of us. A year will go by faster than you think, and I'll be right here when you get back."

I hate him. Oh my God.

My head draws back before I spit in his smug-ass face.

"Fuck you, Hunter. You're a dead man."

Hunter wipes his face, smirking as he comes close. "Your boyfriend's never going to find you because he'll be behind bars. I told you it was better to have me as a friend."

He looks up over my shoulder, behind me, to my parents.

"I'm so sorry this is happening. But I love her, so I know it's for the best."

I scream as he steps aside, and I'm hauled out like a criminal.

Chapter Thirty-Nine

Calder

The engine growls, tires squealing as I take the corner faster than I should making the ass end of the car fishtail. I correct it, knocking into a higher gear as I speed down her street.

My phone rings just as I hit the brakes. Her gates are closed, but there's a black van and Hunter's fucking car in the driveway.

I kick open my door, getting out in the middle of the street, pulling the phone to my face.

"What."

"Check the glove box."

I don't wait to end the call, knowing Roman will. I shove it into my back pocket, stalking back to the car and ripping open the door, making the hinges strain before I lean inside, popping the box open.

My fucking gun.

I open the chamber, gritting my teeth when I see only one bullet before I slide the safety off and tuck it into the back of my Dickies.

All the dark swirls of rage begin to still inside me as one foot steps in front of the other toward her front door. Because I finally understand all of it—my destiny and hers.

"Tragedy awaits you. Death is knocking. And it's on her doorstep."

Yes, I am.

Sutton

MY HANDS DROP FROM MY HEAD AS I crawl toward my bed to hide underneath it.

"Sutton. Can you hear me? It's just you and me, Freckles."

I scowl, looking over my shoulder, hearing Hunter through the door.

"Go to hell, Hunter."

"Now, why would I do that when it's more fun here?"

My body freezes because we're definitely alone. There's no way he'd talk like that in front of anyone else. I sit back on my ass, my hand brushing past my phone.

Oh my God. I swipe the screen, but it cuts my finger because it's cracked from me dropping it. Fuck. I can't get it to work.

"Why did you lie?" I yell, tossing the phone back to the ground.

"Because I had to. Why'd you choose him?"

"Is that what this is about?"

He laughs. "No, you egotistical bitch. But if you're regretting it, I can make all of this easier on you."

I don't answer, looking at the ceiling.

"Because, Sutton, this isn't even the hard part. See, setting you two up was easy. All it took was one little peek in your room and, of course, your panties drawer because that's where all bitches like you keep shit."

What the fuck? My mind is spinning in circles. Why would he want to set us up? Why is this happening? I don't understand.

"Then it was a matter of presenting the plan. I let Tyler Wolfe know his only son was fucking the enemy."

Oh my God. My head swings toward my closet—he took the note. I feel sick. My eyes fill with tears, wishing I could stop him. Just stop him from speaking.

"Then I told him that I could connect you two, in a way that's public record—rehab. And I hid a little white bag of goodies in your room. So, not only will everyone know Calder popped your cherry, but they'll think he's helping you pop pills too."

My head's shaking as my cheeks grow wetter.

"I'll tell everyone you're lying."

This can't happen. They can't send me away...I can't leave him. I won't.

"Tell them the truth. Because that seems to be working so well for you. You can't do anything except watch the O'Bannions blackmail your father while mine is set free as payment. If you think about it, you kind of whored yourself out for me. I guess I should say thank you."

I push to stand, trying to process what he's saying. *What does Hunter's family have to do with the O'Bannions and Calder?* I can barely understand my own thoughts, running my hands through my hair.

I'm trying to hold on to one thought as another crashes down onto me as my chest shakes.

"I hate you. Stop. Just stop it, Hunter."

"Do you want to know the best part, Freckles? Now that you two are broken up—"

"We aren't," I snap as my eyes land on the bag of little white pills.

I stand, swiping them off the bed, yelling my words through ragged breaths and tears.

"There's a flaw in your plan, Hunter. You left the evidence in here. No pills, no proof. Fuck you. I won't let you hurt him."

There's a bang in the distance like the front door slamming, but I don't slow my stride, walking toward my bathroom and opening the baggie as Hunter says, "God. That's even better. Now you can watch him hate you."

I freeze before spinning around, stalking toward my bedroom door.

"Why would Calder hate me? That would never fucking happen. Ever."

Ignore him. Don't listen, Sutton.

"You're so dumb. Do you think he'll still love you when he's arrested for rape? Because a photo of you kissing on the Ferris wheel is gonna be what helps do just that."

"Lies. Shut up."

Walk away, Sutton.

"Is it a lie? Come on…you're smarter than that. There won't be a judge out there that we can't make believe that your drug dealer wasn't grooming you."

My heart stops beating because I don't want to believe Hunter, but I know what these people are capable of. And suddenly, I'm not just afraid of what they'll do to me.

"No. You can't do that. I won't let you."

He laughs. "Yeah, we can. Have you forgotten my last name? Or yours? It was just luck that Tiffany saw you and sent me the photo. Though, lately, that seems to be on my side. Because it's really the pièce de résistance. Don't you agree?"

I can't breathe. Oh fuck, I'm having a panic attack. Stop. Please, God. Make it all stop.

"He loves me. It doesn't matter what you do to us. You can't stop that."

The tears won't stop, and my goddamn feet won't move to run from this door. Hunter laughs again, and I close my hands over my ears, wanting all my thoughts to just stop.

This is my fault. All my fault. I've done this to Calder.

"I don't have to stop anything. Time will. You'll never see him again, Sutton. By the time he gets out of jail, he'll fucking despise the bitch that put him there—you. I hear that place really likes pretty boys too."

It's like I can't focus. My heart is beating too fast, and I can't catch my breath. How did this happen? Tears stream down my face, the saltiness bleeding between my lips.

I love him so much, but it's all my fault. Hunter would have nothing on him without me.

"You might as well be dead, Sutton…because that's what you'll be to him after he lives his life in a six-by-eight prison cell."

My eyes half blink as my body feels like it's curling in on itself. I've lost track of the tears I've cried. I'm overwhelmed by the emotion. I can't speak to fight back or feel anything other than grief. This is my fault. I've hurt the only person that's ever loved me.

The bag in my hand feels heavy as my head drops down toward where my hands have fallen, Hunter's words sounding far away because my mind is numb.

I can't live without Calder. But without me, he gets to live.

No pills, no evidence. No me, no setup.

The plastic tears under my fingernails. I bring the bag to my lips, letting the contents fill my mouth, swallowing as many as I can before I hurry to my nightstand and grab the water bottle left from last night, chugging it back.

Everything drops from my hands as another sob racks my body before I slide down the side of my bed to the ground.

"I'm sorry, Calder. I love you. So, I'll save you."

Chapter Forty

Calder

The front door slams behind me, pulling all eyes to the entry as I walk inside. Everyone stands silent in the living room, fear on their faces—murder on mine.

Two assholes in all black start toward me as Sutton's father begins yelling for someone to call the police.

"Where is she?" I roar, pulling my gun from the small of my back.

The guards put their hands in front of them like they're trying to defuse the situation, taking a step toward me. I look between them as my teeth fucking grind.

All my words are growled. "I said, where's my fucking girl."

"She's already gone, buddy. Let's put the gun down."

"Fuck you. Where'd you take her?"

The guy not talking steps in closer, so I pistol-whip him, sending blood flying as Sutton's mother begins screaming. He falls to the floor, hands on his face, trying to stop the blood gushing from his broken nose.

My gun points at the other dipshit left standing, who takes a step backward. Sutton's mom is still fucking screaming, so I point the barrel at the senator.

"Shut that bitch up before I put a bullet in her fucking head."

She immediately goes silent, shaking as she stares back at me.

"You're lucky I don't take your fucking hands for touching her."

Her face turns to ash as Baron puts his arm in front of his wife. I'd bet it's the single bravest thing he's ever fucking done.

"Now, I'd answer my question if I were you. Or I'll let Sutton choose whether or not you live or die. Because that feels like justice—judged by the daughter you mistreat."

Before I finish, her mother's already blurting out, "We don't know. They wouldn't tell us. It's part of the program."

"Bullshit," I rumble.

"It's true," Baron rushes out, eyes darting to something behind me before he swallows, looking indignant.

My head swings over my shoulder as I lock eyes with Hunter, who's standing by the front door.

"You did this," I spit, turning around. "And like a fucking coward, you were gonna sneak away. Where? Back to daddy?"

His eyes grow wide as I shake my head. He knows what I mean. *He's dead. Just like you're about to be.*

One step after another gathers speed as I lift the gun, feeling the kick as his shoulder's thrown back, hit with my bullet.

Screams erupt around us.

Hunter howls in pain as he stumbles, back hitting the door. I run toward him, raising my arm and bringing the butt of my gun down on his fucking skull.

I'm drowning in a red mist of fury, giving him what he deserves. He's done this to my baby—taken her from me.

"You're fucking dead."

Spit flies from my mouth as my hand comes down over and over, blood erupting underneath each hit as he tries to fight back. But I throw him to the ground, gripping his hair, holding his head in place, knocking the metal into his face.

"This is what you get for what you've done."

Bone cracking under the gun's handle echoes in the hallway, becoming the only sound mixed with my grunts as Hunter stops fighting back.

"She could've died because of your fucking little game."

I hit him harder each time, smashing his face until I can't see him past the blood. I hit him until his body goes completely limp and then after.

I hit him until he's dead.

Hard, abrasive breaths drag from my body as I stand, stumbling backward, blood splattered over my shirt. I heave out as much air as I take in, hovering over his body. I'm staring down, filled with my hatred, fueled by it.

I suck in a breath through my nose and spit on his fucking body before I step away. The noise in the room, all the shit being yelled. The cries. It all begins to reach full volume.

They're going to tell me where she is. Or everyone's going to suffer.

As I turn, bloody and cruel, I see the security guard halfway up the stairs. My eyes shoot back to Baron, who pales, backing away, taking his wife with him.

Fuck.

I drop the gun to my side, feet taking the stairs three at a time, pushing past the fucking guy.

"Baby," I bellow as I get to the top of the stairs.

My hand pushes off the wall as I rush down the hallway, attacked by a sense of emptiness that suddenly fills my body, making my hands almost shake.

"Baby," I yell, coming in front of her door, banging on it. "Everything's okay now. Baby, open the door."

Bust it open.

The thought starts out quiet until it's screaming inside my head. *Bust it open. Bust it open. BUST IT OPEN.*

I throw my shoulder into the door, but it barely moves, so I do it again, and again, groaning as the pain grows with each hit.

"Sutton," I holler, throwing myself into the door a fourth time, feeling it start to give.

I'm a machine, bashing into the door until it opens just enough that I can get my hand in and fucking push. I shove harder just as it gives, making me fall inside past the desk she pushed against the door.

"Sutton," I yell.

But as my eyes lift, I see her.

Oh God. No. No, no, no, no, no.

I scramble, half crawling to her body, lying lifeless on the ground. My hands hover over her, almost too scared to touch her small frame.

"No," I grit out, feeling my chest split open. "No, baby."

I touch her arms, then her stomach, before I cradle her cheek, staring down at her peaceful face. My palm presses to her skin, hoping to feel warmth as I move it over to stroke her hair. Fuck. She's so pale. *Why is she so pale?* I don't understand. This can't happen. *Not my baby. Please.*

My forehead drops to hers. "Wake up. Wake up, Sutton."

Everything inside of me feels broken as I kiss her lips, praying to feel her breath before I pull back, looking at her face. I seal my lips over hers, blowing into her mouth, pulling back to look at her before trying again, but nothing happens.

She doesn't move.

My entire body is vibrating, shaking with the emotion I feel. I scoop her up, gritting out, "Please, baby. Don't leave me."

I tip my head back, holding her lifeless body in my arms as a guttural cry erupts from my chest. I scream until my voice gives. Because all I can do is weep, rocking her, folded down over my beautiful girl. My chest shakes as my voice cracks, and tears pour down my face.

"Not you. It wasn't supposed to be you."

Back in the recesses of my mind, I hear commotion, people yelling, footsteps falling quickly, but I don't care. Because I'm praying.

I'm praying for God to take me with her. To forgive me of all my sins and let me go with her. Please take me with her. Please, God.

"Our Father, who art in heaven—"

"Step away from the girl. Hands up."

"Hallowed be thy name —"

"We need paramedics." … "Step away from the girl or I'll shoot."

Her face flashes in my mind, moment after moment relived.

From the rock I'm seated at, I watch her dramatic little moment unfold, lifting my cigarette to my lips, readied to light it as she whispers.

"I hate you, moon."

"What are you doing here? How'd you get here so fast? I just saw you—"

"I ran."

"Now I'm baptized in you."

"I'm gonna give you the stars, and the moon, and—"

"Love. You're going to give me love."

"I've always loved you—my whole damned existence, even before. And I'll love you after I die. The world will have to dedicate stars to us. Because you will always be the only fucking one for me."

My body shakes as I hug her to me before placing her body back to the ground.

"Forever, baby. I'm coming," I whisper before my voice raises. "Thy kingdom come. Thy will be done. On earth as it is in heaven—"

"Show me your hands."

I swing around, quickly lunging forward. Searing hot pain shoots directly through my chest as all my breath is torn from my body. I collapse, falling backward to the ground. My head falls, facing Sutton.

"I'm coming," I whisper, straining to touch her hand as blood begins to pool around me.

"Medic" is called out, and I feel myself being jerked around, eyes beginning to close as people kneel next to her. But my eyes remain on her. Her beautiful face.

I'm coming. I feel it.

"It's an overdose. Narcan."

We'll have forever now.

I feel cold, eyelids closing longer and longer. They don't want to open anymore. I just want to go. Be with her. I blink one last time, staring at her face, death gripping my shoulder.

A needle is shot into her arm, and I close my eyes.

"Calder."

Baby. She whispered my name, but I can't open my eyes.

Baby, I scream inside my mind, but it's too late…
Everything goes black.

318   JUST *like* HEAVEN

acknowledgments

This is the part where I usually say "Thank you" to
everyone who helped me shape this book. And while
I'm eternally grateful to each and every person, I'd
like to use this section to remind my readers that while
the idea of dying for someone you love is romantic in
fiction—that's where it should stay. In fiction.
If you struggle with thoughts like these in real life or
feel alone, please know that you're not.
Use this resource because you are important to *me* and
so many others:
The Suicide Prevention Hotline.
1-800-273-8255
And if you are like our heroine—innocent, then make
sure you're educated. Because innocent never means
ignorant. Know your body. Know your boundaries.
You're in charge.
https://www.plannedparenthood.org/learn

About the Author

Trilina is a USA Today Bestselling Author who loves cupcakes and bourbon.

When she isn't writing steamy love stories, she can be found devouring Netflix with her husband, Anthony, and their three kiddos. Pucci's journey into writing started impulsively. She wanted to check off a box on her bucket list, but what began as wish-fulfillment has become incredibly fulfilling. Now she cant's see her life without her characters, her readers, and this community.

She's known for being a trope defier, writing outside of the box and creating fictional worlds that her readers never want to leave.

Connect with Trilina and stay up to date.
www.trilinapucci.com
facebook.com/trilinapuccibooks
twitter.com/trilina_pucci
instagram.com/authortrilinapucci
amazon.com/Trilina-Pucci/e/B07BQFYLKB

Printed in Great Britain
by Amazon